SARAH'S LIST

SARAH'S LIST

Elizabeth Gunn

This first world edition published 2020
in Great Britain and the USA by
SEVERN HOUSE PUBLISHERS LTD of
Eardley House, 4 Uxbridge Street, London W8 7SY.
Trade paperback edition first published
in Great Britain and the USA 2021 by
SEVERN HOUSE PUBLISHERS LTD.

British Library Cataloguing in Publication Data
A CIP catalogue record for this title is available from the British Library.

ISBN-13: 978-0-7278-9049-8 (cased)
ISBN-13: 978-1-78029-706-4 (trade paper)
ISBN-13: 978-1-4483-0427-1 (e-book)

This is a work of fiction. Names, characters, places and incidents
are either the product of the author's imagination or are used fictitiously.
Except where actual historical events and characters are being described
for the storyline of this novel, all situations in this publication are
fictitious and any resemblance to actual persons, living or dead,
business establishments, events or locales is purely coincidental.

All Severn House titles are printed on acid-free paper.

Severn House Publishers support the Forest Stewardship Council™ [FSC™],
the leading international forest certification organisation.
All our titles that are printed on FSC certified paper carry the FSC logo.

Typeset by Palimpsest Book Production Ltd.,
Falkirk, Stirlingshire, Scotland.
Printed and bound in Great Britain by
TJ International, Padstow, Cornwall.

ONE

Monday

'Between Camino Del Cerro and Sweetwater, Dispatch told me, on Silverbell Road.' Sarah leaned forward, squinting across the driver. 'Must be almost— There it is. See all the squads?'

Bogey turned left quickly to drive through iron gates standing open, onto a fresh asphalt driveway. He parked to the right of the three black-and-whites that were nosed in behind a passenger van covered with logos. Its ads matched the ones on the new brick building behind it. They all read *Fairweather Farms*, with *senior living* in smaller print below.

A couple of Tucson street cops, new recruits that Sarah didn't know, were stringing crime scene tape around the rear end of the van. The front end was out of sight, improbably buried in the half-open garage door of the handsome three-story building.

'Whoa,' Bogey said. 'Somebody forgot to stop, huh?' For a few seconds, both detectives sat still while their eyes scanned the puzzling scene. Besides being stuck in a half-open door, the vehicle was pocked with what looked like fresh bullet holes, their sheared metallic edges winking in the sunlight.

Two men stood just outside the tape, wearing brown jumpsuits with logos that matched the van. They carried gardening tools, a rake and an edger, and were watching the vehicle warily, as if they thought it might explode.

A few feet away, between the men and the front door of the building, a woman in tan scrubs with the same logo as theirs was standing with her hands over her eyes. She was shouting something. Or crying? Both, Sarah decided as she opened her door and heard, '. . . never saw so much blood in my life! Omigod!'

Sarah said, 'I don't see any blood, do you?'

'Sure don't,' Bogey said, but he unclipped the cover on his Glock.

He was still trying to fit in, she thought. She had watched his efforts, during his first week in homicide division, to get everybody comfortable with his big square face and his name, Zivko Boganicevic. A mouthful for sure, but he'd spelled it for anybody who asked and, if they still looked confused, pronounced it again: Zeef-ko Bo-gan-EESS-uh-veech. By the end of the week they had all begun, at his suggestion, to call him Bogey.

In the shady interior behind the half-raised garage door, Sarah could see the feet and lower legs of more patrolmen. They must be taping an area around the front of the van. She watched as the two outside patrolmen finished stretching their end of the tape. Simultaneously, each man fastened his end to the door frame on his side and stood back, looking for the next order of business. *Looking for Pratt?* Sarah thought. *Where is he?*

Big, loud, hard to miss, Pratt was the patrolman who had called homicide, looking for somebody to take over this crime scene. Sarah had been at her desk when Delaney answered the phone, and she'd heard him tell Pratt to wait for the team of detectives that he would send right away. Delaney had not become head of homicide by being shy about issuing orders – rattlesnakes hid quivering in the cactus, his detectives claimed, when Delaney got riled about an order overlooked.

So where's Pratt?

'You know either one of these boys?' Sarah asked Bogey. It was a reasonable question – Bogey had just made his rating, and he was fresh off the Tucson streets, not a transfer from out of town – he must know most of the guys on patrol.

Like every other detective in homicide, Sarah had heard about the bold collar that got Bogey's application lifted out of the slush pile and put up front in the promotion queue. He was replacing Leo Tobin, who had given plenty of notice about his intention to retire in September, and they all knew one or two detectives who were slogging through domestic abuse or auto theft, waiting their turn for homicide. So when they got a few spare minutes for the gossip that greases the wheels of police work everywhere, they began to ask each other, what kind of juice has this Bogey got?

Sarah tried to steer clear of department gossip, usually, and Bogey's story – the single-handed arrest of five armed men – had a show-boat slant that made her extra dubious. *Why didn't he call for backup?* She would not have picked him to partner with today, but Delaney said, when he assigned her to this oddball street attack, 'Might as well take Bogey along for backup. Good chance to get him started.'

She'd been listening to chaotic radio traffic from the street chase while she worked, and began to play closer attention as the chase cars reported in from a place called Fairweather Farms. So when the call came in for homicide and she got the case, she'd asked her backup to drive and let her monitor radio traffic on the way. But there'd been nothing much going on for the last few blocks. *Well, we'll get the skinny from the patrolmen on site.*

'The short one's Frank O'Neill,' Bogey said. His voice had a little rasp of tension in it – he knew all the experienced detectives were watching him, curious to see his chops. He added the other thing he knew about O'Neill, 'The Irish guy who speaks Spanish?'

'Ah.' That was the other story on the grapevine this week, the new recruit with an edge in *la lengua*. Most Tucson cops, the Anglo ones, quickly acquired the few words of Spanglish sufficient to make an arrest. But this recruit from last fall's class had a father whose job with a major oil refiner had kept him travelling the Mexican states, and afforded his son many school holidays cruising the barrios of outback Mexican towns. O'Neill spoke street Spanish, it was said – he could even roll his Rs.

'The other guy on the tape is Francisco Gomez,' Bogey said. 'Mexican but second or third generation; people call him Franny. He and O'Neill seem to team up often, and the guys say they gossip together in Spanish, sound like a pair of old *abuelas* sitting around the *pueblos*.'

'Fine, then, 'Sarah said. 'You download O'Neill and his gossipy partner. I'll check the victim and see what the staff has to say.'

'Gotcha,' Bogey said. And then, over his shoulder as he walked away, 'Call me if you need any help with that screamer.'

'You bet,' Sarah said. *When pigs fly, I will call you for help.* Back in the day when she was new in homicide, part of the first wave of female detectives in Tucson, men had offered to help her all the time – her male peers had made no secret of their disbelief in her ability to do the job. She had ignored the snickers, bit her tongue to hold back sharp answers, and worked hard to prove she could hold up her end. She was proud now that she was treated as an equal by the men and respected as a leader by the many younger women coming on board.

She unclipped the badge from her belt, aware as she got out of Bogey's unmarked Ford Fusion that they were the only two people in sight whose clothes and vehicle did not identify them. Like the Glock in her shoulder holster, her badge didn't show under her neat jacket. A savvy observer might realize she was too well-dressed for the weather, but this group looked too preoccupied to notice style points.

So she held the badge up for the two gardeners to read as she passed them, and said, 'Wait here for me, please, while I get a look at the body. Is that what's bothering this lady?'

'Tammy? I guess,' the older one said. The name tag on his pocket read *Henry*. 'I know she ain't as crazy as she sounds right now,' he added. 'Must be the first time she ever seen bl—'

Just then the woman cried, 'I'm going to be sick!' and bolted for a door under an arch in the building behind her.

No use following her there. Watching the attendant run toward a bathroom, Sarah noticed for the first time a tiny woman seated on a bench in the shade near the front door of the building. Not in uniform, so she must be a patient. She seemed oddly detached, paying no attention to the activity churning all around her. As Sarah watched, she raised her hands from her lap and scrutinized them carefully as she matched fingers – thumb to thumb, index to index. Her lips moved but no sound came out.

She probably shouldn't be alone, Sarah thought, but I don't have time – is anybody controlling access to this scene? Bogey was already talking to the tape-stringers. She held up her badge and called, 'I'm going aboard here.'

Bogey held up one hand with fingers curled in the 'OK' sign, and made a note. It would have to do for now; the squad stringing tape hadn't brought a posse box evidently, and nobody was controlling access to the van. She gloved up and ducked under the newly strung tape.

The steps slid out from under the chassis when she pushed back the big side door of the van. Luckily the vehicle hadn't penetrated the building far enough to jam the lock. She climbed aboard and turned right.

Somebody had turned on the overhead lights in the garage, but the front of the van was still gloomy compared to the brightness outside. There was indeed a lot of blood, spread over the whole front of the van. And glass – the windshield had shattered and there were shards of glass scattered over the console, the floorboards and the dead man.

He was still in the driver's seat, slumped over the steering wheel, left arm lying on the padded armrest. His shoulders rested on the steering wheel and his right hand had slid forward onto the console.

The entry wound from the bullet that had killed him looked surprisingly small. She leaned over his back, put one gloved finger under his chin and lifted his head a fraction of an inch. They were not going to find an exit wound – the area under his face was clean. So the bullet was still in his head – good; the crime lab might get some news off that.

The smell wasn't bad yet. She took a deep breath to get her olfactory nerves adjusted, so she could ignore it as it got worse.

What was left of the windshield, and the undamaged window on the driver's right, were streaked with blood. The blood streaks, in turn, were festooned with clinging fragments of dust and pollen. She felt an impulse to close the window but quelled it – it was crime scene evidence that the driver's side window was open. *Open, in this weather?* She made a note and went on.

She kept turning left, typing notes on her tablet. Most of the spatter had stayed up front. The chase car must have come from behind, and never quite caught up – even the two shots that had come in through the open window had buried themselves above the windshield. The one lucky shot that killed the driver must have been fired on an inside curve. By the end of her first turn she had a dozen questions in the hasty code she used for first impressions: *Hi-pow rif – ammo 22 or up – w-sh brok, right wind not?? Where casings from (how many) shots?*

Wanting answers, she climbed out of the van and asked the two gardeners, who were still jittering nearby, 'Tell me how this trouble started.' She had scrolled back to what Delaney told her when he gave her the case: 'People working outside heard shots and yelling.'

Usually the story changed considerably in the telling, but today the crew members confirmed what Delaney had told her.

'Shots is what I heard first,' Henry said. He wore an air of being in charge of the whole place. When she'd asked, he said he was head of the grounds crew, which seemed to be this two-man team.

'Yeah, and then a lotta yelling,' the younger man said, 'out on the road.' His pocket said his name was Jacob. He avoided eye contact, had trouble with r's and l's and a nervous habit of scratching his elbow. Sarah noted these quirks as she always did, handy reminders when she had to get acquainted with a group in a hurry.

'Two shooters with high-powered weapons,' Henry said, 'hanging out the rear windows and they shot fast. Yelling and shooting, going bam bam bam . . .' He did his best Tom Cruise imitation.

'About what time was this, do you remember?'

'Uuuhhh,' Henry looked pointlessly at his watch as if he expected it to tell him how many minutes had passed since the van grazed his shins. 'Few minutes after eleven.'

'Good. Thanks.' Knowing the time of death would save some time for the coroner who got this autopsy. They were always overloaded, so you earned some credit with the coroner if you helped speed up the process. Sarah was a careful collector of credits.

'The yelling,' she said, 'could you hear what they said?'

Henry turned his hands over and looked at Jacob, who shrugged. 'No idea,' Jacob said.

Henry added, 'Spanish.'

As she watched them over her glasses, they began to nod, each encouraging the other to go on. Finally Henry said, '. . . And then our van, this one here, came through the gate very fast. We was working over there near the entrance, spreading gravel on the plant beds next to the driveway. That van missed killing the two of us, Jesus, just by inches.'

Emphatic head-shakes from Henry and a little groan from Jacob, who said, 'But it did miss us, but then it didn't stop! Crashed right into the garage door when it was only halfway up. That got it stopped all right, but the motor kept on running.'

'But right behind it – I mean *right* behind,' Henry said, 'the shooters' car come roaring in – and man, it was lucky we'd already jumped out of the way of our shuttle bus or they'd a' got us for sure. Because them bozos wasn't thinking about anything but killing, never looked at a friggin' thing but our van. I never seen anything like it – we coulda been sticks and stones for all they cared!'

'Wasn't for these cops here,' Jacob said, nodding at the tape-stringers, 'we'd a been dead ducks right now.'

'These patrolmen my partner's talking to?' Sarah said. 'They were the ones chasing the shooters?'

'With lights and sirens going soon as they turned onto Silverbell at the light up there,' Jacob said. He got excited, waved his arms. 'And the shooters, soon as they heard the sirens they started yelling at each other. All in that Mex lingo, but it wasn't hard to guess what they were saying.'

'Oh? What do you think they were saying?'

'"Let's get the hell outta Dodge!" Right, Henry?'

'Right. And did they ever – look what they done to our perfect gravel.' He waved mournfully at the trenches in the freshly manicured grounds. 'Three days we been rakin' this place, we had it smooth as a new baby's ass.'

'Even so, I guess we should be grateful,' Jacob said. 'They'd a run over us without battin' an eye if we happened to be standin' in the way.'

Henry waved forlornly at the toppled desert plants all around him. 'Drove right through the yard without slowin' down, see the track? Straight through the fence like they never heard of obstacles, down into the borrow pit and back up onto the road. Tore off back to town about a hundred miles an hour.'

'Any chance,' Sarah asked them, 'you got the make and model on that auto? Or the license?'

'Beat-up Dodge Ram pickup. Club cab,' Henry said.

'Looked old,' Jacob added, 'but they must have some kinda souped-up motor. That baby could move.'

Henry said, 'Arizona license but that's all I got.'

'First three letters XMZ,' Jacob said, earning a surprised look from Henry. 'I didn't get any numbers.'

'Color?'

'Ehh, dirty gray. Or dark blue. Getting back on the road, he just missed colliding with the patrol cars coming in pursuit. Cut in right in front of them.'

'I think we heard some of that,' Sarah said. 'We were on our way by then, listening on the radio.'

'Yeah, well, then didja hear the part,' Jacob could not repress a grin, 'where them patrol cars was goin' so fast they missed our driveway and had to go way up the road to turn around?'

'While you stood here with a dead man in a van, right?' Sarah said.

'But we didn't know that yet,' Henry said. 'What I did know was that motor was still running and I was sure it was gonna explode. So I run over here to turn it off.' He looked back along the driveway he had run, remembering. 'But when I got here somebody was yelling inside the van and doing a lot of thumping.'

'Henry was all set to give the driver hell for reckless driving,' Jacob said, grinning some more. 'But he never got a chance because the passenger was just inside in a wheelchair, yelling and pounding on the door with his cane.'

'Were there other passengers?'

'No, just him.'

'Was he hurt?'

'No, but he was gasping for breath,' Henry said. 'Yelling that the driver was hurt, it wasn't safe in there, we had to get him out.'

'Truth is he was perfectly safe once the shooting stopped,' Jacob said, 'the wheelchair locks into a frame on the floor, he wasn't rolling around or nothing. But it was Mr Ames in the chair, and we all know it's no use arguing with him. So I grabbed the portable oxygen tank that we keep in the van and helped him get the cannula in his nose and around his ears.'

Sarah made a note: *Ames status?*

'And even Mr Ames can't snort oxygen and yell at the same time, so for a couple minutes things quieted down,' Henry said. 'So then I did turn toward the driver . . . for help! Because after all, the passengers are *his* job, not mine. *But—*' Henry made a choking noise and put his hands in their heavy work gloves up to his face.

Till now he had seemed the model of an authority figure, but as Sarah watched, his shoulders began to shake and he made little *mmp* noises. Sarah waited three breaths and then said quietly, 'But you found him slumped over the steering wheel, is that it? Unresponsive.'

Henry said, through his gloves, 'With blood coming out of his eyes and nose . . .'

'You done better'n I did,' Jacob said, trying to comfort Henry. 'I took one look and jumped out of there yelling for help. Lucky thing was right then those three cop cars got back to our driveway. Two of them went on after the shooters but one turned in, and two boys in blue jumped out. So I got them to help me get Mr Ames out of the van.'

'Was he in very bad shape?'

'Nah,' Jacob said. 'He was just havin' a panic attack. I thought maybe he was going to have a stroke but he never shut up long enough to fall over.'

Henry turned sharply, shook his head and made a tamping-down motion with his hands. Jacob shrugged and looked at his shoes.

'OK, so you got him out . . .'

'Yep.'

'And then what?'

'Took him inside. This time of year, we got strict orders – don't leave any of these folks in the sun for more'n a minute or two.'

Sarah nodded; Tucson PD had the same orders. Monsoon rains were drying up but September was still a scorcher – it would be a hundred degrees in this parking lot before lunch. Homicide had recently taken a beating about an elderly bystander who collapsed while a pair of detectives questioned him on the street. All investigators now got reminders with the morning brief: *Get your witnesses out of the sun!*

'Does he need medical attention now?'

'No,' Jacob said. 'Happens this is the nurse practitioner's day to visit. We turned him over to her and she put him on a respirator.'

'But he's still very upset about the shooting,' Henry said. 'Giving everybody hell about it like we could make it unhappen if we tried hard enough. Mr Ames is in about the best shape of anybody living here. But he always wants to be sure he gets his share of everything we got.'

'And gets it first,' Jacob said. 'Never too sick to see to that.'

'So with him out of the way I finally did get the motor turned off,' Henry said. 'I had to go right up there close to . . .' He choked again briefly but went on. 'Blood all over the place and even, God, I guess, must be pieces of his head . . .' He closed his eyes, took a deep breath, opened them and said, 'Shouldn't there be a doctor coming?'

'The coroner will be here soon. Tell me about the victim. What's his name?'

'The vic— oh, you mean the driver? Same as mine but Spanish – Enrique? But everybody around here calls him Ricky.'

'Any idea why somebody would shoot him?'

'Hell no,' Henry said, 'Ricky's a muffin.'

'Must be a mistake,' Jacob said. 'Of all the guys I know, Ricky's the last one I'd shoot.'

'What's his last name?'

'I don't know,' Henry said. 'Ask the manager.'

'All right. What's *his* name?'

'Her. Letitia.'

'That's all?'

''S'what she said to call her. Everybody's first names here.'

Both men shrugged. Who knew what managers would do next?

'Except Mr Ames,' Sarah said. 'Why is he special?'

'Dunno,' Henry said, 'probably because he demanded it. He's a better'n average demander.'

'Right up in the top tier, I would say,' Jacob said. 'Him and his pal Millicent.'

Sarah was thinking, *Where's my crime scene crew?* She asked the gardeners, 'Have you seen a tall patrolman named Pratt, about this wide—' She held her hands up.

'With a hillbilly accent?' Henry's eyes recovered a little luster.

'And freckled all over?' Despite the stressful morning, Jacob began grinning again.

'That's the guy,' Sarah said, thinking, *nobody like Bobby Lee Pratt for warming up the crowd.*

The young gardener pointed toward the entrance and said, 'There he comes now.'

She turned to look. Pratt was coming across the porte-cochère with his hand under the elbow of a tall, handsome woman who walked with a self-confident air. Pratt saw Sarah's nod of recognition and strode toward her with a gleaming smile. So big and all-over-blue, he looked like a uniformed tsunami ready to sweep her across the beige-pebbled grounds that surrounded this elegant building. Sarah got ready to fend off – they were not back in the day and it wouldn't do for the lead detective to be lifted and twirled by the meaty ol' boy from West Virginia. She settled her jacket with a quick shrug and stood tall.

But she relaxed as she saw him stifle his grin. Bobby Lee Pratt had never been the clueless hick it pleased him to imper-sonate, and they had stayed in touch during his years of teaching wannabe law officers down on Kolb Road. He had even treated her once to the standard tour of the training school, with gunshots and lunch. So he knew she had been over plenty of jumps herself and advanced several pay grades, including the big move to detective, in the thirteen years since he'd been her field training officer. He squared up in front of her and said, 'Detective Burke, good morning.'

'Good to see you, Officer Pratt. What have we got here?'

Waving a magisterial hand toward the capable-looking woman beside him, he announced, 'This here's Letitia

Broderick, the manager of this fine senior living establishment.'

She was a bottle-blonde dressed in Business Impermeable, a copper-toned faux-suede jacket over a beige sheath that looked guaranteed to have no natural fibers. Exuding confidence on the gleaming asphalt of her domain, she re-set the tone of the morning. Her face said, *Time I got this mess squared away.*

'I've told her,' Bobby said, 'that you're here to help us sort this out.'

'Sorry for your troubles, Letitia,' Sarah said. She put out her hand. Letitia, instead of shaking, put an elegantly embossed card in it.

'My card has all my numbers,' she said. 'Call me any time, I'm always on duty.'

'Here's mine and I'm always available too,' Sarah said. 'Although you do have to go through this headquarters number to find me, I'm afraid. Do you know why these people attacked your van?'

Letitia looked dubiously at the vehicles and uniforms clustered around her entrance. 'No, I certainly don't. And if you'll excuse me for a moment, I have to find out – why's Millicent sitting over there on the bench all by herself?' She looked at Henry. 'Who brought her out here?'

'Tammy did. She's right over there in the—'

'Here I am, coming right now!' the uniformed aide who'd been weeping when Sarah arrived came running. She had cleaned up a little but her face was still ashen and strained. 'I was just in the—' She waved apologetically toward the bathroom as she pulled up in front of Letitia, who regarded her stone-faced.

'You know Millicent can't be left alone anymore,' she said, quiet and fierce. 'And it's getting hot. Get her inside right away.'

'I know. I will. She just wanted to know about the noise so I came over to see—' Letitia continued to look at her coldly and she bolted again, to Millicent's side.

Abandoning her finger-counting, Millicent looked up and said, 'What's going on, Tammy?'

'Nothing to worry about,' Tammy said, 'the van driver made a little boo-boo, that's all. He ran right into the garage door, can you believe it?'

'Sure I believe it. You can't get good help anymore, everybody knows that.' She shrugged irritably. 'I'm getting hot.'

'Well, I have a magic fix for that,' Tammy said. 'I'll take you inside, whaddya say?'

'I'm feeling too weak to walk,' Millicent said. 'You'd better fetch a chair.'

'Oh, come on, you need to walk, here we go, we'll work up an appetite for lunch.' Overriding the whining objections of her patient, she made small petting gestures and cooing noises till she got Millicent up on her feet and moving toward the entrance.

The manager watched them get into the shade before she turned her purposeful gaze on Sarah and asked, 'Detective, how soon can you get this mess cleared out of here?'

'Well, Letitia, do you know who killed your driver?'

'No, of course not.'

'Then I'm afraid we must investigate his death, and the first part of that process starts right here, right now. So tell me, what's the biggest problem that gives you?'

'My biggest concern is to maintain peace and quiet,' Letitia said. 'I'm very worried about all this noise and confusion. Our clients are here to rest.'

'I understand,' Sarah said. But looking past Letitia she saw the crime scene crew pull in and park their truck and three cars. Half a dozen people began pulling their tools out and asking questions, looking around, impatient to start.

Sarah gestured toward them and said, 'Right now I need to get this forensic team started while the evidence is still fresh – and then you and I can go inside and talk. Before I let them in the van, though, are you ready to step inside and identify the victim for me? Please don't touch anything – and I should warn you, this won't be pleasant.'

'Don't worry about that,' Letitia said impatiently. 'I've pretty well seen everything in this job. But will you please emphasize to all these people how important it is to keep their voices down? Serenity is what we sell here.'

She turned toward the façade of her classy facility, regarded the van still haplessly impaled in it, and sighed. 'God, what a mess.'

Sarah lifted the crime scene tape and Letitia ducked under it. Facing the van, she squared her shoulders and took three decisive steps toward the side door. Sarah pressed the latch and slid the big door open. The two steps slid out from under the chassis, Letitia climbed them, stepped into the vehicle and turned toward the driver's seat.

Then she began to scream.

TWO

Monday

Getting her out wasn't easy – Letitia was a tall, strong woman, and rigid with shock. But Pratt got her right arm looped over his shoulders while Bogey, a head shorter, managed to keep breathing somehow until his stoic cop's face emerged from Letitia's left armpit. Somehow, the two cops adjusted their different heights in order to work as the manager's crutches.

Sarah took hold of both her hands and walked backwards out of the company shuttle saying quietly, 'Look at me, Letitia, look at me now,' assuring her it was going to be all right, they would stay right with her and here – 'just here, do you see it?' – is the first step down.

The crime scene crew, who really had seen it all, set up the legs on a gurney without being asked, and Gloria, the light-hearted photographer who usually floated above the fray, silently reached around Sarah to help hoist Letitia onto her ride. Then the scientists went back to unloading their stuff while the three law officers wheeled the manager toward her front door.

As soon as they got her into the shade of the porte-cochère she began to revive. She caused more trouble then, trying to sit up, protesting that she was *all right now*, she'd be *fine*. But Pratt, who under all his vamping was a sublimely pragmatic street cop, just pushed her flat, saying, 'Lie still, we got no sides on this thing,' and they rolled on.

Once inside the building, Sarah left Letitia with the two policemen and hurried out to her crime scene crew. They had started without a briefing since, as Gloria said, 'Our uncanny instincts told us to start with the guy whose eyes were leaking blood.'

Six feet tall and solid, an ex-basketball scholarship jock

from UCLA, Gloria had swallowed the disappointment of not making the Olympic team and toughed out a work/study program to get a degree as a criminalist. Once out of sweat-pants, she'd 'decided to *spruce up*,' she said – dyed her hair copper to match her skin and poured her streamlined body into the tightest pants she could zip up. Some of the Tucson crew still thought she was 'kind of off the wall'; Sarah appreciated her bounce and her admirable work ethic.

Sarah climbed aboard with the three scientists and scrolled through her notes to give them a run-down on the chase and shooting that preceded the scene they were working on.

'So there's not much doubt about cause of death.' She looked around the charnel house the front of the van had become. 'We're looking for reasons. A carload of bandits thought there was something on this van worth killing for. I haven't seen anything that precious so far, so anything out of the ordinary . . .' She paused, looked around the blood-smeared massacre confronting them and shrugged. 'Well . . .'

'Gotcha.' Gloria swept her south-LA deadpan around the gore. 'If we see any trolls we'll call you right away.'

'Can't say we don't have plenty to work with,' Lois muttered, and the three techies went after it, Gloria shooting pictures, Lois lifting latent fingerprints and Sandy taking swabs for DNA tests.

They paused only to dicker over spaces. Sarah stood wher-ever they nudged her to, doing her best to see everything while she stayed out of their way. She did another complete three-sixty-degree inspection and shot some pictures on her own phone. The four of them worked on, uncomplaining, as the crowded space got hotter and the smell got worse.

After half an hour she told the crew, 'I'm going back in to talk to that manager now, and Bogey can take his turn in here to get a look at this.'

Gloria paused from aiming her digital flashes. 'You mean you brought along this Bogey I been hearing about? The one they say bagged all them gang-bangers single-handed?'

'Yup.'

'Well, why didn't you say so? Ooh, now I'm excited! OK if I pat his butt?'

'You might want to hold off,' Sarah said, 'until you've watched a few of his moves.'

'Now why would I need to do that,' Gloria said, swinging her camera back to the streaks on the shattered windshield, 'when I got a good buddy like you whose nose for fake heroes is legendary?'

'Even for more of that flattery I can't tell you what I don't know,' Sarah said, 'So far, he's been quiet and polite.'

'Aw shee-ee.' This time Gloria actually lowered the camera. 'A well-behaved detective? Girl, I got no previous experience that enables me to deal with *that*.' She climbed into a second-row seat to try some overhead views. 'Present company excepted, of course.'

'Uh-huh,' Sarah said. 'Take your best shot.' She stepped out of the grotesque scene in the van into a sparkling bright morning and stood still a moment, enjoying a tunnel vision view of the perfectly groomed entrance across the parking lot. *If I don't turn my head*, she thought, *this still looks like a wonderful place to retire to.*

Then she pivoted forty-five degrees and walked through a noisy, confusing snarl of TPD vehicles and forensic equipment, to where Bogey stood with digital devices in both hands. He was still interrogating the tape-stringing street patrolmen who had been first responders, recording their answers and taking pictures of the scene.

She asked him, 'Anybody over here know what this is all about?'

'Not a clue,' Bogey said. He had filled out the printed incident forms he carried in the car, entered their names and badge numbers along with the few facts he'd been able to elicit – partial plate numbers of the attackers' car, and fragments of shouted threats.

Relaxed now that the next layers of law enforcement had taken the situation out of their hands, the street cops were signing off on their comments before going back on patrol. They knew they would probably be called on later to repeat the few facts they could recall about today's event, and the more experienced ones had already commented that none of their evidence would be enough to identify the killers or

provide a motive for the driver's murder. Their careful work
this morning might never be brought to court or even be
discussed again. But the street patrolmen were cheerful – they
had done their part well, none of them had been hurt, and the
incident had made the shift go faster.

'Your turn in the van, Bogey,' Sarah said. 'Take your
time. When you're done there, come and find me inside – I'll
be talking to the manager.'

Feeling sweat begin to trickle down her sides, she headed
back to the lobby at a moderate pace. The thermometer outside
the heavy front door of Fairweather Farms read ninety-one.
And it isn't even noon yet. What's happened to Fall?

The building was cool and dim inside. A few couples moved
quietly about, mostly elderly people at some stage of debility,
being helped by younger, spryer people in Fairweather Farms
uniforms. Other clients walked on their own, some quite brisk,
others with canes or walkers. They all looked engaged and
intent, like a mid-morning crowd anywhere, but slower. Posters
and kiosks offered schedules of activities, tennis and swim-
ming, reading and quilting, card games and cooking classes
and trips.

The quiet busyness of life here had already absorbed the
noisy interruption of the wrecked van, formed a kind of mental
crust around it and gone flowing on like a stream around a
boulder. Whatever the problem was, these faces said, somebody
else would have to deal with it.

A helpful stranger pointed the way to Letitia's office. It was
quietly elegant with wood-paneled walls hung with industrial-
strength art. Letitia sat behind her big clean desk with her
door open, trim and collected as if she had never had hysterics
at the sight of her company van turned into an abattoir.

Clearly, she was a trooper who had earned the manager's
badge she wore so proudly. It seemed to be her policy to
encourage chatty visiting, and she was a wizard at remembering
the names of all her drop-ins. A woman in tight ginger curls,
carrying a toy poodle that matched her hair, was asking about
the relative merits of different bridge clubs as Sarah approached.
When Letitia had explained the different skill levels of the
players, the poodle carrier walked away and a bejeweled

woman stepped up to ask an anxious question about this even-
ing's Trivial Pursuit game. No, Letitia assured her, she would
not be too slow and hold everybody up. 'Listen, Angela, don't
you worry about that! We're just one big happy family here.'
A warm chuckle, and then, 'Nobody's in a hurry, we all take
our time and enjoy each other's company.'

Letitia was good at this, she made everything seem easy
and nice, with her warm voice and kindly, confident tone.
Then she turned her head and saw Sarah, and for a few seconds
the façade seemed about to crumble. There was a flush of
embarrassment and a sharp little intake of breath. But the
trooper recovered fast.

'Ah, there you are,' she said. 'Come in. Sit down, won't
you?' Flustered, but going for cordial, her stock in trade. 'You
must think,' she shook her chic hairdo and delivered an ironic
shrug, 'that I'm some kind of a weenie.'

'Not at all,' Sarah said. 'I'm always glad to be reminded
that most people don't have the hard shell we have to grow
in homicide.'

'Well, how kind you are. It was just . . . seeing poor Ricky
like that—' She shuddered. 'I always say I deal with everything
in my job, but I guess . . . compared to you . . . I really lead
a pretty sheltered life, don't I?'

'I certainly hope so. Sheltering is what we get paid to do.
And we'll hope to help you get back to that routine soon, but
first I have to ask a lot of questions. Are you able to start
now?'

'You bet. Let me just close this door.' She pulled it shut
quietly enough, but it seemed to be an agreed-upon signal –
the constant flow of visitors stopped, nobody knocked. 'I don't
know if I can help much, though – I'm just as mystified by
this crazy attack as everybody else,' she said as she sat down
again.

'But you can tell us a lot. You know the people here and
we don't.'

'Well, sure – and I think it's good to talk about it right away
while our memories are fresh. Get everything you need to
know out in the open so we can all *move on*.' Her mind seemed
to work that way, entirely in positive terms. Her determined

cheeriness seemed a little disingenuous, but it was good to see she wasn't going directly on the defensive as so many witnesses did.

Her driver's name was Enrique Lopez. He was part of the large well-established Hispanic minority in Tucson, and had worked for Fairweather Farms for six months, Letitia said, 'almost as long as we've been open.'

'Is that all? You seem remarkably settled into your routines,' Sarah said, 'for only being open half a year.'

'Oh, well, we're part of a chain, you know—'

'No, I didn't. You have other places in Arizona?'

'Four others right here in Tucson. And half a dozen in Phoenix.' She handed over a card with names and addresses. 'So that makes it easier. The operations aren't identical, but we share a good many features – we're senior living facilities, we don't do nursing care. Our purchasing and accounting is done at the corporate level, and it's not unusual for personnel to move from one installation to another.'

'Did you?

'Yes. I was assistant manager at Hanging Gardens in Phoenix for three years – that's a bigger place, twice the size of this one – and then I worked as catering manager for almost a year at the Sheffield House across town, so that I could be available to help with questions while this place was being built.'

'So you already had this job lined up while you did that.'

'Exactly. And you see, by having my hand in the mix from the beginning, I pretty much had my systems in place before we opened.'

'Interesting,' Sarah said. It wasn't, particularly, but Letitia's brisk responses seemed to demand that reaction. 'You don't use surnames here much?'

'Hardly ever. Clients don't either – we all use first names.'

'Except Mr Ames?'

'Well, he said he was accustomed to more formality, so of course we accommodated him.'

'I'd like to talk to Mr Ames. Will you set that up for me?'

'Mmm . . . that's not going to be easy. Mr Ames is not very outgoing.'

'Oh? Well, if you don't want to introduce us, I'll just knock on his door and go in. I'm not shy.'

'Oh, please.' She made a pleading gesture. 'I'll do it. Just don't be surprised if he's a little rude.'

'I interview a lot of murderers, Letitia; I think I can handle the disappointment if Mr Ames doesn't like me.'

'I suppose you can. You find us all a little amusing, don't you?'

'No. I just want you to understand that I'm a licensed criminal investigator, and the fact that I'm a woman is irrelevant.'

'I hear you. I'll check his schedule for medical appointments. Aside from those of course he'll be available – I'll let you know.'

'Good. He doesn't allow you to use his first name?'

'Says he's used to formality so he needs it to be comfortable.' She shrugged. 'Go figure. Most people like it that we're kind of easy-going and homey.'

'But Enrique was too hard to say?'

'What? Oh, you mean the nickname. Yes, some of the staff had a hard time figuring out how to say it, they started calling him Ricky and he didn't object so I just . . . went along with it.'

'I see. I'll need all Enrique's stats, of course, full name, age, social security, health records, driver's license . . .'

'Well . . . of course. But most of that information is kept in the accounting office in Phoenix, so I'll need some time.'

'I don't understand. Wasn't he hired here?'

'Umm . . . yes.'

'And you must train and supervise here, right?'

'Of course.'

'So you must keep some employee records here?'

'No. We have one bookkeeper here, who keeps daily records and submits a daily report – but even that office is closed today because Amanda had to take a personal day. But she'll be here tomorrow and I'll have her put in a request for Ricky's stats first thing.'

'You can't just pick up the phone and get the information?'

'It doesn't quite work that way. It's a big company and . . . But Amanda should be able to get all those records by, oh, what's today? It's Monday, isn't it? So I should think . . . if she puts in a request tomorrow . . . that we can have everything you need by close of business on Friday.'

'Letitia, you don't understand – this is homicide, we don't wait for information.' She waved the card Letitia had given her. 'Which one of these numbers is headquarters? I'll call myself and get what I need.'

'Please don't do that,' Letitia said quickly. 'Just give me a couple of hours. I'll call and explain the circumstances, and I'm sure if I explain it's police protocol I can get all the data you need right away.'

'Well . . .' Sarah looked at her watch. 'It's lunchtime, so . . . Two hours after lunch is three o'clock – can you get it by then?'

Letitia looked haggard for a moment but then summoned a cheery smile. 'Sure. These people are demon record-keepers up there, they're always after me for faster replies. So now I'll ask *them* to show *me* some moves.'

The phone rang on her desk. She raised her eyebrows, surprised by the interruption. Then she lifted it and answered brightly, 'Letitia!' The murmur on the other end sounded apologetic. But Letitia, still smiling, said, 'Fine!' and got up and opened the door.

Bogey stood erect in the doorway with his neutral expression facing into Letitia's high beams. There was a moment of mutual puzzlement until Letitia trilled, 'Hello, Officer.' She evidently had no memory of his time as her left-hand crutch, helping her out of the van.

Bogey nodded, muttered, 'Ma'am,' turned ten degrees toward Sarah and said, 'there's something in the van I thought you might want to see.'

'Oh?' Sarah looked at Letitia, whose smile had begun to urge, *Let's do some questions with this officer.*

'Before they tow it away,' Bogey said. His left eyebrow twitched.

'Right,' Sarah said, getting up, moving to the door. 'See you at three, then, Letitia.'

They didn't say a word as they padded softly along the quiet hall toward the entrance. Their silence made it easy to hear the woman in tan scrubs on the far side of the lobby – it was Tammy, wasn't it? – still plaintive, not entirely recovered from getting sick outdoors. She was asking another woman in the same uniform, 'Patsy, do you know what's happened to Amanda?'

'Why, isn't she in her office?'

'No, and it's strange – I talked to her in there before I took Millicent out for her walk and she said that I should come see her at lunchtime, that she had something funny to tell me. But now the light's out and her door's locked.'

The two officers marched silently on to the exit. But as soon as the front door closed behind them, Sarah turned in the blazing sunshine and told Bogey softly, 'That's really quite interesting, what that woman just said.'

'Is it? Can you tell me in the van? Because the tow could get here any minute, and the driver's side door of this van is also very interesting.'

THREE

Monday

The coroner and his assistant had the body bagged and were bringing it out of the van on a gurney. They said they didn't need any help, so Sarah and Bogey stood aside as the forensics team maneuvered it down the steps. While they waited, Sarah told Bogey what was interesting about the bookkeeper named Amanda.

'According to Letitia she's off today, but Tammy just said she was at work this morning. We need to figure out what's going on with Amanda.' Bogey listened respectfully, but his eyes kept wandering up the steps.

As soon as the gurney was out of the way they climbed back inside. The three techs were just finishing up, Lois and Sandy packing samples, Gloria taking a few last pictures of the empty driver's seat, working fast and, as usual, talking a blue streak.

'This is kind of like one of those old Agatha Christie mysteries, isn't it?' she asked, blazing away. 'Big shoot-out at the old folks' home – you don't see that every day, do you?'

She had evidently decided the new guy was worth a second look, she wanted to get a little chat going with Bogey. Ordinarily Sarah would have helped. She sympathized with Gloria's often-expressed need to 'get a little action going in this cowboy town.' But right now she wanted to hear what Bogey thought was interesting about the driver's side door of the van, and Delaney had just texted that the tow was on its way. Sarah knew the tow yard got paid by the trip, not the hour, which meant the driver would be hell-bent to hook up and haul away. So she just said, 'For sure,' and Gloria's opening gambit went nowhere.

Sarah began helping Lois move DNA swabs out to her car, and Bogey asked Sandy, 'Can I help you?'

Lois paused in the middle of muscling boxes and said, 'Sarah, did you hear what the Doc said about the driver's clothes?'

'What? No,' Sarah said. 'Is that what's in the bag? Let me see.'

'No, wait.' Lois moved the big paper bag farther out of reach. 'Just listen a minute. He said he wasn't going to strip the body here, said he'd send me the clothes to check after the autopsy. So you can check them at the lab later, OK? But this' – she held up the paper bag, already showing blood stains – 'is the jacket that was hanging over the back of the driver's seat. Do you want to check it before I take it to the lab with my stuff?'

'Yes. Wait, I need gloves.' She patted her jacket pockets. She'd discarded the ones she'd worn earlier when she went inside to talk to Letitia. 'Damn. Gotta get some from the car.'

'Here,' Bogey said. He handed her a pair and gloved up himself. He held the bag open and she pulled out the brown windbreaker. 'Must belong to the driver.'

'Probably,' Sarah said. Holding it carefully to avoid a sticky spot on the left breast, she looked on the front pocket. 'No, I guess not – the name on the pocket is . . . uh . . . DeShawn.' She looked around, saw Henry resetting a cactus nearby, and called across the yard, 'Henry, is there somebody working here named DeShawn?'

'Sure,' Henry said. 'He's the usual driver.'

'What?' Puzzled, she looked at Bogey and shook her head. 'Henry, will you come over here for a minute, please?'

Henry frowned, sighed, stuck his shovel upright in the loose dirt and walked across the yard to the van. When he stood by the steps looking up at her, she said, 'What do you mean, the usual driver?'

'Just what I said.' He shrugged. 'DeShawn Williams is the maintenance man who usually drives this van.'

'Why didn't he drive it today?'

'Well, I'd better not say much about it or it'll turn out to be my fault,' Henry said, aggrieved about some slight she didn't understand, 'but I *heard* he was in an accident.'

'An accident? Here? Before this one with the van?'

'Not here. Sometime last night, off-duty, in his own old

rattletrap. He got T-boned in an intersection down on Broadway. He's in St. Mary's Hospital with many broken bones and in a coma, according to my friend who's an orderly there.'

'Um . . . Sarah?' Bogey said, 'we can talk about this after the van's gone, but right now . . .'

'You're right. That tow is always late except when you want it to be, isn't it?' Another shrug; Bogey didn't know. She dropped the jacket back into the paper bag and told Lois, 'I think this does belong with your crime scene stuff, but I'll get it back to you later. I need to ask Letitia about this usual driver named DeShawn.'

'Suits me,' Lois said, and lugged the last of her boxes out to her car.

Sarah turned to the gardener and said, 'Thanks, Henry, that's all for now.'

Henry shrugged again and went back to his damaged plants, looking seriously ticked off. *Working up a real grudge about something*, Sarah thought as she watched him go, *but I don't have time for his snit today.*

'OK,' she said when she and Bogey stood, alone together at last, facing the gore, 'now will you show me what's so fascinating about the driver's side door?'

'The driver's window was open,' he said, 'even though it's a hundred degrees outside and the A/C was turned on high.'

'I know,' Sarah said, 'that was number one on my list too. We can't ask the driver why he opened the window in this weather, but maybe Mr Ames will know something?'

'Mr Ames didn't sound very helpful.'

'True. But I want to talk to him anyway. I've asked Letitia to set it up for me. Anything else?'

'Yes. I took a walk around the outside of the van with O'Neill and his partner while I was talking to them. They look at cars all day; they're good at spotting things. There are seven bullet holes in this van, that we've found so far. Three in the rear – probably lodged in the chassis somewhere. And two above the windshield, see? Which is puzzling, since they're inside. But I was waiting to ask Banjo—'

Bogey pointed with gloved fingers at the two holes above the windshield.

'From the way the metal's bent, I'm sure you're right, this is an entry hole. The shooters must have managed to get alongside at one point and the bullets must have come in through the open driver's side window, hit this spot above the windshield and buried themselves in the insulation. When we get back outside I'll show you that the metal outer layer is undisturbed. You can see that all the shots that hit the van very consistently buried themselves in the vehicle. They had power enough to penetrate one layer of metal, but not enough to go through two.'

'So we've still got all the bullets, right here in the vehicle. Now if we could find a casing . . .'

'I've got one.' He pulled a baggie out of an inside pocket. 'Henry found it in the driveway and gave it to me.'

Sarah held it up in the bright sunlight, squinting at the rim, and read, '"223 Rem." OK, twenty-two caliber, and it looks like,' she squinted again, 'made by PMC.' She added it to the satchel of evidence she was saving for Firearms and Toolmarks.

'Right. But. On the outside of the driver's side door, there are two more fresh bullet holes that don't quite match the others in size and shape. That's what I wanted to show you. Shall we step out and look?'

When they stood together on the hot asphalt outside the driver's door, he said, 'Don't you agree? These entry holes are almost a match, but a little smaller, and see how the metal's heaped up on one side? You think maybe the same ammo but the second shooter had a different gun?'

'Or the same gun and ammo with a different angle of entry? Fired from a greater distance?'

'I suppose it doesn't make much difference, they're still in the door and they didn't kill anybody.'

'Well, it doesn't make much difference to us, but it might matter a lot to lawyers sometime in the future. If we get lucky enough to catch this pair of hoodlums and they want to prove both shooters are guilty of murder . . . So let's take some pictures of these entry holes, and we'll give those to Banjo too.'

She was pleased with him and said so. 'Very good detective work, Bogey. It'll take an expert to confirm it – to my eye these look about the same as the ones in back of the van. What's amazing,' Sarah said as they climbed back in the van, 'is that it matches what the coroner said – apparently the driver died from just that one lucky shot through the head that came in through the open window. He had no other wounds that Cameron could find.'

'The ballistics guy hasn't looked at this yet, has he?'

'No. I got a message from Delaney on my phone – Banjo heard the crime scene was inside the company shuttle and said there was no use trying to dig out ammo in a space as crowded as this one was going to be. Said he'd rather do his chores down at the impound yard tomorrow after the other techs were done.'

'Ah. You think he'd let me keep him company if I promise not to touch anything?'

'We can ask him – he's a reasonable guy.'

'His name is Banjo? Really?'

'It's a nickname. He moonlights in a bluegrass band. Don't worry – he's very good at his job. And I expect he'll be glad to let you watch – he enjoys showing off his skills.'

'Good. How do I—'

'I'll call him and set it up for you. Let's see, what time is it? I'm due back in Letitia's office soon to get the stats on Ricky. You want to come along? Shall we take another look at that jacket? I'm not sure I'm ready to give it to Letitia, but I know I don't want it to go down to the impound yard.'

'Sure.' He pulled the brown jacket out of the bag and held it up. 'It's got bloodstains all over the front but I don't see any holes. I wonder why it was even along in the van? Surely the driver didn't need a jacket in this weather.' As he turned it over his arm, he said, 'There's something heavy in that inside pocket – shall I see what it is?'

'Sure.' She stepped out and put her day pack on the gravel by the bottom step, checking that all the snaps were closed, getting ready to go. She heard the sound of the zipper as he opened the pocket. Then Bogey said, 'Oh!' And after a moment, 'Sarah, come back.'

When she stepped back up he was sitting in one of the seats with the jacket heaped in front of him. 'Close the door,' he said.

She slid the big door closed, stepped closer, said, 'What?'

Bogey lifted the jacket and showed her a banded pile of twenty-dollar bills. And another. And then two more.

The usual driver had a tidy pile of cash in his coat.

'The first thing we have to do is protect ourselves,' Sarah said, ten minutes later. 'Damn lucky we happened to be together when we found this money. Hang on, I'm calling the boss.'

Delaney's first question was, 'How much?'

'Eighty-four hundred dollars.'

'Oh. So not a major bank heist.'

'But quite a bit more than pocket change for a maintenance man.'

'And enough to interest those shooters if they come back around.'

'That's what I'm thinking. Any word on the chase?'

'We got an all-points out, everybody's looking. They went to ground fast. No trace of an old Dodge Ram pickup with the license numbers your gardener saw.'

'And here we sit with the money they must be after.'

'Anybody see it but the two of you?'

'No.'

'Keep it that way. Put the money back in the jacket pocket where you found it, zip it up and wait. Hang on a minute till I see who's around to send . . . yeah, Ray and Ollie can come and collect it.' Thumps and voices, then he was back. 'OK, they're on their way with a receipt which you will all sign before they take the cash. You got that?'

'Sure. But listen, boss, I expect that tow truck to be turning in here any minute, and you know how they are about not wanting to wait—'

'Sarah, listen to me. If that tow truck driver gets there before our guys, tell him you just found what looks like a pipe bomb and you're waiting for the disposal guys to come and disable it, so he should stay back in the driveway and wait until the experts handle this thing.'

'OK. Good idea.' *Brilliant, actually.*

'How wrecked is that vehicle, can you lock it?'

'Uh . . . I suppose so.'

'Lock the doors and don't open for anybody till our guys arrive. Text me when they get there. Stay frosty, the guys are on their way.'

'Ten-four,' she said, falling back on the old code because it sounded sufficiently laconic. *Don't I always stay frosty?*

She told Bogey, 'Delaney says lock up. This vehicle's got the new system, but we still need the keys. Have you got them?'

'No. You mean you don't?' He looked at the empty ignition switch. 'Who else would have – maybe Henry?' He looked across the yard to where the gardener had been replanting a cactus. The spade stood alone, stuck in the dirt near the sprawled plant. 'He must have gone to coffee. Shall I go find him?'

'No! We're sticking together till this money's gone. I'll phone Letitia.' She asked Letitia to send Henry out with the keys. 'Right away, please,' she said, making it urgent but not, of course, panicked – Detective Sarah Burke did not do panic.

She dithered, though. It was not possible to pace in the small space afforded by the Econoline, but she sat down and got up repeatedly and looked at her watch a dozen times in ten minutes. But then, oh damn, the tow was at the gate – but before she could jump out and head him off he was cut off by one of their old maroon unmarked Crown Vics, making a snappy turn through the open gates alongside the tow truck. Two sets of screeching tires, and there was Ollie's genial grin showing in the Ford's driver's side window.

Ray jumped out of the passenger side and hopped on the running board of the banged-up tow truck, in a padded vest and gloves and some kind of crash helmet, looking like Mad-Dog Raimundo, Taker of Crazy Risks. Sarah watched as he gave the driver a quick-and-dirty about the possible pipe bomb. She watched him urge the driver to wait there while he and his partner got this murderous little nuisance cleared away, and saw the driver's expression change from whaddya-want to whatever-you-say. Ray jumped off the tow truck and back into the department Ford wearing his Mad Dog smirk.

But now here – oh rats, rats! Here came Henry trotting with

the keys – too late, wrecking the story! – but Bogey erupted out of their ruined vehicle and ran to him, waving his arms in a *wait* gesture. He grabbed the keys and said something sharp that sent Henry sprinting in alarm back to the entrance of Fairweather Farms. It was amazing how fast they all became shameless liars in support of the imaginary pipe bomb, and how well it was working.

Ollie pulled their vehicle up tight against the crime scene tape and the two detectives sprang out of the car. Ray carried a first-aid kit he'd grabbed off the wall by his workstation, with a big red 'Caution' sign he must have pulled out of storage and plastered on the side during the trip. Sarah slid back the side door and let them in just ahead of Bogey, who waved the keys over his head, then lowered them and said, 'Do we still need these?'

'Sure,' Sarah said, 'lock up while we count. Then we'll give them to the tow truck driver when we turn the rig over to him. Ollie, you got the receipt?' They all signed and then settled down to the counting job. When they finished they put the money and receipt back in the pocket of the brown windbreaker, zipped it up and dropped it into the fresh evidence bag that Ray held open. He closed it, stapled it, attached a label with the date and time and they all initialed that.

'There, by God, that ought to secure the chain of evidence,' Ray said, and put it in the trunk of his car.

As he climbed out of the van, Ollie said, 'All due respect, but isn't this kind of a big whoop to raise over such a puny amount of cash?'

'If it weren't for the chase I'd agree with you,' Sarah said. 'But one man is dead and two or more shooters are on the run, so . . .' She turned her hands over. 'We don't know yet what the connection is to the shooting, but there has to be one. How else do these few dollars get so much juice?'

FOUR

'Well, here you go,' Letitia said, handing over a Manila folder, 'the whole nine yards on Ricky Lopez.'

'Let's see. Birth certificate, social security. Medicaid? You don't pay a living wage?'

'We pay about ten percent above average for these jobs. But Ricky had a live-in mother and there's a hoard of needy relatives who move in and out, so he was on food stamps and AHCCCS.'

'I see. Tip declaration – they still pay taxes on their tips?'

'Right. Banks get bailed out but service personnel pay taxes on tips. We don't stand over them and count the change, needless to say.'

'Uh-huh.'

'Still makes you mad, I see. Me too. But the law's the law. Look, they even faxed me a copy of his birth certificate,' Letitia said. '*That* was a surprise.'

'Because he was born in Pima County?' Sarah said, looking at the document. 'You thought he was an immigrant?'

'No, I knew he was local,' she said. 'But his age – forty-two! I thought he was somewhere in his mid-fifties. I wonder why he looked so old?'

'You didn't get all the facts about him when you hired him?'

'I didn't hire him. When the time comes to staff a new place the company sends a professional team, they notify the local unemployment office and run ads on social media, and in about a week they hire the whole crew, check the records and start the training – hold classes on company policies and benefits, issue uniforms, put them all on a bus and tour a couple of our other facilities. Meanwhile I do three days' intensive brief of department heads and then *they* start training staff.'

'It sounds very efficient.'

'It is. Premium Eldercare has been building these places for over twenty years and they've pretty well smoothed out the rough spots.'

'OK. So where's his driver's license?'

'Here.' Frowning, Letitia pulled a printed copy out of a basket by her elbow and laid it on top of the pile. *Why does she look so distraught?*

Sarah studied the picture, briefly thinking, *He did have a nice face.* She scanned the rest of the picture for a few seconds, then sat up suddenly and stared at Letitia. 'Did you know his driver's license had expired?'

'Of course not. I'd never have sent him out in the van if I knew.'

'But you knew it this morning when we talked, didn't you?' Sarah said, remembering, getting angry. 'That's why you pulled that silly caper about Amanda having the day off. She was here in the morning, wasn't she? And you sent her somewhere out of my sight.'

'I thought I just needed a little time to get to the bottom of the license situation,' Letitia protested. 'I told her there must be an extension on file, a temporary license to carry while he corrected some problem. When I asked Ricky, he told me he was fine to drive. I said Ricky would never play a trick like this on me, there must be something in his wallet – have you found that, by the way?'

'No. Usually we look for that early on, but there was so much blood, and the van was heating up fast – so we said we'll get it out of his pants when we get them from the coroner. But see here, Letitia, this is a homicide investigation, serious business. It's a crime to lie to the police in a homicide case, an obstruction of justice!'

Which was perfectly true and also total bullshit, Sarah thought, watching sweat break out on the manager's upper lip. *If I had a dollar for every lie I've listened to in this job I could retire.*

But she was seriously annoyed that Letitia had caused her to waste time, trying to find out why Amanda came and went in her job. Angry at herself too, for letting Letitia think, even for a few hours, that a police investigation could be manipulated.

'What else are you lying about?' she demanded. 'Did Ricky have a record? Is Lopez even his real name?'

'Yes, of course it is – Ricky was thoroughly checked out, like everybody else on the starting crew. He was a totally respectable citizen – his license only expired three weeks ago. He tried to renew it then, but he failed the eye exam. So he was saving up for new glasses, he intended to get them next payday and then renew the license.'

'Sounds like you knew all about this.'

'No! As soon as I heard about the accident, I told Amanda to call for Ricky's records, and that's how I found out about the license and his glasses. I should have checked properly before asking Ricky if he'd drive the van, but we were desperate for a driver. The next thing I knew I was getting chewed out by the Phoenix office for having a driver with an expired license.

'I told Amanda that someone must have known. And Amanda said that she bets Henry knows. Because she knew, we all knew, that Henry and Ricky were buddies. They worked together before, at one of our smaller Premium Eldercare places on the east side. So I called Henry in, and Amanda was right – Henry knew all about Ricky's license problem.'

Letitia looked at her ceiling light and took a breath. 'I was furious, of course. Henry's been my right-hand man here and I thought I could trust him with anything. I told him that and you know what he said?' Her eyes blazed indignation; she needed a scapegoat and had just fastened on one. 'He said, "You didn't ask me before you sent him out in the van, and once he was gone I thought you were better off not knowing." Is that a lame excuse or what?'

'So that's why Henry's in such a bad mood.'

'Yes. He hates being put in the wrong. Plus he's really devastated about Ricky getting killed. And even though it's illogical he blames DeShawn for not being in the van where he belonged.'

Sarah sat back, glanced at her notes to get reoriented, and said, 'What else can you tell me about Ricky as a person?

Was he good at his job? Did you like him? Why would anybody
want to kill him?'

'You bet I liked him – we all did.' Letitia's chin quivered
and she closed her eyes; when she opened them and tried to
go on her voice broke. 'It must be just a terrible mistake –
Ricky was a real sweetheart.'

Sarah waited a couple of heartbeats before she asked, 'Henry
called him a muffin; is that what he meant?'

'Yes. Ricky will be sorely missed around here. Not just by
the staff – all the guests depended on him too. He had the
perfect personality for a place like this.'

'Kind, you mean? Compassionate?'

'All of that. Ricky had . . . empathy, is that the word I want?
A special knack for dealing with this particular clientele.'

'You mean Fairweather Farms is different from the rest of
the chain?'

'A little bit, yeah. It was built for the top of the market,
has all the amenities and it's not cheap. It's designed for
quite successful people to retire to. These movers and
shakers get to a stage where they need some things managed
and they can afford it – so lucky, you might think. But
retirement for some people . . . it's kind of love/hate. This
may be hard to understand, but they're used to doing things
their own way, so sometimes getting helped makes them
grumpy.'

Tell me about it, Sarah thought, remembering her mother's
dour face at last night's dinner.

'And dissatisfaction can turn into depression in just the
blink of an eye.' Letitia was warming to her subject now. 'I
think of it as the bear in the nearby cave, always lurking,
ready to pounce.'

'But you're saying Ricky had special tricks to fend off the
bear?'

'Yeah – well, not tricks exactly – he just had a knack for
putting himself in other people's shoes, knowing what would
make them feel better.'

'Like what?'

'Oh . . . like one day here when Millicent's dementia was
worse than usual, and she kept saying she wasn't hungry,

Ricky wheeled her over to the dining room, saying, "Madge is making her chicken noodle soup today just for you, Millicent – she remembered how much you liked it before." And talking so sweet, you know, about Madge in the kitchen cutting up the mushrooms for the special soup, that by the time he was tucking that napkin on Millicent and spooning it into her we all wanted chicken noodle soup, and Madge was out in the kitchen telling the dishwasher she made this soup special for Millicent.'

'But she didn't . . .?'

'She makes it every Tuesday,' Letitia said. 'Rain or shine.'

Sarah's phone dinged. She saw it was Delaney and stepped out in the hall to pick it up. 'How's it going on the chase?' she asked him. 'Any sign of the shooters?'

'No, they must have holed up someplace. I've got all cars looking but – what?'

She had been making impatient sounds. 'There are some things about this crime scene that seem pretty odd. I think we've stumbled into something out of the ordinary here and we should talk about it.'

'Oh? OK, soon as you're done there, come in and talk to me. Listen . . . why I called? One of the autopsies scheduled for tomorrow got cancelled; the coroner can put your new victim in that slot if you or your backup can attend. What do you think?'

'Well, not much doubt about the cause of death, so I'm not in a hurry for his verdict,' Sarah said. 'But come to think of it, didn't Banjo say he'd like to take a look at that van tomorrow?'

'What? Yes, he wants to dig out those bullets before they get dusty, he said. What's that got to do with—'

'Tomorrow? You sure he said tomorrow?'

'Yes, he said tomorrow. Why do you care?'

'Well, see, Banjo already agreed to let Bogey observe—'

'What? Why would Bogey be watching Banjo? I don't get it.'

'Bogey says he had considerable experience with AR15s and their ammo in Iraq, and the holes in this van look familiar to him so he'd like to see the slugs that are in the driver's side door and figure out why their entry points don't look like the rest of the shots.'

'Since when do we need his opinion? Seems to me we've been getting along all right with whatever Banjo tells us.'

'Well, boss, maybe he just wants to show us he's got some extra expertise with high-powered ammo, nothing wrong with that, is there?' She felt her bile rising; why did everything have to be so freaking hard, always an argument? 'And if he and Banjo could give us a read on the guns and ammo while I was doing the autopsy,' she said, a little louder than necessary, 'maybe for a change we could show some speed here, get a skitch closer to nailing these crazy shooters who for all I know are still roaming around this neighborhood, perhaps close to me as we speak.'

Two seconds of silence were followed by a small cough, and then Delaney said, 'So is that a yes? You want to do the autopsy tomorrow?'

Back in Letitia's office, Bogey was saying, 'Your usual driver named DeShawn – one of the guys on the maintenance crew told me some of the staff call him "Romeo." What's that all about?'

'Well, DeShawn is very handsome, so I suppose . . .' She patted her hair thoughtfully. 'One of the problems to watch out for in a small operation like this one is that jealousies crop up . . . any little sign of approval or somebody getting extra attention . . .'

Bogey looked amused. 'They thought you liked DeShawn best?'

'If they did they made it up – I never show favoritism. But some of the clients, I think – he does know how to please the ladies.'

'Is he still in St. Mary's Hospital?' Sarah asked her.

'Oh, yes. For some time, I'm afraid.'

'Still in a coma?'

'Yes.'

'So in intensive care?

'Yes. Poor guy got clobbered last night by an old Jeep going fifty miles an hour through a red light. It was hit-and-run, and the driver got away. We're not having our best week here, automotive-wise.'

'For sure. I'll just keep checking till he wakes up. We're most anxious to talk to him.'

'I suppose. Although I don't suppose he can help you much, since he wasn't driving when these shooters attacked.'

'Well, but the money was in his jacket. Aren't you alarmed to find your driver carrying that much cash? Do you know why he was?'

'No. I suppose he might have been gambling and got lucky.'

'Do you really think that? Why would he bring his winnings to work with him?' Sarah gave her the look the squad called the Full Dubious, which usually turned even seasoned liars into babbling jerks.

Letitia just gave a blithe shrug and said, '*I* don't know. Why does anybody do anything?'

'Doesn't it seem more likely he was running a small cottage industry on the side? Maybe dealing a little pot to some of the guests?'

'Good heavens, no. Please don't go spreading that idea around – this company is very particular about image. What we sell here is care for a vulnerable segment of the population. They want peace and quiet! We take great care to guard our squeaky-clean reputation.'

'I'm sure you do, but now you have this van full of bullets and a dead driver, and we have to account for those, don't we?'

'Well.' She took a deep breath. 'Yes, I suppose we do.'

'So let's start over. Was DeShawn hired and trained with the rest of the crew; will they have all his stats in Phoenix too?'

'No to the first question, yes to the second. DeShawn's a replacement; I hired him myself when the original van driver quit to follow a girlfriend to New Mexico.' She held her hands up in an 'I surrender' gesture. 'Even great company policies can't always protect against private lives. But yes, I sent all DeShawn's stats to Phoenix as soon as he passed his ten-day probation period.'

'So you can get them back for me right away?'

'Yes.'

'How did you find DeShawn?'

'Luck. I had just listed my request at the unemployment office – a little reluctantly, you know, because they don't always get the sharpest knives in the drawer, but when needs must . . . and then DeShawn walked in off the street with a commercial driver's license and a letter from his last employer that said he was capable and trustworthy. Usually I'd say this is too good to be true so it must be false. But he had nice manners and the first two people who rode with him expressed total satisfaction so I put him on.'

'And you're still happy with that decision?'

'Yes. DeShawn has invalidated every cynical rule I ever heard about how careful you have to be with walk-ins. From day one he had a good attitude and did whatever I asked.'

'Which was what, besides driving the van?'

'He's on the Maintenance crew – not a glam job. Unclogging sinks and toilets, readjusting all the TV sets and thermostats that the guests constantly screw up and then complain don't work. Moving furniture, vacuuming. His hours in the van are probably the most fun he has at work.'

'And was he a good driver? Did he satisfy the guests?'

'Oh, indeed he did. Quiet and careful, helpful with boarding and getting off. Well-spoken young man who never gets lost and treats the rolling stock with respect – what more do you want? I already put him in for a merit raise as soon as he's completed his first six months.'

'Sounds like you're good at shaping up staff.'

'Well,' she squared her shoulders, pleased, 'I'm a good explainer, and I treat everybody with respect. I always say we're just one big happy family here.' Letitia gave a fierce little chuckle. 'And if that isn't true when they come to work, it by God is before many days have passed, or they don't stay here with me.'

'OK, you're cleared to tag along with Banjo Bailey tomorrow,' Sarah told Bogey as they drove away from Fairweather Farms. 'Meet him at the impound yard at eight-thirty. Wear old clothes, that place is not fancy.'

'Yeah, I know what salvage yards are like. My brother restores old Model T Fords, he's always scavenging for parts, and I go along sometimes to help him hunt. I suppose I'll find Banjo where I find the van, huh?'

'And he'll probably be the only one around with Prince Albert facial hair and a long white pigtail.' She looked at her watch. 'Let's do one more stop before we quit for the day. I'd like to get a look at that usual driver who carries unusual amounts of cash.'

They got back on I-10 and were soon parking in the lot at St. Mary's. 'I like the way Tucson's developing, don't you?' Bogey said. 'The outskirts grow and grow, but the core is still small and easy to reach.'

'My partner hates it,' Sarah said. 'He says they tore down all the old fun stuff and the replacements are square and uninteresting.'

'He was fond of some of the barrios, was he?' He cleared his throat and squared his shoulders. 'You got a room-mate with privileges too, huh?'

'Yes.' *Little do you know. My boyfriend, my mother and my niece, all in one house. Let's not go there just now.*

'I'm on my third try.' Bogey looked mildly embarrassed. 'But cops work such awful shifts, and now I'm finding out detectives are even worse, we never know when we'll be done. My roomie and me, we text each other all day and still mess up our dates.'

'And then stay home and have a real whopper of a fight, right? I had a husband for six years and that's how we handled the stress.' She was just chatting to establish comradery; actually, although he wasn't ugly, she couldn't imagine moving in with Bogey – didn't find him attractive, maybe because his hazel eyes grew colorless in some lights and made his face look expressionless. There was nothing wrong with his demeanor, though – after a day together in a bizarre crime scene she was ready to tell Delaney that his new detective had passed several stress tests. 'There's a parking spot,' she said, 'by the red pickup.' And then thought *he even puts up with my backseat driving* – a fault her own family had often complained about.

In the lobby Sarah asked for DeShawn Williams and was told he could not have visitors. She showed her badge and explained how little their mission resembled a visit. Presently they were standing beside a bed on which a comatose man lay almost completely swathed in bandages, one leg suspended from a wheeled device that hung from an overhead track. They were accompanied by the head nurse on the floor, a monumentally calm woman in scrubs and a hairnet whose name, Judy, seemed entirely wrong for her. She said DeShawn had been in and out of surgery twice since last night, had been critical for his first ten hours but was now upgraded to serious.

'He's improved a lot in the last couple of hours,' she said.

'But isn't this a long time for him to stay in a coma?'

'Well, that's induced. His surgeon won't let him wake up till sometime tomorrow, when the worst of the pain will have eased. He sustained several fractures and a massive concussion; he's got a lot of healing to do.'

'His collision was hit-and-run?'

'Yes. But luckily there were witnesses nearby, and the ambulance got him in here quickly. You want the name of the traffic officer?' She pulled it up at her station in the hall and handed the printout to Bogey because Sarah was already talking to traffic division, arranging to have a copy of the accident report faxed to her PC at headquarters.

When the nurse was called away they stood together looking down at the patient. He had been lucky in one respect; except for a scrape on his right eyebrow and cheekbone, his face was undamaged.

You might get a black eye, but nothing's broken above your shoulders. And you look as if that would matter a lot to you, Sarah thought. A light-skinned African-American, he wore his hair trimmed short and his beard clipped in an elaborate pattern that emphasized the handsome line of his jaw. His mustache was narrow and did the same favor for his full-lipped mouth.

Watching his peaceful drug-induced slumber, Sarah grew thoughtful. The much-maligned opioids that filled so many column-inches of daily newsprint with tales of calamity, at this moment were blessing DeShawn Williams with hours of peace in which to heal.

They talked about him, on their way back to headquarters.

'I can see why his fellow staffers called him Romeo,' she said. 'How much time, do you figure, does he spend every day in front of a mirror, grooming all that glamour?'

'Quite a bit. He really is pretty, isn't he? I bet he was teacher's pet all through school. It isn't getting him very far, though, is it? Driving a van in an old folks' home?'

'Well, it took him far enough this week to get upwards of eight thousand dollars in his pocket.'

'Kind of a lot for a rent boy, don't you think?'

'Yes,' Sarah said, thinking about the hard line of his jaw. 'Anyway, I'd be more inclined to connect this guy to today's shooters, wouldn't you?'

'Yes. And I'm pretty sure they're selling drugs, not sex. DeShawn's fancy whiskers wouldn't impress those bandits. Where do you suppose they got to, by the way? We don't seem to be any closer to catching them than we were this morning.'

'I mentioned that to our boss,' Sarah said, 'a time or two.'

'What did he say?'

'He doesn't like to be reminded. We're supposed to know all the hidey holes in this small accessible city that you like so much.'

'We never really know them all, do we? You going to the autopsy tomorrow?'

'Yes. But I don't expect many surprises there – the man had his brains blown out.'

'But maybe I can learn a thing or two if I get a good look at that van.' Turning into the skewed parking lot at South Stone, he asked, 'This your car?'

'Yes. Call my cell when you finish in the yard, will you?'

'The doc won't object to a phone call in the lab?'

'I'll turn it off in the lab – leave a message if I don't answer. We'll probably finish with the autopsy early, though, and if we do I'll go back to the senior living center and talk to the elusive Amanda. I need to see if I can get her to tell me anything about the little pot-smoking club I'm pretty sure DeShawn has been running there in his spare time.'

*   *   *

The house on Bentley Street smelled like beef and onions, but there was no cook in sight. It was Monday, which used to be one of Aggie's nights to cook, but these days you never knew. Sarah could hear the Rival Sons rocking Denny's upstairs bedroom – she thought it was 'Do Your Worst,' but the sound was turned so high the lyrics turned to screaming mush.

Sounds like an uprising, she told herself. *Better get out of my work clothes and investigate.* She almost said aloud, *Lucky I'm a detective.* This summer her family had formed this nauseating habit of trying to put a humorous slant on everything as they tip-toed around the tar-pit of Aggie's depression. *Playing some game called 'Just keep chuckling till it goes away,'* she thought as she climbed the stairs. *Makes me want to gag.*

She knocked and got no answer, decided *she can't hear me*, and turned the knob. Denny was at her desk, bent over a math book and work sheets. *Making noises like a wrecking crew but she's just doing her homework. Be patient.* Sarah smiled before pointing to her ears, and Denny killed the music.

'Smells like dinner but there's nobody around,' Sarah said, 'so I thought I'd ask?'

'No prob,' Denny said. 'Gram had all the stuff out for meat loaf and was just starting to chop the onion when I got home. But she looked so fagged I told her I'd finish it and I think she's taking a nap.'

'Good girl. What's left to do?'

'I put in two baking potatoes, big enough to split. Will you nuke a frozen veg and set the table? I'd like to finish this math before dinner so I can watch "The Big Bang Theory" after.'

'Sure. Thanks for doing all that.'

Denny was taking Aggie's lingering illness in stride the way she took most things, Sarah thought gratefully as she hurried down to her bedroom. From Denny's twelve-year-old perspective Aggie was very old, so her debility was not surprising. Sarah remembered the capable ranch wife her mother had been, not so long ago. Watching her descent into wan indifference was painful.

It had come on in stages. Helping her mother through post-stroke recovery three years ago, Sarah's resources were already

stretched thin when her haplessly drug-addicted sister disappeared, leaving Denny, her nine-year-old daughter, in peril on
dark city streets. Sarah found her and brought her home, but
suddenly adding two needy family members to her responsi-
bilities, Sarah felt obliged to cut her new lover loose.

'You don't want to get mixed up in this mess,' she told him.
But she had reckoned without the passionate attachment of
Will Dietz, who said, 'What I really don't want is to live
without you, so let's figure this out.' She had admired him
since he was her first boss in homicide, and loved him since
she befriended him after his near-death injury on the job. As
they helped each other surmount the problems of their made-up
family, their love and trust had grown deep as the bone.

The three adults pooled their financial resources to buy an
old house on Bentley Street, its marks and scars compensated
for by a little casita across the patio for Aggie and an attic
room of her own for Denny. Aggie's fears of being a burden
quickly faded when she saw she could help rescue her shame-
fully neglected granddaughter. And Denny, who had been
getting through middle school by figuring out her own schedules and stealing lunch money from her mother's deadhead
boyfriends, nimbly converted her survival skills into helping
with the housework and making no waves.

It wasn't always pretty, but Sarah's determination and Will's
fix-it skills had kept annoyances from ever reaching crisis
level. Dietz continually tinkered over sagging steps, broken
molding, and missing door handles, Sarah painted walls in
desert colors, and together they had almost saved enough to
remodel the kitchen, which they all thought of as their most
serious problem, until this summer.

In June, a serious case of flu rendered Aggie bedridden for
two weeks and convalescent for two more. The other three
rallied to help, feeling quite proud of their teamwork, and in
July, Aggie was pronounced recovered by her doctors. But she
never quite got her bounce back. Still listless in August,
she continued to lose weight, resigned from her bridge club
and quit going to weekly lunches with friends. Creeping around
the house in her oldest clothes, she took frequent naps in her
casita and came to meals looking woebegone.

Sarah was 'cranking up her courage,' she told Will, to arrange for a joint visit to Aggie's primary caregiver.

'I know she won't like it, and Ma can be an alligator when she gets mad. But somebody's got to help me figure out if this is depression or the onset of dementia. And what to do about it – if there is anything to do.' And even Will, the pragmatic fixer who hated to talk about feelings, said at once, 'You're right. I've been wanting to say, we need to do something.'

Now as she stepped out of their bedroom in cool shorts and T-shirt, she saw Aggie coming across the patio, wearing rumpled jeans and carrying a pamphlet.

'Ah, you're home, good,' Aggie said. 'Have you got time to look at this catalog with me?'

'Sure,' Sarah said. 'Is it something you want for the house?' She and Will had always encouraged Aggie's suggestions, but lately she'd seemed indifferent. Now she had one of the home-improvement catalogs they constantly got in the mail, open to a colorful page.

'Well, I've been thinking about some kind of a barrier we might put up between our yard and the one behind us. As long as the Dietrichs lived back there I never thought about the fact that we really had nothing between us but an alley full of weeds. All right, wildflowers. But now we have this chatty neighbor who keeps being so *friendly* . . .'

'He's bothering you?'

'Always waving and calling out the cheery hello.' Aggie curled her lip. 'Has lots to say about the *weather.*'

Well, no wonder you're upset. We certainly don't want any loose talk about the weather. Then she thought, guiltily, *it must be hard to be the one who stays home alone.*

'I count on sitting out on my patio.' Aggie frowned at the pictures in the booklet. 'And I want my privacy.'

'Of course you do. Let me see what you've got there.'

'Well . . . see these white building blocks? Like bricks only bigger, and you stack them up however you like. But if you think that's too expensive we could always just put up a fence.'

'A fence.' Sarah tried to keep the horror out of her voice. 'You mean wooden posts and . . .'

'Could be wood, I guess. But you have to dig post holes for them, don't you? I was thinking of the metal poles that you just pound into the dirt. And then you fasten the wire on with metal clips . . . of course I couldn't do all that by myself, I'd need Will's help with that. Whereas with these white blocks, I could stack them up myself, a little at a time . . .'

'Well, if we have to have a barrier there I think I'd like a hedge better,' Sarah said, hating the idea as soon as she said it, already dreading the need to water and clip. But at least it would look better than a fence. Then a smell of well-done beef reminded her she had a project in hand.

'Hey, I think that meat loaf smells almost ready. Why don't you come in and tell me some more about these building blocks while I dish up?' she said. She walked into the kitchen with her arm around her mother, exclaiming how good the food smelled.

Then she heard Will Dietz pull into the carport, the quiet sounds he made closing his car door, taking his badge and weapon out of the hatchback and walking across the patio to lock them in his shop. Her mother was sitting on a stool across from her, moving her hands to illustrate an idea for a barrier. Taking an interest in something for the first time in weeks, Sarah thought. *Is it possible we ignored Aggie's depression long enough, and it's going away?*

Well then, maybe, to keep the momentum of her recovery going, it would be smart to take her complaint seriously, and see if they could help her fend off this pesky neighbor.

FIVE

S arah slid into her workspace a half-hour early Tuesday morning and went to work at once. She had been primary on the Fairweather Farms case for a whole day but had not had time to pull her scattered notes into the organized list she liked to work off as a case went along. She dug scraps of paper and small items out of her day pack and purse, spread them on her desk along with her tablet, and began to enter them in the random order in which she'd encountered them.

The first half dozen items read:

1. van stuck in garage door?
2. Tammy hysterical – did she see anything besides blood?
3. ammo in van – how much/what?
4. dead driver – bio?
5. window open – A/C working
6. need interviews with Amanda, Henry, Mr Ames

By the time the rest of her detective division came to work she had set up a folder marked 'Fairweather', entered the list in it, and sent a copy to her home computer. She would add to and amend it as long as she worked on the case. Everything went in – descriptions of the scene as she had first seen it; names of people as she encountered them; and items collected – name cards, interviews, clothing, money, the pictures on her phone. Also questions, comments, irritations, and insights.

Delaney would set up a numbered case report with a coherent account of the crime and its investigation. All the detectives who worked on the case would have access and add to it as they went along. This list was her own, not meant to work for anybody else. When she had taken it as far as it could go

today, she closed her computer and went back outside, got in
her car and drove to the morgue.

Swathed and slippered in pale blue plastic, Dr Cameron
was already bending over the body in operating room five.
Sarah saw him through the heavy glass door as she entered
the building and hurried to robe up, thinking, *Let's hope we
can make short work of this autopsy. The man was shot in the
head, what more do we need to know?*

The first half hour made her think she was right, because
the doctor, after cleaning up the discolored and misshapen
head, went right to work with the bone saw. He was reversing
the usual order of autopsy – usually, he'd open the body and
inspect all the organs first. But today he made the cut across
the cranium, from ear to ear, and folded down the flap of
hair and forehead over the face. Then he made the cut across
the eye ridge, lifted out a wedge of skull, and looked in
at the brain.

'Too much blood to see anything yet,' the doctor said. 'You
ready, Josh?' His assistant installed a pipette on a tiny hand
vacuum, and soon the fractured brain lay revealed.

'Just like the picture,' Cameron said. Off a side table next
to the gurney he lifted, carefully, by the edges, an X-ray photo.

'What's that?' Sarah asked. It looked like a snowstorm filled
with bits of gravel.

'It's this brain, filled with tiny pieces of the bullet that hit
him,' Cameron said. 'It happens sometimes – a bullet travelling at high speed, it hits soft tissue, ricochets off the inside
of the skull, fragments and the pieces fly all over the place.
We're going to have to be very careful lifting this brain out
of there, Josh.'

They spoke in little grunts and murmurs, communicating
knowledge Sarah envied as she watched, and presently
Enrique's brain lay – mostly intact, with a few outliers – in a
metal dish.

'Brain cell pudding, that's what we have left here,' the
doctor said, nudging a bit around the edges with a wooden
paddle. 'All the good thinking parts reduced to mush in about
a second. But here at the bottom there's a couple of things
the bullet didn't reach. Not every day you're going to see a

cross-section like this, Sarah – you might as well learn something. I haven't seen this view for a while myself; let's see if I can remember . . .' He dropped the paddle, took up a pipette and pointed. 'See this fat round part? That's the cerebellum, where the messages come in from the body parts, lets you know if you're cold, if you're standing straight.'

Sarah stood up straighter.

'And here's the medulla oblongata, that's the piece that controls your breathing, all your automatic functions – helps you sneeze, fart, belch—'

'What a splendid part.'

'Try getting along without it. Now, if we were looking for a bullet in here, we'd be sorting more carefully, but no need for that today.' He set the dishful of brains aside and turned back to the corpse. 'Let's get on with this.' He picked up the biggest scalpel and began the big V-shaped incision to open the trunk.

'You're going to do the whole autopsy? I thought since we know what killed him, you'd probably skip the rest.'

'I thought so too, but I asked for a quick-and-dirty on the blood work I sent in yesterday, and the report they sent back suggests a serious pre-existing disorder.'

'What's the difference if he's dead?'

'Maybe quite a bit. Delaney's note said you wondered why he turned the A/C up to the max and then opened the window, and I have a hunch about that. Stand back now, there's going to be some spillage.'

In another flurry of muttering, sawing and four-handed cooperation, the doctor and his assistant removed a ribcage and liver, and cleaned out more fluid.

'Now,' Cameron said, 'stand here so I can show you the kidneys. They look quite normal, but the tests show high calcium and creatinine levels, and now, see the ureters? Almost completely blocked. He must have been having trouble urinating – does anybody know if he said it was getting hard to piss?'

'I can ask, but – why do I care?'

'Because, see this section of skull?' He held up the wedge of bone he had removed from the dead man's head. 'I'll confirm this with X-rays of some of the long bones, but this is what I was expecting to see: bones that look moth-eaten and fragile. They're full of holes and hairline fractures.'

'Why were you expecting to see that?'

'The blood tests showed high levels of creatinine and calcium. His symptoms are about what that would indicate.'

'Symptoms? The man had his brain blown apart.'

'Yes, he did. But in addition to that, I'm quite certain he had multiple myeloma. And the symptoms include fatigue, confusion, nausea, dizziness – he should not have been driving the company van.'

'And you think that's why he opened the window?'

'Probably. Got dizzy, opened the window to get some fresh air, just in time for these merry bandits to come along and shoot him in the head.'

'Of course, the window wouldn't have prevented that if it had been up – but with the window down their ammo went right through the windshield.'

'So I heard. Oh, speaking of that' – he reached under his operating table, pulled out an evidence bag – 'I promised that amazing photographer of yours that I'd save this victim's clothes and not let them get thrown in the trash. So why don't you take possession now before I forget them again.'

'Oh, thanks. Let's see, I have to fill out a transfer form to keep the chain of evidence clear and unbroken.' She dug through her day pack for the tag as Cameron issued a passionate denunciation of the bureaucracy that dogged the criminal justice workplace.

'Yeah, well,' Sarah said, 'it's like what you said about that medulla whatchadiddy – try getting along without it. Gloria Jackson isn't my scientist, by the way – she works at the crime lab. Why do you think she's amazing?' she asked him as she signed the tag and handed it to him.

'She looks like she belongs in a Hollywood musical but she has rigorous standards; she really does very solid forensic work.'

'Good-looking women aren't supposed to have rigorous work standards? Dear me, what primitive bias is this?'

'All right, all right. You think she's amazing too – I've seen how you look at her.'

Sarah smiled and said, 'Well, she makes me feel optimistic.'

'About what?'

'The human race – she's so enterprising.'

'She makes me feel prurient,' the doctor said. 'She's the sexiest woman I've ever seen.'

Sarah stared at him, speechless with surprise for a couple of seconds, then quickly said, 'She admires your work too.'

Cameron blushed with pleasure, then scowled and said, 'How'd we get on this ridiculous subject? Any word on the shooters yet?'

'Not a sign of them since they drove away from Fairweather Farms. They're probably across the border by now – they've had time to get all the way to Chiapis if they want to.'

'I wish I shared your optimism about that,' the doctor said. 'What worries me is that a lot of these hoodlums, lately, seem to want to stick around Tucson.'

'Oy vey, let's not get into border issues, we'll be here all day. How do you get along so well with all this standing on cold stone floors?' Getting ready to change into street shoes, Sarah sat cradling one foot in her hand, 'My feet hurt for three days after every autopsy I watch in here.'

'Who says I get along so well?' Cameron said. 'I have ridiculous bills with my podiatrist – if only he gave bonus gas points like my grocer I could be driving for free.' He looked cheered up, though. It must please him to know someone admired his work.

Sarah pondered the conversation with Cameron as she drove back to Fairweather Farms. Gloria evidently had something going with the good doctor, but didn't realize it – all she'd ever expressed about him was admiration for his expertise.

Sarah told herself to steer clear of that puzzle, and turned her mind to Cameron's autopsy report. The shooters had gone to a lot of trouble to kill a man who was already dying – if indeed he was the target and not DeShawn. They could hardly have known his medical condition, but did the victim know it? If he did, had he shared the information with his colleagues? Had Henry been helping him cover up his illness? Thinking

she already had more leads than she could decide how to
follow, Sarah nevertheless went back to the senior living home
to find the elusive Amanda.

The two gardeners were once again working in front of the
building. The gravel was all smooth again, and they were
replacing the last of the plants that had been damaged
yesterday. Jacob gave her a cheery wave, but Henry went on
tamping down dirt around a bush and did not look up. He
seemed to have developed some lasting grudge against her –
or was it fear? Her impulse was there was something he was
holding back and to confront him about it. But her watch said
three-thirty, so she decided to stick to the errand she'd come
to do. She wanted to speak to Amanda first, and then Tammy,
and Mr Ames if there was still time.

Inside, she asked the first uniformed woman she met how
to find Amanda. 'Look down the hall there past Letitia's office,'
the woman said, pointing. 'It's the door with a sign that says
Supplies.'

Sarah turned left and padded along the dim, quiet hall. As
she passed the open doorway of a room marked *Library*, a
crackling elderly voice from inside called, 'Hold up there, you
– policewoman!'

Sarah stopped and looked inside. Half a dozen couches and
deep chairs with tables and lamps sat in front of bookshelves
less than half full of books. Across the room, a white-haired
man in rimless spectacles beckoned and said, 'Come in here,
girlie.'

Standing her ground, she said, 'Are you Mr Ames?'

'Yes,' he said, and fixed her with a flinty stare. 'You the
policewoman that's been asking about me?'

'Yes,' she said. She came into the room, pulled a card out
of the holder clipped to her belt and handed it to him. 'Detective
Sarah Burke, how do you do?'

'Well, what do you want? I don't like to have people asking
about me in public, drawing attention like this. What in blazes
do you want?'

'I need to ask you a few questions about the attack on the
van you were riding in on Monday.'

'Yes, what about it? Damn disgrace if you want to know

– it was even in the paper! And the name of this place, very bad publicity. I don't like that at all. I've spoken to the manager, made it clear I expect better performance from now on. I pay top dollar and the least I expect to get is peace and quiet.'

She decided to ignore his ridiculous complaint and asked him, 'Why did the driver open the window?'

'What? Oh, the window – damn foolishness. It was when they first started chasing us. He thought he knew them. I think he recognized the old pickup. Ricky had friends all over the south end of town; he grew up here and he was always joshing with somebody. So when the first bullets hit the van he thought they were paintballs or something. He rolled the window down and shouted something in Spanish. Laughing!'

'He thought it was all in fun?'

'These people are so childlike, aren't they? Then one of the bullets came in through the window and hit above the windshield just in front of his face. I saw his eyes in the mirror, suddenly terrified – he stamped on the gas then and I realized we were running for our lives.' He sighed. 'Poor Ricky almost made it.'

'Why didn't you tell this to the police when they took you out of the van?'

'I couldn't breathe! Thought I was having a heart attack. I finally got the attention of that young simpleton on the yard crew, and he got me hooked up to the oxygen tank. Saved my life! Should have tipped him, I suppose. Ah well, another time.'

'How do you imagine that management might have prevented this incident, Mr Ames?'

'They should be more careful whom they hire! That DeShawn – it's all very well his helping with the smokes and the great wines, and you can't fault his work ethic, but some of his friends won't bear scrutiny.' Ames stretched suddenly, self-indulgent as a cat, and said, 'Go away now, dear. I'm tired; I need to rest.'

Feeling grateful that she didn't have to deal with Mr Ames every day, Sarah walked further along the paneled hall until she found a half-open door marked *Supplies*. The space she could see was brightly lit and smelled like ink. She tapped on the door and walked in.

The room was smaller and plainer than the manager's quarters and had no easy chairs. Every inch was crammed with useful items. One wall was all shelves full of paper and printed forms, plus a counter that held two printers and a fax machine. Another wall was floor-to-ceiling pegboard hung with menus, calendars, weekly schedules of events, and samples of fabric, paint, and tableware. Most of the floor space was occupied by a big well-organized desk filled with two computer monitors, another printer and labelled baskets of correspondence.

Alone in the middle of this businesslike clutter, in the only padded chair, sat Amanda, a small, pretty girl with soft brown eyes and a dimple. Sarah shook hands and sat down on the well-worn folding chair in front of the desk. She pushed a stack of paper aside to make room for her tablet and went right to work – the room did not encourage small talk.

Amanda said her last name was Petty, and reeled off relevant numbers for phones and email – no fancy printed card for her.

'Looking around your office,' Sarah said, 'I'd say you have more than enough to do.'

Amanda raised an ironic eyebrow and said, 'You think?'

'You print all the weekly schedules?' Amanda nodded. 'And the menus?' Amanda put a thumb up. 'How often do they change?'

'Once a season. But the busiest part of the job here is the correspondence with prospective customers. We do a lot of outreach to selected lists, and we're quite aggressive in our follow-up after tours. Letitia does the phoning and conducts the tours but I do most of the letter-writing.'

'Yet despite this busy schedule you manage to take a personal day when you need it?'

'We get four a year with pay. Anything more has to be negotiated.'

'I see. So now tell me, Amanda – did you or did you not come to work here yesterday morning?'

Amanda cocked her head sideways, regarded Sarah with a mildly humorous expression and said, 'That's a funny question to get confrontational about.'

Sarah waited, and after a few seconds Amanda said, 'Yes, I did.'

'But you left soon after you arrived?'

'That's right. Because Letitia was having a problem about some records and soon after I got to work she sent me to straighten it out.'

'Sent you where?'

'Um, actually I went home and made phone calls from there.'

'Why? Does the phone work better from your place?' When Amanda merely shrugged, Sarah continued, 'And why did I get two different stories about where you were? Letitia said you were taking a personal day, but Patsy said she talked to you in the morning but couldn't find you later.' Sarah looked at Amanda sternly over her glasses. 'Were you just hiding out at your place so I couldn't find you while I chased my tail around Ricky's no-good driver's license for a few hours?'

Amanda blinked thoughtfully for a few seconds and finally said, 'If you've got the whole thing figured out, why are you ragging on me about it? I was just following orders.' Far from apologetic, she actually looked annoyed.

'I was just doing my job too,' Sarah said. 'The difference is I was trying to find the truth, and you and your manager were doing your best to cover it up. Is that the understanding you have with her – whatever lie she wants to tell, you'll swear to it?'

'Oh, now, come on, that's putting it pretty strong. Letitia got wrong-footed by that expired license and I didn't think it was any crime to give her some help to get to the bottom of it.' The dimple had disappeared and Amanda's warm brown eyes had turned cold and hostile.

Sarah's phone chirped. For a second she thought about letting it go to messages – a cute cuddle-bunny who was also the company drudge, who demonstrated a lively sense of irony but expressed unstinting loyalty to her superior – this was not an interview you wanted to interrupt. But she couldn't resist a peek at the text message. It was from Bogey and read, 'Call ASAP got new puzzle.'

'Gotta take this,' Sarah said, and stepped into the hall punching buttons.

In the middle of the first ring, he said, 'Boganicevic,' somehow contriving to make it sound short.

Sarah said, ''Sup?'

'Remember the dashboard that we didn't touch when we first walked into this van?'

'Sure. Because it was covered with blood and fingerprints that the techs were still sampling.'

'Yes. And then we found the money and it kind of blew everything else out of the water. But Banjo got the vehicle connected to a power source a few minutes ago, so I quick-powered up my tablet which was almost out of juice. Fooling around the console made me realize I'd never looked in the glove compartment, so I did that. Took everything out, and there behind all the documents was one of those little plug-in things . . .'

'A thumb drive?'

'Yeah, that. Just now I plugged it in and read what's on it. As much as I could. The top line says 2459 West, the middle two lines look like nicknames for street drugs, and the bottom line is just four numbers, eight four zero zero.'

'Well . . . the top one sounds like an address, doesn't it? But on which street?'

'Don't know. What I noticed is the bottom number is the same amount as the money we found in the jacket yesterday.'

'It's a dead drop,' Sarah said in Delaney's office later. 'Must be.' She had driven to the impound yard, read the message with Bogey, and called her superior. Delaney said yes, bring it in right away.

She walked in without a word, handed him the thumb drive and watched as the message scrolled out on his monitor.

Four lines here:

2459 West
Shine 24
Snow 48
8400

Now she faced him across his desk, talking fast. 'The middle two lines are street nicknames for popular drugs. I checked with our undercover unit and they say shine is probably fentanyl mixed with some useless substance like baking powder, and snow is likely cocaine. The numbers to the right of the formulas appear to be confirmation of the number of pills, or however they're expressing doses. And the bottom line, of course, is a price quote.'

'It does look like it, doesn't it?' He fiddled while he thought – rubbed his hands together, pulled on his ears. 'But – why the thumb drive, do you think? So risky, easy to lose . . .'

'But totally off the grid. You get the message, you wipe it, it's gone. Off the planet, like it never existed. Unlike an email or a text, there is nothing left to be traced.'

'That's the good news *and* the bad news, isn't it? Slick but risky. Lose the message before you've memorized it, it's gone forever.' He tapped his nose a while. 'Tell me how you think this one works.'

'The buyer leaves one of these thumb drives at an agreed location with the order on it – he must be the middleman who's buying for the members in this little club. The device gets picked up by the usual driver of the Fairweather van, who's got this side job working for the seller. A day or two later, maybe at the same place, maybe not, he leaves confirmation that the order's being filled – just like Land's End, you know? I think that's what we're looking at here. You see it includes the location for the delivery and the cost.'

'Ah,' Delaney said, and did his thoughtful dry wash. *He's beginning to enjoy this case. Something different for once, more fun than discipline reports and budget overruns.* 'So then the buyer picks up the product at the agreed spot, and the price gets paid in cash . . .'

'To the driver's jacket pocket, that's where we found it. Sweet hiding place, huh? Kind of like *The Purloined Letter.*'

'The what?'

'In school, remember? Edgar Allan Poe.'

He shook his head.

'The letter was in plain sight,' Sarah reminded him, 'in such an obvious place that nobody looked at it.'

'Oh, yeah.' He laughed. 'I remember complaining to my mother, "Why do I have to read this dumb story?" It's so far-fetched, I said, it could never happen. But here it is, you say, working just fine. Until now.'

'Because this time the usual driver got hit in traffic and landed in a hospital bed. Which threw a monkey wrench in the works, big time.' Sarah stared at the message a minute, thinking it through. 'Because nobody delivered the goodies. So the company goons came out to set things straight.'

'Uh-huh.' Delaney tapped out a march on his sunburned nose while he thought, and finally said, 'Right there's where I begin to question your theory.'

'Because?'

'What Ollie said. It's too much firepower chasing too few dollars. It seems to me you've got two different stories here and they don't fit together.'

'Well . . . maybe. But right now I'm worried about the first part of the story. Because like it or not, there's a dead man in the morgue, a car full of shooters still at large, and the man they must have been after is just waking up at St. Mary's.'

'I hear you. And that usual driver – what's his name?'

'DeShawn Williams.'

'OK. I guess he's not likely to escape for a while but we need to get him identified as a suspect and in custody right away. So you get on the phone quick before the Court House closes, and get a warrant for his arrest.'

'But if he's under arrest we'll have to put a guard on his room, won't we?'

'Yes. Conscious or not, if he's under arrest he's got to be under guard. And it might take a couple of days to get him into the hospital ward at the prison, so we're going to have to pop for twenty-four-hour guards for a while. Damn, this late in the day – I hope the chief's still here. While he's putting the guard squad together I'll put the arm on one of our guys to cover the interim, and he can be your backup when you serve the warrant. Who's around that can take an all-nighter without squeaking?'

'Jason Peete,' Sarah said. 'He's between girlfriends, he always wants the money and he has energy to burn.'

'Good. Let's get at it.'

Jason was a fresh eye on the Fairweather Farms case – fresh on the case, that is, otherwise somewhat worse for wear. He had spent the last two days buried, literally, in the bermed storage unit of a big house in the foothills of Oro Valley, where a bloody murder-suicide had ended the apparent happiness of the owners. All the horrified neighbors and family members he interviewed assured him they had never known a happier couple.

'Please let me drive,' he said. 'I've got a head full of ugly pictures I need to blow off. Rush hour traffic in Tucson should be just the ticket.'

'Fine by me,' Sarah said. 'Knock yourself out.' After thirteen years in the department, she had pretty well worn down the rough edges of resentful male colleagues, so she no longer insisted on driving her own car when she was primary on the case. And Jason was a buddy – they had developed rapport in the course of several shared cases. He hadn't heard any details about the Fairweather Farms shooting, so this was the chance they needed to get on the same page. She relaxed in the passenger seat and let him deal with the motorized barbarians on I-10 while she filled him in.

He loved the story about the company van that nearly killed the gardeners, and the fantastic chance of the driver getting shot and losing control just in time to bury the corporate vehicle in its own garage door.

'God, you can't make this stuff up, can you?' he said. 'But how come we're serving the warrant on the guy who wasn't there?'

She told him about the money.

Jason said, 'Aahhh,' and nodded his shaven head contentedly. Money made it all add up – or it would soon. The crazy chase and the van stuck in the garage door were not so flat-out looney if money was at stake. All of Sarah's fellow officers could cite casework showing that when it came to crime, money was almost as big a motivator as love.

On the second floor at St. Mary's they went to the nurses' station, where Sarah was pleased to learn that Judy, the unsinkable head nurse she had met here before, was on duty and would answer a page. Stoic as always but keenly attuned to the suffering all around her, Judy guided them down two long halls toward the room where DeShawn was waking up.

During the walk Sarah explained the warrant she was about to serve, and her need to place the patient under arrest. Judy agreed to help communicate with the patient if he seemed strong enough to respond without jeopardizing his health.

'But you understand my first responsibility is to the patient,' she said, as they walked through the big double doors into the Intensive Care Unit.

'Of course,' Sarah said. 'And mine is to the safety of the community, so we have to try to fit—' She stopped talking because Judy had abandoned her in mid-sentence.

Inexplicably, Judy had grown the bristling look of a junkyard dog and was walking quickly toward a thin young man in scrubs, who as far as Sarah could see was blamelessly pushing an empty wheelchair into a room three doors away.

'What are you doing?' Judy asked him. 'I didn't order that.' She reached the blue-clad attendant while he was still in the doorway, peered into his face and demanded, 'Who are you? What are you doing on this floor?'

He swiveled the chair and pushed it hard into her, knocking her down. He looked around, saw the two detectives staring at him, and in one fluid motion he released the chair and turned to run. But Jason had pulled his taser off his hip, stepped forward to get a clear field of fire and shot the stranger in the chest as he turned.

The jolt threw him writhing to the floor, yelling in pain. As he went down, just before Jason jumped on top of him, Sarah noticed that his arms were covered with crude and violent tattoos. *An orderly with jailhouse tats?* He landed near Judy, who was struggling to rise.

'Judy, stay down,' Sarah said, not too loud because this was a hospital, but urgently because another man in dark blue scrubs was coming out of the room the wheelchair man had been going into. He had his right hand in his pocket.

Sarah just had time to wonder *what's he got in his pocket?* when he pulled it out. He twirled something that gleamed in the light and looked like a shiny snake, or – then his hand stopped moving and the snake became a knife.

Jason was on Sarah's left, busy cuffing the man on the floor, who was resisting, rolling around. Judy was on her knees between Sarah and the man with the knife. He was big and well-built, moving straight toward Jason, who was too busy to think about his unprotected back. Judy must not have heard Sarah's warning. She was getting up in between Sarah and the moving man. There was no clear field of fire for a taser shot and no room here for mace. Sarah had her Glock in her hand in one smooth second and she said, 'Put the knife down now or you're dead.'

He turned sharply toward her voice. She wasn't wearing a uniform, so the weapon surprised him. Sarah watched him hesitate, stop moving for a second with both hands in the air in front of him, his dark eyes shining and his thin-lipped mouth open, sucking air.

His partner was on the floor squealing like a pig, saying Jason was killing him, kneeling on his legs like that. The knifeman ignored the two men struggling on the floor and kicked Judy aside. She fell flat with a grunt and rolled away, and her assailant strode through the cleared space toward Sarah.

'Drop the knife now!' Sarah made her voice mean and sharp, hoping to startle him into rationality. But as she watched his eyes and his hands, she saw in a despairing instant that the macho arrogance he wore like armor was leading him to make the wrong decision. He grew a smirk that said, *What the hell, she's a woman, she's not gonna shoot.*

He lunged with the knife in both hands, the blade coming down at her taut and shiny, and she pulled the trigger.

SIX

The roar of the shot in the confined space made her deaf. She felt in her gut what she could barely hear – shock waves echoing down the hall.

The bullet hit her attacker in mid-leap, and in one incredible mini-second she saw the light go out of his eyes. The force of the point-blank shot blew him over backwards. It knocked the knife out of his hand, too, and the gleaming blade nicked her forearm and kneecap, going down. He landed with a smacking thud and lay motionless, his feet six inches in front of hers.

Sarah felt vertigo for a terrible few seconds, and willed herself to stay erect. When the world stopped whirling, she stepped forward and crouched by his chest, feeling behind his ear for a pulse.

Nothing. She stood up, drew a shuddering breath, and watched bright red drops of her own blood fall on the dead man's face. That was the image that stayed with her – his pale face of no obvious ethnicity, growing younger as the contempt went out of his features and her blood spattered on his softening cheeks.

For the first time, she noticed his pale hair, tightly curled in short dreadlocks. *Odd*, she thought, *you don't see many blondes in dreads*. He seemed to grow younger as she looked. *God, he's really just a boy.*

Then Judy was beside her with a stethoscope slung around her neck, saying, 'Here, let me see . . .' in a strange muffled voice Sarah could barely hear. Sarah pointed at the man on the floor and said, 'I checked, I couldn't find . . .' and Judy said, 'What?' Both deafened by the shot, they stared at each other, each shocked by the faint surreal voice they were hearing.

Judy crouched over the body on the floor, listened to her

stethoscope a few seconds, shook her head and said, 'He's gone.' She stood up, yelped at sudden pain, said, 'Oh, my hip,' and stood rubbing it. Then her eyes fastened on the blood dripping off Sarah and she said, 'Let me fix your cuts.' Sarah felt a cool swab on her wrist and knee, the brief sting as it penetrated the wounds and then bandages going on.

Jason propped his still-protesting prisoner against the wall and began talking to him. Sarah vaguely heard him say, 'Quiet down now, this is a hospital. What's your name?'

'Ow, ow, you hurt my legs.' His prisoner made a tragic face. 'Gimme something for the pain.'

'Your legs are all right; they'll stop hurting soon. What's your name?' But the man began to mumble and then lapsed, or pretended to, into a semi-conscious state. Jason abandoned the effort to identify him, stood up, and asked Sarah, 'You OK?'

'Yeah.' She pointed to her ears. 'Deaf.' Then she said, 'Better call Delaney,' and began patting her pockets, forgetting she'd put her phone in her day pack.

'I'll do it,' Jason said. 'Jeez, I'm almost deaf too. Damn Glock sounded like a cannon in here, didn't it?' He looked down at the body on the floor as he dialed, and then back at his prisoner, who was slumping toward the floor. 'What the fuck did we walk into here? Who are these guys, do you know?'

'No idea.' She slapped her forehead as a terrible thought struck. 'God, I hope this guy didn't use that knife on the driver we came to—' But Jason was already talking softly into his phone.

Turning, Sarah saw that Judy had just remembered her patient too. She had left off rubbing her hip to hobble, groaning, toward Room 278. Sarah faintly heard her asking, 'DeShawn? Did that man cut you, or just rip out all your . . . Oh, dear, he made a real mess, didn't he? Let me get some help in here and we'll fix you up.'

So calm. She makes it sound like housekeeping chores. Sarah yawned a couple of times to pop her ears and get some of her hearing back. She tried to monitor events in DeShawn's room while she stayed busy in the hall, going through the pockets of the man she'd shot. The other pocket, that didn't hold the knife, had something else heavy in it, didn't it? She felt cold metal and pulled it out: a ring of small burglary tools, thin metal devices for opening locks. *I've killed a common thief*, she thought, feeling oddly diminished. She sealed the cluster in an evidence bag, dated and timed it and dropped it in her day pack, thinking, *Too late to charge him, but I'll turn them in anyway.*

She could hear DeShawn babbling questions – he was deeply confused, his life support ripped off by a stranger. Then he'd been abandoned for a quarter of an hour while a small war apparently took place outside his room. His body hurt all over, so much he couldn't say, when Judy asked him, what hurt worst. But in the next few minutes the kindly nurses Judy summoned soothed his injuries and calmed him down, and his charm began to come back. He thanked everybody who came to his bedside, so sincerely that they began to empathize with him – they asked Sarah, does he really have to be handcuffed to the bed?

'Yes,' she said, 'I'm afraid he must.' But she helped them find the most comfortable position for his arms, and the nurses added padding for his elbows. They put nutrition and a seda-tive in his IV and began to call him their favorite criminal.

Sarah found no wallet on the body of the dead man, no store receipts or bar tabs – the pocket that had held the knife was empty. He wore briefs under the blue scrubs, nothing else but cotton socks under his Nike racers. 'Wait, though, what's this in the shoe?' She pulled it out from where it was wedged between the tongue and the laces, a torn slip of notebook paper with a name in block letters: Russell Sexton.

She asked Jason, 'Your man got any ID on him?'

'Haven't found anything yet,' Jason said. He was down on the floor again, busily patting down his man. 'He's not being a bit of help.' He added, over a howl of protest from his pris-oner, 'Relax, I'm too busy to make love just now, Baby Cakes. But you wouldn't be the first genius I ever busted that tried to hide his goodies in his drawers. Look here!' He stood up crowing, waving a set of car keys.

'Oh, good for you,' Sarah said. 'That'll have all their clothes and ID. I found some keys too, see? Burglary tools, actually. Soon as we get some help in here let's go find that car and see where it leads us, won't that be fun?'

Firm footsteps came through the swinging doors then, and Delaney said, 'Sarah? What happened?' He scanned the scene quickly, saw Jason's prisoner slumped against a wall in cuffs, Sarah's opponent stretched on the floor in a pool of blood, and Sarah standing there blinking in bandages. 'You hurt bad?'

'Nah,' she said, 'scratches.' Trying to look better organized, she straightened her shirt. 'It happened so fast, boss, he came right at me with this weird knife . . .'

'But you did what you had to do, good for you. You just got these cuts, you're not shot?'

She shook her head. 'I'm deaf is all. Am I yelling or – no? He didn't leave me any other choice, boss. I warned him twice but he wouldn't stop.'

'I hear you. Jason, you're all right?'

'Not a mark on me,' Jason said, holding his arms out, flashing a dazzling smile. 'Both these wingnuts were high, boss – this one I've got here isn't even talking to Planet Earth.' He stooped to prop up the chin of the man he'd hit with the taser. 'See?' He dropped the head and it flopped back against the wall, the shoulder-length dark hair hiding his face. 'I was too busy getting the cuffs on this dude to help Sarah, but I saw her fire, she was right under that knife. I can testify it was an absolutely righteous shot. Good thing she was quick or she'd have been dead meat.'

Judy came limping out of DeShawn's room and added her endorsement. 'Of course it was justified,' she said in response to Delaney's question. 'That crazy man knocked me down twice. If Sarah hadn't shot him I believe he'd have killed us all.'

'With this ridiculous-looking thing? This is what he was carrying?' Delaney pointed, but did not touch the weapon on the floor. 'I hate these trick knives. What's it called?'

'A balisong,' Jason said. 'Here, you want me to—' He held up an evidence bag and started toward the knife, but Delaney said, 'No, don't touch it!'

Both his detectives looked at him, startled. Sarah said, 'What?'

'Crime scene unit's coming right behind me. I'm sorry to mess up your hall for a while longer, ma'am,' he told Judy, 'but we have to get everything measured and photographed.'

'Oh, boss, listen,' Sarah said, 'we can do that ourselves. It's just these few square feet – I can do the whole thing with my phone.'

'You crazy? This isn't just some little thing like jaywalking. Two wounded and one fatality, in the intensive care unit of the hospital? You're damn lucky it hasn't already turned into a mob scene.'

'But that's what I mean, we don't want a lot of people milling around in here—'

'The crime scene unit does not mill around. As you well know. Step aside, here they come now. Good, the steno's here to take your statements. Why don't you three step out in the hall there?'

Which they did, for the next hour, fidgeting in the hall outside the double doors, stopping to peer through from time to time as they fed their stories to Polly, the young newbie with the clipboard and all the forms. Inside the ICU the work went on, weighing and measuring, testing and charting and taking dozens of digital pictures.

Gloria was the first criminalist out, pulling her wheeled camera cart. She paused to give Sarah a squeeze and murmur, 'Don't let the bastards make you sweat, hear?'

Delaney had concluded that the usual arrest procedure was out of the question for DeShawn – he was already dozing off again, courtesy of the drugs in his IV. Declaring the twice-injured ex-driver a person of interest, Delaney clipped the arrest warrant to the chart at the end of his bed and arranged for his transport tomorrow to the prison hospital on Kolb Road. The two extra detectives he had brought with him took charge of the car keys Jason had just found, and the body of Sarah's attacker.

Then he turned to Sarah and said, 'Ready to go?'

'Well . . . I feel bad about leaving such a mess behind,' she said. 'Blood all over the floor, and every call light in the hall blazing – shouldn't I stay a while and help out?'

'Detective, this is an ICU, remember?' Judy said. 'The blood on this floor is probably the least vile substance we'll deal with today.'

So they shook hands and Sarah said, 'Thanks for the bandages.'

'My pleasure,' Judy said. 'Thanks for saving my life.'

They bagged the casing for the bullet she had fired, and found another bag for the weird knife that had come so close to killing her. 'Why does anybody carry one of these things instead of a good strong switchblade like a respectable criminal?' Sarah said, holstering her weapon, strapping on her day pack.

'I have no idea,' Jason said. 'Is that going to be on the quiz?'

'You better believe it,' Delaney said, 'that and everything else that happened here today. So hold your sarcasm, you two, and remember the story you just told that steno. This incident is probably going to have the shit queried out of it before it's done. Let's take it seriously.'

'OK, I'm serious,' Jason said. 'Am I riding back with Sarah?'

Delaney said, 'No, you ride in with the meat wagon that's coming to pick up your prisoner. Forget about guarding the one we got in bed in there – I got another man coming for that job. You check your prisoner in at County and you're done for today, but see me first thing Monday morning – we'll debrief your taser technique. Congratulations on using it, by the way, you saved yourself the big shitstorm Sarah's got to face. OK, Sarah, you need to follow me downtown.'

'Don't I need to sign off on the body on the floor, though?' she asked Delaney. 'At the morgue?'

'Not your problem,' Delaney said. He had been through this ritual with many a nerve-wracked officer before, and he knew it wasn't going to get any easier. So without wasting time on sympathy, which risked an emotional response, he asked her if she felt up to driving, which predictably made her declare that yes, she could drive, she even had a license. Then he led her downtown to turn in her weapon and shield.

She knew the process was totally routine. She had helped explain, to other officers after other shootings, how reasonable and necessary it was. But now that it was her turn to go on leave she hated it, felt insulted, and wanted to cry out at the injustice of being judged by people who hadn't even been on the scene when it happened.

Eyes bright with unshed tears, she confronted the lined face of Chief of Police Fabian Moretti, whose Sicilian features wore his usual expression, firm resolve overlaid with inexpressible sorrow. 'Zorba the Wop,' Jason called him. 'He was born looking sad.'

Just before he signed the order that put her on paid administrative leave until further notice, he patted her shoulder and mumbled, 'I know how you feel.'

She was not sure she believed him because she wasn't sure, herself, how she felt. *Angry, breathless, glad to be alive, spoiling for a fight, longing for peace and quiet – take your pick.*

She left her two superiors there in the chief's office, assuring them she was fine to drive home. *Still a little deaf if the truth be told,* but that was surely temporary.

The lights were coming on all over town. It was just dusk, not even full dark yet. That seemed amazing, but her watch agreed with a wall clock that it was still a few minutes before seven. Shouldn't it be midnight, at least?

She had phoned home as soon as possible after the shooting and told Aggie, 'Please go ahead with dinner and don't wait up, I'm in a situation here that's going to take some time.' She didn't want to talk about the shooting until she was home with them. She knew Will would tap his sources at the County Attorney's office, and get the bare bones of her story, but she trusted him not to tell her mother and Denny much before she got home.

They were all in different rooms, busy doing work to convince themselves they were not just waiting for her arrival. As soon as they heard her car turn in they came to the kitchen, Aggie to warm up her dinner, Denny to set up her place at the table and then sit next to her, close enough to occasionally touch her arm, pat her shoulder – she had a need to touch. Will brought her a glass of wine and then her slippers, saying, 'Let's get those shoes off.'

She said, 'Doesn't that look good,' and sat down in front

of a plate of food. With a forkful of sweet potato halfway to her mouth, she put it down and said, 'I'm on paid administrative leave because I had to shoot—' And then the tears she had not been able to shed at the station cascaded down her cheeks. She covered her face with her napkin and wept for a full minute while her family circled around her, making little comfort sounds and patting her shaking shoulders.

When she could stop crying she wiped her face and blew her nose, got a fresh napkin out of the holder on the table and cleared her throat. Took a swallow of ice water and said, 'I want to tell you how it happened, so whatever comes out in the news tomorrow you won't let it bother you – you'll know the truth.'

'No hurry, honey,' her mother said. 'Eat your dinner while it's hot.'

'I can talk while I eat. Don't we always?' She ate a bite of pork chop. 'I'm lucky to have all of you to talk it over with.' She ate some peas. Sat a minute, chewing and thinking, and began. When the food was gone and she had finished her story, she said again, 'He didn't leave me any other choice.'

Denny cleared away her plate and said, 'You were awesome, Aunt Sarah.'

Aggie said, 'Thank God you're home safe now. Oh, Sarah. Oh.'

Will said, 'How about a dish of ice cream?'

Later, in the warm quiet of their bed, he held her close and told her, 'Remember this extra part I've got in my hair? I think I know exactly how you feel tonight.'

They had fallen in love during his long recovery from a near-death shooting, and she well remembered how his hands had trembled when she shook them to welcome him back. He and his partner had killed three men fighting their way out of that ambush, were both wounded multiple times and spent a long time in recovery. 'Listen, Sarah,' he spoke softly into her ear in the warm dark, 'what you're feeling now . . . it will always hurt, but after a while it will be more like an ache than a pain.'

'That's good to hear. It's still . . . killing a person, it's a terrible thing to do, isn't it?'

'The worst thing you'll ever have to do, no question. But you had to do it, Sarah, remember that.'

She made herself stop gritting her teeth and lay very still until her muscles stopped jerking. There was one more thing she needed to say, that she knew she could never say to anybody else. Wasn't sure she should even say it to him, but she blurted it out quickly. 'I'm sorry I had to kill that man, and I hope I never have to do it again, but I have to tell you there's another side of me that's glad I was able to do it.'

Will made a sound in his throat, somewhere between a chuckle and a groan. 'I'm glad to hear you say so. That's the only upside – that now you know. All the hundreds of times we go over it in drills, practice and practice, and every time you wonder if the day actually comes when it's necessary to kill somebody, will I be able to do it?'

'Yes. Now I know.' The words came out blurry; she was too tired to talk any more.

Will made one more soothing sound, 'Mmm,' and stroked her gently, and they slept.

Sometime in the still-dark hours of early morning, she dreamed the attack over again. Not exact – it began with a feeling of dread. Something just out of sight was threatening her and then out of the darkness the glittering eyes appeared, and the knife coming at her, gleaming. In her dream she begged, 'Oh no no please no,' and then she must have said some of that out loud because she was sitting up in bed, sweating and crying. Will's arms were around her, he was trying to soothe her with soft words. Then she was fully awake and embarrassed.

'I'm sorry, babe. Shee, so sorry I woke you.' She found a tissue, wiped her face, blew her nose. Got out of bed, went to the bathroom without turning on the light because she felt bad enough without seeing her face right now. Washed her hands and face in cold water and scrubbed hard with a towel, trying to get rid of the sick feeling that she had done something unforgivably wrong. Still in the dark, she came back into the bedroom and stood by the bed shivering, feeling utterly bereft. Will came with her robe and put it on her, pulled the sash tight and slid her feet into slippers.

'You had a bad dream,' he said. He rubbed her hands. 'Take your time, let it go away. Would you like some cocoa?'

'Oh . . .' She took a long, deep breath while she got ready to tell him that hauling her tired body to the kitchen for hot chocolate in the middle of the night was the last thing she wanted to do, but suddenly the idea blossomed in her brain like a beautiful flower and she said, 'That would be nice.'

He even made the cocoa. 'You better watch yourself,' she said as he poured it into mugs. 'You're beginning to act like the tooth fairy.'

He laughed and spilled some cocoa, said, 'Oh, damn,' and then finished pouring while she mopped it up. When he set the pan down he cocked his head and raised one eyebrow – a daffy libertine tooth fairy now – and said, 'Would you like some brandy in this?'

'I better not. I'm a little unstable,' she said, and then, 'Oh, what the hell. Sure, I'd love some brandy in this.'

He measured an exact ounce in the shot glass and poured it in, and poured another for himself. The aroma coming off the hot drink stopped being merely delicious and became sublime. After the first sip, she sat very still on the stool and let the pleasure travel over her taste buds and down her throat, easing the tightness in her warming trunk. A second sip sent gratification spreading slowly, no need to hurry, through all her remaining molecules out to her fingertips and toenails. She said, 'I believe you got this recipe just right.'

'Good,' Will said, and settled more securely on his stool. His complexion improved, too, which made Sarah realize her crying had upset him more than she'd had time to notice.

She touched his arm and said, 'This is hard for you too, isn't it? Did you have dreams after . . .?'

'Yes,' he said abruptly, his eyes on the sink drain. 'And I'm sorry, Sarah, but I can't talk about that.'

'That's OK. Listen, you warmed me up, you made the cocoa. It's what you do that counts, you don't have to talk.' Now she was patting his hands, because he looked so devastated.

'I just . . . I'm not as good with words as you are. If you need to talk, though, there's nothing wrong with that. We have counselors, they always offer.'

'I know. I don't think I want to talk to anybody in the department. They always say it doesn't put a mark against you, but I think it does.'

'Oh, the hell with that. If you need it, go ahead and talk. The important thing is to do what you need to do to get over it, not let it mess up your head. Promise me you'll do that, will you?'

'Yes. Whatever it takes, I'll do it.'

They finished their drinks and went back to bed, and to her surprise she went back to sleep and slept soundly till morning.

Maybe she did still need to talk, though – she was undergoing emotions she didn't fully understand. At first she thought the guilt she'd felt this morning, after the dream of the eyes and knife, was guilt about shooting a man. But as the morning passed she realized she didn't feel guilty about that at all – she had just done what any competent cop would do. And it wasn't guilt she was feeling, it was shame. *Because I begged that lowlife . . .* So as she cleaned the kitchen after breakfast she told herself, *You didn't really do that. That was a dream.*

It still felt shameful. *That must be in my head now, the craven hope that I can dodge the next challenge. That's why I dreamed it that way. What if I lose my nerve over this?* She shook herself. *Maybe I do need to talk to somebody.*

Moretti had cautioned her not to come to the workplace or discuss the case with her fellow officers. 'You got that?' he'd said when she'd been in his office. 'I know you'll be anxious to know how the case is progressing, but you must keep hands off. There'll be an official hearing down the line somewhere, and you can say anything you want to say about this incident then. In the meantime, keep out of it and let the system work.'

She knew better than to argue with the Chief of Police, but back in Delaney's office she'd said, 'Boss, there are things you don't know that you're going to need.'

'Finish the incident report,' he'd said. 'You can do that at home, can't you? After I've read it I'll be in touch. Maybe not tomorrow, but soon. Be patient, Sarah. I have to follow protocols.'

'I know you do. I don't mean to make more trouble for you than you've got already. I just feel like—'

'I know,' he said. 'Go home.'

At home with her family, after she'd told her story she said, 'Now I'm not supposed to talk about the case. But it's the only thing on my mind right now, so I hope you'll understand if I keep talking about it. I don't think I can avoid it.'

Will said, 'No, you can't. Just don't do it in public. I have access to most of the computers in Arizona. I'll bring you everything I can find and of course we'll talk about it.'

To help finance the many family needs they had agreed to carry together, Will had retired from the Tucson Police Department as soon as he was eligible, and gone to work as an investigator for the County Attorney's office. Sarah had never thought much about his second-dipping job, except to love the Blessed Second Paycheck. Now she began to see what a great stroke of luck it was that his job gave him wide access to what she had always called 'the punitive wing of law enforcement.'

'Tell me about it, Will,' she said. 'You get to stick your nose in everything, do you? How much do you, you know, know?'

'Sarah, now,' Will said, holding up a hand, 'I'll do what I can to keep you from dying of curiosity, but we gotta keep it legal.'

'Sure, sure. But you can't expect me to stand right next to the candy store and not even sniff. So please be thinking about this: the man I just killed – who is he and what was he doing there? I mean, obviously he and his buddy were there to grab DeShawn. But what did they want him for and how did they find him so fast? It all says good connections, a big network. But it comes armed with nothing but a tricky knife and a wheelchair? And back to what Ollie said, why are stone killers chasing this two-bit drug deal?'

'Stop,' Will said, looking grave. 'This isn't the time or the place.' He rolled his eyes sideways and Sarah, looking around, saw her mother and Denny watching her, Denny with rapt attention and Aggie looking about ready to faint.

'You're right,' she said. 'Let's see what's on TV.'

Aggie came in from her casita Wednesday morning and floated an idea. 'Sarah, it seems to me you should try to think of this

leave as a chance to do some of the things you never have
time to do.'

'Like what?'

'Well, for instance, you used to read a lot. Why not get
your library card limbered up again? I could make a list for
you to choose from, and we can talk about it.'

'OK. You remember a lot of book titles, do you?'

'Sweetie, I probably could give you fifty just offhand without
looking anything up.'

'Wow. Impressive.' *Look at her, all smiles. I should have a
disaster more often.*

'Besides, it's September,' Aggie went on. 'Almost the right
time to plant bulbs. Wouldn't it be grand to have tulips coming
up by the kitchen door next spring?'

'Ah, Mama, tulip fever strikes again, eh?' She told Denny,
'That's what your grandpa used to call it.' She told her
niece how often Aggie had campaigned, during Sarah's
childhood, for bushes and flowerbeds to brighten the austere
practicality of the farmyard. Sarah's father had always
promised to bring in his plow and tractor and make it
happen, 'as soon as I have the time,' but the ranch work
always intervened.

Sarah asked her mother, 'Have you got a catalog for tulips
too?'

'Just happens I do.'

'I've got an edger,' Will said. 'Let me know when you're
ready and I'll dig a trench.'

Denny said, 'And hey, Aunt Sarah, any idle hours you can't
fill, I can always use a little help with math.'

'Oh, math help from Aunt Sarah, won't that be the day,'
Sarah said. 'You went past me like a rocket early last year.'
Given enough home support to allow full concentration, Denny
had uncovered a talent for math and shot right to the top of
her class. She was beginning to talk about a degree in one
of the hard sciences, staying vague about how she intended
to wedge it in alongside the career in law enforcement she
had been aiming at for years.

But she could use a little attention to body parts, Sarah
decided, noticing how much her niece was filling out. *Those*

pants are too tight, and it's time she got out of braids. I'll take her to my stylist and get her a hairdo.

After Will and Denny got away to work and school, Sarah spent an hour over catalogs with Aggie and they ordered bulbs online. Then she said, 'Now, since I have the computer all warmed up, I'd like to get on with that incident report I promised Delaney, while it's fresh in my mind. Will you be OK till lunchtime?'

'Oh, indeed,' Aggie said. 'Time for my morning nap.' Sarah watched her cross the patio, thinking, *How long has she been dragging her feet like that? I wonder if I could get that stopped?*

She opened the daily diary that she kept at work, read the last cryptic entry: 'Headed to St M's w/Jason, to del arrest war DeShawn Williams, set up squad for 24/7 guard until trans to PiMa Co pris hosp.'

Reading it over, thinking, *so much for good intentions*, she pulled up incident report #96532 and began to type the story of yesterday's events.

It was hard to type the killing onto the page. Revising the first paragraph for the third time, she told herself impatiently, *harder to write it than it was to do it.*

I need to describe exactly how he looked, coming out of that doorway so furtively with his hand in his pocket . . . she drudged on, setting up the scene, hoping she was being clear enough about their mission to the hospital and the shock of what really happened. She had consistently expressed the event in her mind that way – *what really happened.* Now as she typed it for what she hoped would be the last time, she stopped, read the phrase over and recognized it as the evasion that was bothering her. *Happened, my ass. Like some mysterious third force was in control? Let's suck it up here.*

She went back again, reopened the report, and watched the plain words scroll out on the page. 'This is my recollection of what I did when I was attacked in the hall at St. Mary's Hospital yesterday.' Read it over and told herself, *Now you're cookin'.* After that she detailed every move made by the five people in the hall, from the time she came through the door to the ICU with Jason and the nurse.

She posted the account to the department database, then

copied it again to her diary. When she finished, she closed her laptop, gently patted the lid, and said softly, 'There you go.'

She took a big drink of ice water and walked out to find Aggie, sitting quietly in the shade outside her casita.

'You look pretty comfy,' Sarah said, and then sotto voce, 'Any sign of the pesky neighbor today?'

'The weatherman? That's how I think of him. No, he hasn't been around today, so far. But you'll meet him soon, never fear. He'll be thrilled to have a new friend to report to. "It'th a nithe bwight Mawneen, ithn't it?"' She imitated his weather commentary.

Sarah cringed. It wasn't like Aggie to do cruel imitations. This neighbor must have really tried her patience.

'I'm raging hungry,' Sarah said. 'OK if we have ham and cheese sands for lunch?'

'Fine.'

'And after that would you like to go shopping? I need new tennies to wear around the house and so do you – the ones you're wearing don't seem to fit right.'

Aggie had vaguely agreed shopping might be fun, but as they finished lunch she said, 'The shoes I've got fit fine if I lace them up right, but I don't because my feet are sore.'

'Why are they sore? Have you ever told me this? Sit here in the sunshine so I can see.' She spent the next few minutes with her mother's feet in her lap. Aggie had corns, bunions, at least one bone spur that she could see. 'Ma, your feet are in terrible shape. We need to get them taken care of – why haven't you said something?'

'Well, I've had so much wrong with me lately, it seemed like it was just one doctor's appointment after another . . .'

'So you figured you'd just go limping bravely along till you were completely crippled, is that it? What happened to the mother who used to say the first thing to try after you fall off a horse is to see how fast you can get back on the horse?'

'I was younger then,' Aggie said. 'Is doctoring my feet your way of getting back on your horse?'

'I haven't thought of it that way but it's not a bad idea.'

'I suppose. I hope you're not going to try to fix everything that's wrong with me while you're off work. There's a lot about old age that can't be cured.'

'What we can't cure we can mitigate. I happen to know a very smart guy who swears by his podiatrist. Let's see if we can get an appointment next week, and *then* we'll go shopping for shoes.'

'Don't worry about me going crazy at home,' she told Will in their bedroom that night. 'I'm way behind with family chores.'

'Is that right?' Will said. 'So you're not in any hurry to hear about the message Banjo sent to Delaney today? Banjo's keeping me in the loop.'

'What?' Sarah threw her arms around him. 'Will, tell me everything you know about that message right now.'

'This feels pretty good,' Will said, nibbling her ear. 'let's canoodle some more before we talk.'

'I've been a whole day in this house with no news, Will Dietz,' Sarah said, dropping her arms, 'don't mess with me.'

'OK, OK.' Ever the nimble lover, he pulled a sheet of text out of his shirt pocket and read it to her. 'We dug all the slugs out of that van, found three or four in fair condition, and the gardeners found three more casings. I'm working on all of that evidence now and should be ready to lay it out for you Friday morning. Let's say ten a.m.'

'Delaney's going, and taking Bogey and Jason along,' Will said. 'Delaney thought you'd want to know.'

'Do I have a great boss or what?' Sarah said. 'Why are you leaving? I thought we had something going on here.'

'We do,' Dietz said. 'Come to bed.'

SEVEN

Sarah and Aggie spent Friday morning scoping out the best spots around the yard for the tulips, daffodils, and half a dozen other spring blossoms whose gorgeous pictures they had not been able to resist.

'We kind of went crazy over that catalog, didn't we?' Aggie said.

'Now don't get buyer's remorse. We've hardly spent anything on this yard since we moved in and we're going to love watching these beauties come up.'

'I'm thinking we may not love getting so many bulbs planted in one fall season.'

'Hey, this is Arizona. We don't have to worry about freezing till Christmas. And don't forget, we have Will Dietz to help.'

'He did make that offer, didn't he? And I'm just wimpy enough to hold him to it. Let's draw the rest of the iris into this patch by the carport and have lunch.' They were making a chart on squared graph paper, using colored pencils to code for the half dozen blooms they had chosen.

'It looks beautiful on paper,' Aggie said, admiring their handiwork back in the kitchen. 'What if they don't all come up, though? We'll have cleared off all the gravel and we'll end up with bare spots.' Having finally won the landscaping battle she had been waging for four decades, she was now beset by doubts.

'We'll go out to Desert Survivors and buy some of those colored grasses to fill in. Ma, we're finally planting the flowers you've always wanted, why are you going all negative on me?'

'I'm sorry, I think I've kind of got out of the habit of being optimistic. Is that the phone?' She grabbed it off the wall. 'Why isn't it working out here?' She stood holding the wall phone while a ring tone sounded from the family room.

'It's my cell,' Sarah said. She quit spreading mayo and sprinted to the dining table in the bay window. 'I didn't expect it to ring today so I left it on the – oh, it's an email from Will.' She read the first sentence. 'Well . . . it's a forward.' After a quick scan, she added, 'No hurry about an answer. I'll study it after we eat.'

As soon as the meal ended Aggie said, 'Let me clean up. You've got police business on your mind now, haven't you?'

'All the time now,' Sarah said. 'Turns out there's nothing like a paid vacation to make you think about your job.'

Will had forwarded an email from Banjo Bailey, with a note that said, 'There's plenty to think about here, and we can talk about it tonight. But I thought you'd like to see the science ASAP.'

Banjo's message read, 'The casings we retrieved from the grounds at Fairweather Farm are all .223 REM, hollow point, made by Winchester. We could not lift any fingerprints off the casings.

'Most of the bullets we got out of the chassis were too squashed to be useful, but the two we pried out of the insulation over the windshield were in fair condition. There was some distortion, but I can declare with about ninety percent certainty that they were fired by a Colt AR-15, one of the early models. The two we have here are the Colt AR-15 SPI and the BushMaster XM-15. Lands and grooves were close but not an exact match on each of those. A colleague in the Phoenix crime lab has an M16, recently acquired after a robbery that was successfully interrupted. It's an early version of this rifle that was made for the military. That's a long shot as there are very few in civilian hands now, but just in case, I'm going to borrow it and try a comparison. If that's not a match I'll keep looking. Be patient, there are a lot of AR-15s out there. Meantime, materials and photo studies are available here and all hands are welcome in the lab if/when you have questions.'

She read over Banjo's report twice, sat back and stared at the newel post on the stairs to Denny's room for ten minutes. Nothing popped up. *An old model of America's most popular rifle. Standard-issue ammunition.* It felt like an odd fit with the mad-dog driving and shooting the gardeners had described. She scrolled back in her diary to the account on the day of the killing, the way the gardeners described the attack car, hot on the chase, oblivious to anything but their quarry until the police cars turned onto the highway with sirens screaming.

Then, according to the story, the shooters took off right away, yelling at each other. *No, yelling to each other.* She remembered asking, 'What did they say?' and Jacob saying, 'No idea.' *Both men shrugging and Henry adding, 'Spanish.' Jacob nodding yes, and later mentioning Mex lingo.*

She sat up straighter in her chair then, comparing that memory with the new one that kept coming back to her – her own red blood dripping onto the face of the man she had just killed. The wan face with the sneer going out of it, softer and younger than when it first came at her alongside the knife – a face, she clearly remembered, devoid of obvious ethnicity – but probably northern European in origin – German, Polish, Hungarian? *Anyway, not a Hispanic face.*

Frustrating. Every new piece of information she got seemed to move her farther from a coherent answer to the puzzle of Enrique's death.

She decided to take a break. Made a cup of tea and carried it out onto the patio. The heat was tolerable in the shade, and she thought a change of scene might help her quiet the jumble in her brain. She pushed a lounge chair into deeper shade and stretched her legs out, sipping tea and telling herself to quit gritting her teeth. But she was too accustomed to being indoors and busy on a weekday. Sitting still, watching birds at the feeders on a Friday, made her antsy instead of relaxed. Maybe I'll read through all my notes again, she decided, and opened her laptop.

'Hi there!' The jolly male voice sounded so close it made her jump. She couldn't see him, at first; the borders of their big back yard were thickly filled with tall trees, cottonwoods and white birches, with desert willows filling in the space below. She finally spied him, standing just at the south edge of the lot, framed by leaves and smiling broadly. He was a barrel-shaped man with stumpy legs below his knee-length shorts. He wore round wire-rimmed glasses and had a lot of curly brown hair. She couldn't tell his age – usually one of the first things she guessed about a newcomer.

'Hello,' she said – a tepid hello, since she didn't know who he was and wasn't feeling sociable. 'Should I know you? You live around here?'

'I'm your neighbor,' he said, nodding, smiling, and then pointing behind himself, 'back there.'

'I see.' *I think I'm beginning to. This must be the weatherman.*

Nodding as if they'd just agreed to something important, he said, 'Isn't this a nice day?' His lisp was very severe and there was something else, a kind of childish naivete.

'Indeed it is.' *A speech impediment is not the weatherman's only problem, is it?*

'Stanley?'

The call came from behind the clump of Texas Ranger bushes that marked the lower edge of Sarah's yard. A woman's voice, not strong. Not angry, either, just a little anxious, as if she'd been searching for him.

He turned his head in the direction of her voice and said, 'Right here, Mama.' His voice stayed pleasant, even complacent, but to Sarah he rolled his eyes to the sky and shook his head in a gesture that said, 'She's such a fusser.'

Sarah got up and walked to where the woman stood peering over the bushes. 'Come in, Mrs – I'm sorry, I don't know your name.'

'It's Pettigrew,' the little woman said, 'Jean Pettigrew. And this, if he hasn't told you, is my son, Stanley.' She was wearing a bib apron with a ruffle around the bottom, over faded jeans and a knit cotton shirt. Her short grey hair was permed in tight curls around her head. She cleared her throat and said, 'I hope he hasn't been bothering you.'

'No, of course not,' Sarah said. 'We were just chatting about the weather.'

'Oh? Well. One of his favorite subjects. Um . . .' Her hands were busy making uncertain gestures. 'Stanley's been anxious to meet you. Somebody told him you and your husband were both on the police force, and he's very interested in that.'

Stanley said, 'It's quite un . . . un . . .'

'Unusual,' Jean said.

'I know what I want to say, Mother,' Stanley said, and then turning to Sarah, 'Unusual for couples to join up together, right?'

'Oh, there are several married couples in the force,' Sarah said, hoping to head off an argument, 'but they mostly met each other at work, I think. They didn't join together. And actually' – *this ought to take his mind off the weather* – 'Will and I are not married.' She smiled, and asked Jean, 'How long have you been living in the Dietrichs' house? I haven't seen you before.'

'Oh, I've seen you lots of times, but you always look busy, so I never wanted to stop you to say hello. It's the Pettigrews' house now; I bought the place. Just Stanley and me, we're the whole crew.' She smiled at him fondly, edged closer and nudged his elbow, and he quit sulking at her and smiled at Sarah.

'But you have an older woman living with you,' Jean said. 'Somebody's mother?'

'Mine. Yes. And my niece, Denny. She's twelve.' She considered a minute and decided to follow her hunch. 'We all had special needs, so we moved in together to help each other out.'

Jean Pettigrew's smile brightened and she said, 'You see, Stanley, we're not the only ones with special needs.' She sent Sarah a conspiratorial nod. 'We all find ways to cope, though, don't we?'

'We certainly do. We should get together and share some of our coping secrets, one of these days,' Sarah said, standing up, gathering her laptop and cup. 'But right now my break is over, I must get back to work.' Aware she was being less than cordial, she smiled, managed part of a wave with her hands full, and added, 'Nice to have met you both.' She hurried back into the house.

Behind her, she heard Jean say, 'Snack time, Stanley!' From inside her open house door she watched them make their way back across the ditch to their own house. Dimly, she heard Stanley ask if they could have ice cream for a snack, and Jean reply that there was no ice cream, but she had a perfect orange they could split.

When Denny came home from school Sarah invited her mother and niece to the dining room table and poured lemonade for everybody. Seated in comfort in the bay window, she shared her afternoon's discovery, that the 'pesky neighbor' Aggie had described, the 'weatherman' interrupting her afternoon siestas on the patio was a special needs person with a serious lisp and some mental limitations.

'But he's got one big asset, a loving mother providing home care.'

'Oh dear,' Aggie said. 'I wish I'd known. I'm afraid I've been quite unfriendly toward that man. He just – his talk seemed odd and it put me off.'

'I was pretty awkward with him too,' Sarah said, 'until I figured out what track he was on. I guess we all get defensive when people don't conform to our expectations.'

'You'd think by my age I'd be past that, but apparently not.' Aggie pondered, tapping one hand with the other, and added, 'His mother has a hard row to hoe, doesn't she? He must limit her social life quite a bit.'

'I suppose so. And she has the job for life,' Sarah said.

'Maybe I'll ask her to have a cup of tea, if I see her out there.'

'We could do that. Both of them, of course. Some day when there's time.'

'Yeah. Before the bulbs arrive.'

Denny schlupped up the last of her lemonade through a noisy straw and said, 'O boy, you bought some of those new LED bulbs, huh? Can I have one for my desk lamp?' She stared at their sudden laughter and said, 'What's funny?'

They brought in the charts and showed her where they meant to put the bulbs. She was delighted and declared her eagerness to help. Unlike Aggie, it never occurred to Denny to worry about the work. What she wondered was why they thought planting bulbs would interfere with asking the neighbors to tea.

'But then she's never had a backache, has she?' Aggie said, talking to Sarah while Will and Denny did the dinner dishes. 'Twelve is really a wonderful age.'

'In so many ways. Sometimes I wish she didn't have to grow up. I'd like to keep her just as she is.' She looked at Aggie, at work on a quilting square under the light. 'I don't suppose you ever wished that when we were growing up, did you? You were so busy, you must have wanted us to grow up and help.'

'Oh, no mother's that busy. There were some ages . . . I remember thinking nine was perfect, for you and Robert both.'

'My brother went through a lovable stage? Really?'

'Now don't start that. You and Robert each had several stages where I wanted to keep you as you were. But Janine – I was always praying for Janine to grow up. I still am.'

In this house, Denny's mother is our special need. We're all waiting for Janine to grow up and come home.

The story of the shooting appeared in the Sunday *Star*. It got only a few column inches but was featured prominently, above the fold, on the front page.

Aggie made a funny noise, a kind of angry gasp, when she discovered it. Sarah, making French toast in the crowded kitchen, heard the sound and looked at her in alarm, afraid she was choking. When she saw her mother, standing at the counter, slide the front page under the sports page, she knew at once what the trouble was. She went on resolutely dipping bread slices into beaten eggs and turning them on the griddle, but the morning had darkened for her. She had to work to keep her voice steady as she called her family to pick up their plates.

They sat down at their accustomed places at the table in the bay window, and tucked into the good meal, making happy noises over toast with maple syrup and the bacon Denny had so carefully broiled. Sarah barely tasted her meal but chewed like a soldier so as not to ruin the treat for the others. As soon as she finished, though, she walked out and slid the hidden front page off the bottom of the pile of newspapers and stood at the counter to read it.

'Well,' she said when she finished, 'it's not terrible.' The very fair and balanced if not quite accurate account began, 'Two Tucson detectives were attacked in the Intensive Care

Unit at St. Mary's Hospital Tuesday as they delivered an arrest warrant to a patient there.' No mention of the fact that Jason was never attacked, but the head nurse was – that it was the attack on Judy, in fact, that had started the incident.

Would she ever be able to explain that to a skeptical board of enquiry? She read it again, wondering – did it seem like . . . *like I just got hysterical and fired my weapon?* Even knowing that was not the case, she thought, *If I was reading this without any prior knowledge, would I wonder why the police had to shoot a man who only had a knife?*

Still, it was not a negative story. It said two police officers had been attacked and had responded appropriately. Delaney must have been consulted and had defended his crew with a straightforward account. She had no cause to complain.

Absurdly, it was her picture at the top of the page that really bothered her. She had not worn the uniform to work in half a dozen years, since she made the detective rating. So why had Delaney chosen that old photo to publish? She'd always hated the way she looked in the hat, had kept it off her head as much as possible. But there it was, squashed on good and tight for some official portrait, making her look, she thought now as she always had, like a dweeby traffic patrolman.

Denny looked over her arm, stared, and said, 'Well, you're safe on the street, Aunt Sarah. Nobody will recognize you from that picture.'

It was just Denny being Denny, clever and humorous, but for a few seconds Sarah wanted to tear up the paper. She tightened her grip on the page she was holding and clamped her jaw shut. Then Will was beside her other shoulder, saying, 'What have you got here? Oh, it's the . . . well. Can I have it next?'

She handed him the section.

'Why don't we all sit down,' he said, 'and have another cup of coffee? Bring the whole paper over, will you, Denny?'

Sarah got busy pouring second coffee, Aggie began to denounce the state tax plan featured on the front page, and the moment passed. Denny got the funnies and giggled over Dilbert while Will read Sarah's story carefully, handed the page to Aggie and said, 'It's not bad, Sarah.' So then Aggie was able to read it without having a tizzy, and in fact said, as she put it down, 'Yes, you can live with this, can't you, sweetheart?'

'Sure,' Sarah said. 'I lived with that damn hat for seven long years, I can stand another day.' And her whole family laughed happily, because Sarah was being a good sport, bringing up that ridiculous hat. As if it could possibly matter to a woman who had just saved her own life by shooting a man.

EIGHT

Sunday–Tuesday

The rest of Sunday passed, as Sundays do – some chores, some shopping, a movie Denny liked and the three adults agreed was terrible. They were all together for the entire day, so it was possible for Sarah, at times, to forget she was on leave. Reality came crashing back Monday morning, when Will and Denny got off to work and school and Sarah stayed home. Aggie went back to her usual routine, too, taking her own sweet time to get dressed and eat breakfast in her casita.

Sarah carried a second coffee to the little desk in the bedroom, sat down in the merciless silence and opened her laptop. She brought up some notes about ongoing cases and began cleaning up the language and shifting them into folders. Always great to get the files cleaned up, she told herself as an hour passed. When she was growing sleepy with boredom her cell phone rang. She picked it up before the first ring ended and Will said, 'Sarah, this has got to be quick, so just listen. Banjo got the M16 he was waiting for and tested it first thing this morning. I don't know what this means to your case yet, but I just got word it's not a match with those bullets he dug out of the van. But close, he says. So he's still looking for the right M16.'

'Oh, good. Not bad anyway. Thanks, Will.'

'Talk to you later,' he said, and was gone. Never a chatty man and really in a hurry today. *Oh, I'm lucky to have him just as he is.*

She went back to work and made rapid progress on the file sorting for half an hour. When her cell chirped, she picked it up absent-mindedly and said, quickly and quietly, 'Burke.'

'Hey there,' a warm-sorghum voice said, 'how's my favorite investigator today?' There was a lot of noise in the background, loud arguments, a crying child and a barking dog.

'If this is Sergeant Bobby Lee Pratt,' Sarah said, slowing down and warming up, 'how I am is delighted. To what do I owe this nice surprise?'

'Heard you had a spot of trouble.'

'I did. Quite a big spot. More like a splash.'

'What's your schedule like today? Got any time to visit?'

'Time is what I have the most of right now, Bobby. You know I got put on leave?'

'Yup. And I was proud to hear you got through the whole first day without having a spasm. But, uh, I get off this shift about three. Any chance you'll be home?'

'If you're coming to see me, I'll be home, absolutely.'

'Then look for me right around three-thirty.' A click and he was gone, back into one of the chaotic street scenes he so enjoyed keeping under control.

She smiled, remembering the key role Pratt had played during that crazy first day at Fairweather Farms. She'd been doing her best to sort out the looney-tunes crime scene when Pratt appeared, smiling benignly with the manager in tow, and order began to emerge out of bedlam.

She abandoned her file-sorting and started to get her thoughts organized again. She wanted to be ready to give a clear account of the shooting to the unshakeable Bobby Pratt. Going over her notes jogged her memory and she added one more item to the bottom of her growing list: to ask DeShawn about the Russell Sexton name she had found in the shoe.

She was still hard at it when Aggie came in the back door. Sarah paused in her work to tell her mother they were due for company later.

'You look a little nervous,' Aggie said. 'Is this man going to be judging you?'

'Oh, no, he's just coming to help, he's not entitled to oversight – in fact, I outrank him now. Amazingly enough.' She blew a stray hair out of her eyes.

'Why is it amazing?'

'Well, he was my field training officer when I started, and that's kind of like first grade, you know. There are things you never forget. Like did you like your teacher.'

'Did you?'

'Boy, did I. He was so patient – but firm, too. He'd say, "You have to get this right, don't try to fake it, your life is at stake."'

'Brr.' Aggie shivered. 'I'm glad I didn't hear that. I was anxious enough as it was. Any time you were on a night shift, that first year you were in uniform, I got very little sleep.'

'Poor Ma. I'm sorry I caused you to toss and turn.'

'I was sure you were going to get killed on a night shift. My daughter, out there in the dark with the crazies. And now you finally have your big disaster in the middle of a sunny afternoon.'

'Yeah, that's law enforcement for you – full of surprises.'

'But you say this trainer was kind to you?'

'So good I couldn't let him go, for a while. The first month after he signed off on me, I must have called him a dozen times. I'd say, "I should have asked you how you . . ." Something or other, and he would go over it again, taking his time, even though a lot of it was surely a repeat. He does a lot of bullshit joking – it's his way to get people to calm down. But underneath the foolishness he's a good, thoughtful cop who likes to help people.'

'Wow. I don't hear you talk like that very often.'

'No? Hmm. I guess I am pretty critical. The job requires precision.'

'I suppose.' She got up. 'Stay where you are, I'll do lunch. Roast beef sands OK?'

'Perfect. I'm going to finish this and then I want to run out and buy a couple of bottles of his favorite lager.'

'I'm looking forward to meeting this teacher.'

Pratt had changed into civvies, so when Aggie answered the doorbell she got the full Door-full-of-Denim impression. Bobby Pratt in jeans and sneakers looked even bigger than he did in uniform. His blue denim shirt blocked out most of the clear blue sky behind him; his canvas-clad feet obscured the doorsill. And he was ready with his country-slicker charisma, bending over Aggie's hand to say hello.

As Sarah came out of the kitchen carrying a cheeseboard and two longnecks, she heard him say, 'Are you the Super Mom I've heard so much about? The one that used to ride in rodeos?'

'Oh, well . . .' Aggie said, but was soon persuaded to show
him the picture on the front wall, of her holding a blue ribbon
aboard Monty, her favorite barrel-racer the year before she got
married. As soon as she'd said enough self-deprecating things
about rodeo queens she declared nap time and retired to her
casita, giving Sarah a little satisfied nod on her way out.

Sarah settled with Pratt at the round table, with the snacks
and Sam Adamses. She opened her laptop and told her story,
reading off the monitor at the spots where she wanted details
to be accurate: how many feet away was he when he started the
lunge? And the balisong – how big a blade? Humbly, she
confessed how opposed she had been at Delaney's insistence on
getting a crime scene crew out to the hospital to measure and
photograph everything.

'Why wouldn't you want a crime scene crew? You know
that's the best protection you can have.'

'I know it now, Bobby. Somehow at that time I thought it
was important that we manage the whole thing by ourselves.'

'So the citizens shouldn't find out we got killers on staff?' His
brutal use of the k-word took her breath away for a second and
then revealed the hilarious wrongheadedness of her trying to
keep the shooting in-house. 'What, you went into brain-freeze?'

'I guess. Been years since I had to actually use that Glock
to shoot somebody – there's a lot of stress, you know?'

And Pratt, who according to legend once brought a four-
man burglary crew to their knees begging for mercy as they
put the handcuffs on each other, said, 'Uh-huh.'

'OK, of course you know. But we were being very calm
and helping each other, everything was going fine until Delaney
arrived, and I guess I just wanted to go on making nice with
my pals.'

Pratt enjoyed that explanation a lot, rocked back in his chair
and had a belly-laugh, slapped his thighs and then high-fived
Sarah as they laughed together. It was good to know she hadn't
thought anything that crazy for almost three whole days.

'I just wish I knew who he was, the one I shot,' Sarah said.
'Jason took some car keys off his prisoner but I haven't heard
what's become of the car.' She jotted a note on her desk pad to
add the keys to her list. 'Gloria says the blood work's done so

they must be searching for a match on that, and the DNA report is due soon, so maybe we'll get a name before long.'

'Before you jump out of your skin, you mean? And Delaney must be about ready to question the survivor, isn't he? The one Jason used the taser on. Had to get him de-toxed some to get any straight answers, I heard.'

'Yeah, so far he's acting more like a recovering boozer than a druggie, they say – just babbling. This case is very odd, Bobby – the harder we work at it the more confusing it gets.' She told him about the money in the pocket of the jacket.

'And the shooters chasing the van – our guys got after them right away, but they didn't catch them that day, and even though they had a good description of the vehicle and a partial on the plate, nobody ever caught them. That car went to ground very fast and never surfaced.'

'So a good organization, seems like.'

'Right. Bigger than just one carful of shooters, anyway. And right there is where we have questions. Ollie brought it up and now it's bothering the rest of us. If these guys are so tough and frightening – oh, and so well-organized – what are they doing with this little two-bit drug deal?' She told him about the dead drop and the money Delaney had in his vault.

'Yeah. See what you mean.' He made a tidy sandwich of crackers and salami. 'But look at it the other way around, Sarah. You think maybe your little two-bit drug deal could be having a growth spurt?'

'Oohhh?' She turned sideways in her chair and watched a hummingbird come to the feeder outside the bay window. Pratt waited. 'You mean somebody like these international wise-guys maybe decided to muscle in—'

'Something like that.'

'Why would they?'

'I don't know. I don't *know* anything yet, except – these people are here, they're raising hell, and I think you should keep them in mind.'

'Well. OK, I'll do that.' She barked a short humorless laugh. 'I might need a quick review course in big-time bad guys.'

'Ah, you know enough. How much do you know about the guns?'

'AR-15, Banjo thinks.'

'Uh-huh. But now, just before I came over here, I was told Banjo thinks maybe they were M-16s, the early version of that rifle that was made for the military. You know all about that, do you?'

'Not really. I haven't encountered it in a crime scene before.'

'Well, when the M-16 was first produced it could fire semi-auto or full auto, based on the position of a selector switch. Current production for the military is now semi-auto, one shot per pull, or a three-round burst. Again, based on the position of a selector switch. Sales to civilians now, though, are all semi-auto – one pull, one shot.

'There's a lot of buzz going around lately that says these bad guys that attacked the van at the old folks' home were firing at least in bursts and maybe full auto – just bam-bam-bam-bam, I heard.

'So if the ammo you've got matches one of these early guns, Sarah, you have a rare set of criminals here – there are very few of these old military guns in civilian hands these days.

'By itself, that might not be so interesting, but together with the balisong, it begins to narrow the field.'

'It's been my experience,' Sarah said, 'that most law enforcement people talk about that knife as the favorite of the idiot fringe. Something for the silly set, Delaney called it.'

'Oh, yes.' Pratt showed all his teeth in a grin. 'Except when it ain't.' He ate some salami rolled around a hunk of Vermont cheddar, and frowned at his napkin. 'For instance . . . Guys on the robbery squads say lately they're hearing from victims that they got robbed by people like nobody they've ever seen before, mixed squads of very mean guys, mostly from Russia and Ukraine, and they sometimes hook up with those Salvadorans that are causing so much grief in Mexico, preying on the caravans and all that mess at the border.'

'Oy vey.'

'Yeah. Global bad guys we're getting now, ain't that a hole in the boat? According to the poker game they robbed last week, these guys are not just after the money, they like to hurt people. Lately there's a lot of lore out there, about bad guys who speak thuggish versions of four or five languages, cross over borders like they aren't even there.'

'Have you noticed,' Sarah said, 'that rumor is often exaggerated?'

'Sure. I discount most of what I hear by about thirty percent. But I keep hearing stories about the guns, that these mean robbers have some old M-16 rifles. And the last liquor store they held up said one of them had one of those trick knives.'

'Damn.'

'Yeah.'

'But' – Sarah pulled her nose, shifted her feet around fretfully – 'if your mean robbers are the guys chasing the Fairweather van I've got about a million questions. Because they don't fit with anything else I've heard or seen, till this one thing that just happened to me at the hospital.'

'Uh-huh. But that one thing has kind of stuck in your mind, hasn't it?'

'Yes, it has,' Sarah said. 'Stuck right there, day and night.' She wasn't going to tell Bobby Pratt about the dream. But she had a feeling he knew all about bad days' nights.

He put his hands on his bare knees and powered his bulk out of the chair. 'Good to see you so well situated here, you and your family on this nice quiet street. You got Will Dietz folded into your household now, huh? Very smart move.'

She smiled, surprised. 'You know him?'

'We go way back. High time he had a little luck.' He put on his big canvas hat and peered down at her out of its shady folds. 'You got lots of friends in the department, kid. You'll get through the hearing just fine.'

'Thanks for coming by, Bobby. It was good to talk.'

The house was very quiet after he left. Sarah spent five minutes wishing she had a recording of their conversation, so she could play it back when these days off got too long, as she knew they would.

I could make a memo now . . . and add a couple of things to the list. She opened her laptop and began typing her memory of the conversation.

Aggie came in quietly, saw how fast her daughter was typing, went back in the kitchen and started a salad for dinner. Denny came home from school, got an absent-minded hello from her intensely typing aunt, and said to Aggie in the kitchen, 'This is supposed to be my night to cook, but I've got homework up the yazoo, is it OK if—'

She got another wave-off from her grandmother and disappeared upstairs. The house was soon reverberating with the screaming rock music that facilitated math homework for Denny. Even through a floor and a ceiling, it briefly distracted Sarah, but she was winding down anyway. In a few minutes she titled her entry, set up a new file for it, and signed off. In the kitchen, she said, 'I never meant to stick you with all the cooking, but Pratt said some useful things.'

'No problem.' Aggie gave a short laugh. 'I believe I just invented a new dish. I think I'll call it Salade au Refrigerateur – doesn't that sound elegant? I put in everything I could find that was at all appropriate for a salad. If we have this and a cheese omelet, that'll be enough, won't it?'

'Sounds wonderful. Shall I do the omelet?'

'No, that's ready to go too, as soon as Will gets home. You can set the table and make toast.'

Feels like we're back at the ranch, Sarah thought. *Ma's giving orders, and I'm doing as I'm told. This recovery from depression may not be an unmixed blessing.*

Delaney called Tuesday morning and said, 'The hearing hasn't been scheduled yet. That means it'll be another week, at least. But I've got a couple hours this afternoon and I'd like to spend them with you, going over the issues I think will come up in the hearing.'

'You want me to come to the station?'

'Well – yes, I'd like to do it here where we have all the recording equipment and could even make a video if we wanted to—'

'That sounds good,' Sarah said, thinking of yesterday, how much she had wanted her conversation with Pratt recorded.

'But we can't have anybody saying we tweaked the evidence, so I want to make this clear before we start: we're just going to confirm the times and distances we established there in the hall at St. Mary's. That's all we're doing, making sure we're all on the same page with that evidence. We're not tweaking anything, do you understand that?'

'I understand it,' Sarah said. 'Will everybody else? Because this meeting won't stay private for a nanosecond.'

'I don't intend it to. I cleared it with the chief and I'm going to repeat it to everybody including the trainee who brings the chalk and erasers. This is just to be sure that we're all on the same page about times and distances, so we don't stir up some freaking come-to-Jesus investigation just because somebody forgot the details.'

'Good,' Sarah said, thinking, *chalk and erasers?* 'Shall I bring my notes?' She faked a cheery voice because this rehearsal for a hearing that everybody assured her was nothing to worry about was beginning to worry her quite a bit.

He cleared it with Moretti? The chief whose last words to her had been to caution against discussing this case with anyone in the department? Was it at all possible that these two superior officers were now primarily concerned with covering their own asses? Afraid they had a detective on staff who might be thought by some to have used excessive force?

Were they in danger of forgetting that she was Sarah Burke, the careful drudge? The one who kept her desk in order, could always find everything in her files, never came late to the meeting? Didn't she rest secure in her squad, knowing her colleagues relied on her for reminders, asked her for help with backup info they should have looked up for themselves, ironically called her Detective Do-Right?

'I want to get Jason in on this too,' he was going on, 'and he's got a deposition at three, so we'll need to start at one sharp. Can you make that?'

'Absolutely.' She was talking on the kitchen phone. As she hung it up on the wall, she saw that her arms were covered with gooseflesh.

Delaney sounds anxious. Why is he anxious?

If her superiors thought she might have used excessive force why wouldn't they say so and give her a chance to defend herself? In Delaney's homicide squad, teamwork was every-thing. The unspoken compact was they gave him their best work and he defended them against any blame that might float in from a demanding world. Was that going to change now?

Seized by a sudden need to move, to use her muscles to work off the worry building inside her, she went out and stood in the middle of the patio, looking around for the likeliest place to start digging. Hadn't Aggie said how pleasant it would be to have tulips coming up by the kitchen door next spring?

She walked across the brick patio area to the shed where Will kept his tools. It had been entirely his domain until now, a small wooden structure with shingled roof and ship-lapped siding, and a Dutch door like a barn that closed with a padlocked hatch. She'd forgotten where he said he kept the key – had to search, found it hanging from a nail under the eave. The way the nail was placed, with just enough haft to hang the key easily, its tenpenny head big enough to keep the keyring from falling off but not big enough to be an obstacle, spoke so eloquently of Will Dietz's thoughtful nature that for a moment she held the key to her lips.

Inside, neatness reigned. The garden tools all hung together along an end wall. She chose a shovel and a spade, not knowing which would be better, and found some gloves that almost fit. After the first attempt to break ground through the gravel, she came back in the shed and took down the rake.

Aggie came out of her casita as Sarah was making her first try with the spade, having already given up on the shovel. She had raked a large pile of gravel out of the space between the house wall and the edge of the brick patio. It was heaped at the east corner of the south wall. She had already stumbled over it twice.

'How's it going?' Aggie asked.

'Not so good.' Sarah said. 'This dirt . . .'

She was trying to break up ground that had the consistency of gravel-infused granite. The result, so far, was hard to see on the designated flower bed, but woefully obvious everywhere else. A good deal of dust from the ground she could not move was clinging to her sweat-covered arms and legs. Insects, usually so scarce in Tucson, had come out of the bushes and were feasting on her body, loving her dank aroma. In a little more than an hour, she had transformed their usually serene back yard into a disordered heap of tools and gravel.

'Maybe we need to water it a little,' Aggie said. 'Soften it up?'

'Good idea,' Sarah said. 'Where does Will keep the hose, I wonder?' Ever since they'd moved into this old house, she had used all of her spare time making small improvements to the interior – painting walls, hanging drapes, shopping yard sales for side tables and extra chairs. Will had done all the outside work, she realized now, trimmed the bushes, raked the gravel and swept the walks. He had never asked for any help and she, consequently, hardly knew how anything worked.

'I'll figure out where to hook this up and dampen down a section before I take a break,' she said, wheeling the heavy roll of hose on its carrier around the corner from where she found it. 'Why does he keep it under the bougainvillea, I wonder? Have we got a lot of hose thieves in the neighborhood?' She showed Aggie her scratched arms as she stood holding the hose end, rubbing her tired back, and asked her mother, 'Where's the outlet back here?'

'Um,' Aggie said, 'I'm not sure there is one. Come to think of it . . .' She looked at her daughter sadly and asked, 'You're getting pretty sick of this tulip-and-crocus idea already, aren't you? I should never have asked you—'

'No! Jesus, Mom, why do you have to make every little setback into a tragedy?' The words were out before she had control. The frustration of not being able to make any of her gardening ideas work had piled on top of the grievance she was already feeling about her layoff from work. Punishing the person nearest to hand, she had blurted out her impatience with her mother's depression.

Immediately contrite, she dropped the hose and walked toward her silent, white-faced mother. 'I'm sorry, Mom. Nothing's working and I got so hot and frustrated I just lost it.'

'Please don't hug me,' Aggie said. 'You're soaking wet.' She uttered a little hiccupping sound and then a chuckle.

Sarah began to laugh too, peering ruefully at her dirty legs and bleeding arms. 'You enjoy watching your daughter screw up, do you?' she said, and then something about that question triggered her memory of the mess she'd come out here to get away from. She cried out in distress, 'Omigod, what time is it?' She'd left her watch in the kitchen so she wouldn't get it dirty.

'Eleven-fifteen,' Aggie said. 'Why?' She watched in amazement as Sarah turned and ran toward the tools by the kitchen door, shouting, 'I have to get this mess cleaned up right now!'

She stopped, turned with her hands in the air and cried, 'I can't clean it up! I'm due downtown at one o'clock and I have to take a shower!'

'Yes, you really do,' Aggie said. 'You go on and take care of yourself and leave this to me.'

'You can't move any of this. It's all heavy stuff. Promise me you'll leave it alone and I'll clean it up when I get back.'

'Yes, all right, I promise. Go on now or you'll be late.'

Sarah did as she was told again, grumbling, 'What was I thinking?' as she hurried into the shower. She winced and complained when the soap and hot water hit her scratched arms. When she was clean and dry she dithered for two minutes about what to wear, wanting to cover her arms and still be cool. Finally, talking to herself, she put on her seersucker suit and mesh pumps. Hair and makeup she could always do in ten minutes flat, but today she needed five extra minutes to clean her fingernails. Then she used three more minutes to print a copy of her notes from Pratt's visit.

Five blocks from home, her stomach rumbled and she remembered she had not had lunch. She found a power bar in the side pocket of the door and ate it, telling her body to pretend it was steak.

She made it to South Stone with five minutes to spare. By the time she walked into Delaney's office, she was once again Detective Sarah Burke, dependable sidekick, reliable finder of lost files. Cool and collected. An officer of the law.

NINE

The small meeting room looked unusually elegant, freshly vacuumed and set up with ice water and glasses. *Ah, but we'll have it looking lived-in before long,* Sarah thought, as she and Jason pulled out chairs and unloaded notes, dark glasses, two digital tablets, a purse and a stack of mail. An office tech was fussing with a projector and a laptop on a side table.

'You look rested,' Jason said. 'Really getting into this paid leave business, huh?'

'That's right,' Sarah lied, 'just drifting in the hammock looking up at blue sky.' Her arms were still throbbing from the bougainvillea cuts.

Then Delaney strode in, all business, and plopped down a folder at the head of the table.

'Lot to go over,' he said, 'let's get started.' Jason's eyebrows went up; his smooth face and handsome shaven head inclined one degree toward Delaney and seemed to ask, *Who's holding you back?*

'I want to begin where the incident began,' Delaney said. 'Alice, you ready?' The steno touched a key, and a chart appeared on the screen across the room. It was a computer-drawn depiction of fifty feet of the ICU at St. Mary's Hospital, on squared paper with distances indicated along the top and sides of the graph.

'The first picture shows the dimensions of the north section of the Intensive Care Unit where the attack occurred,' Delaney said, 'and the positions of the three people who walked into it together on Friday.' His laser pointer danced over the stick figures labelled a, b and c, and a legend at the bottom of the page that named them. 'First, do you both agree that this is where you were, relative to each other, as you came through the doors? Jason, you were farthest left, like this? And you were in the middle, Sarah?' He recited the distances he wanted established – between the stick figures, then from the figures to the third door in the hall, drawn in red. Nodding, the two detectives watched his red dot. 'Both good with this? Next picture, Alice.'

The figures were all in the same places but there was an addition, a stick figure for the man in scrubs pushing a wheelchair.

'And that man in scrubs,' Sarah said, 'could have pushed his chair on into that room without a cross word from me. He looked perfect to be exactly where he was. But Judy really knows her turf, she spotted him right away for a fake. Tore into him like a sheep dog and got knocked down for her pains.'

'OK, next chart, Alice,' Delaney said. 'This is where we need you to clear up a few things, Jason. We established that you were thirty feet from the suspect when he knocked Judy down, but I don't believe you tased him from that distance, did you?'

'No. We spent one whole winter and spring wrangling over which taser to buy, and most of the following summer training with it. So we've all got those parameters drilled into our brains – ten to twenty feet of clear space with nobody in it but your target bad guy. That's what it takes to make the taser man happy, right? Turns out it's hard to find in real time, so we don't use it as much as we expected.'

'Which is why we're all so pleased when it works,' Delaney said. 'This shot of yours went just about as advertised, didn't it?'

'Textbook. I took one big step toward him as he moved away from the chair, and there it was, as fat as butter, the perfect shot. I didn't know he was high, so I didn't even worry that the shot wouldn't work.'

'Oh, I forgot about that,' Sarah said. 'Some of those drugs can make people immune to the jolt, can't they?'

'So I hear,' Jason said. 'But I think my guy has been pickled for so long that he's about ready to fall over from any little nudge. He didn't go totally disabled the way some do, but that first jolt put him on the ground all right.'

'Yes. Each take-down is a little different, isn't it? Now let's move along to the second half of this incident. Alice?' A new graph appeared onscreen. 'You were putting cuffs on your prisoner when the second man came out of the room your man had been headed into, right? Is this about right for your position – left of Sarah but somewhat ahead?'

'Yeah. Little further ahead, I think – maybe ten feet. Well, to tell the truth we were rolling around some. Tased or not, this dude doesn't like to get tied up. He had a kind of panic reaction to restraints.'

'So you had a pretty busy time, finishing the arrest?'

'Fair to say, yes. I think he must have been tied up a few times as a child and maybe had some bad stuff done to him because he went totally apeshit. Tried to bite me – almost made it once. I don't ever want to meet this guy in the dark – he's dangerous.'

'But then you couldn't really have been watching Sarah when she shot the second man, could you?'

'Well . . .'

'Think about it. Were your eyes really on Sarah when she fired that shot? Or were you watching the man you were tying up?'

'Um. Put it that way, I suppose I must have been watching my prisoner. But I was aware of my surroundings and I heard Sarah warn her attacker. Twice, actually, wasn't it, Sarah?'

'Yes,' Sarah said. 'But he's right, Jason, you were busy with wheelchair man on the floor there, and weird knifeman was heading straight for your unprotected back. So I drew my gun, there wasn't time for anything else. I thought when he saw the Glock he'd believe me when I told him to drop the knife.'

After a long moment of silence, Jason said, his voice as dry as the desert outside the window, 'My God, Sarah, is that really what happened? The knife guy was headed for me?'

'Yes. He'd been busy in DeShawn's room, remember, tearing the patient out of his IV hookup, but he heard his partner yelling with pain from the taser. So he abandoned the guy they came to get and came out to help his partner.'

'But then he ran into you first?'

'No, at that point he wasn't even looking at me. He spotted

you on top of his partner and started toward you right away. I saw him heading for your back and pulled my gun and told him to put the knife down or he was dead.'

'No shit?' Jason said. 'He was headed for me?'

'Yes. You couldn't see him because you were on the ground with the one you were fighting.'

'So then instead of planting his fancy knife in my nice wide-open back he kicked Judy out of the way and went after you?'

'Yep. That's when I warned him again, and he did pause, for a couple of seconds. But I saw him decide that I must be bluffing. He got that sneer that the real bullies get; I could see him decide that no woman was ever going to shoot him. So he lunged at me with the knife held in both hands, straight-arm, like this.' She showed him. 'He was really close by then so I had to shoot him.'

Delaney, who'd been swiveling his head from one side of the table to the other like a man at a tennis match, said, 'All right, this sounds very credible now.'

'Does it?' Sarah said. 'You think the establishment is going to accept my word when I say the victim was a male chauvinist pig who couldn't believe a woman could hurt him, so I had to kill him?'

'You've still got a week or so,' Delaney said, watching her carefully. 'Maybe in seven days you can think of a better way to say that.'

'I'll try.'

'Good. So now do you two agree? You're both firm on this recollection of how the two shootings went down? You'll need to make a few amendments to your written reports in the case file. Can I count on you to revise them so they match this account? Jason, you won't change your story any more after this?'

'I haven't been changing my story, Captain,' Jason said, starting to bristle. 'I'm just doing the best I can to recollect all the moves we had to make to survive in that very confusing situation.'

'I know but—'

'You make it sound as if I'm trying to hide something.'

'I never said that,' Delaney said, getting pinker. Sarah began wishing for the lunchbreak she knew they weren't going to get. 'But your story has changed from the original in the course of this conversation and I want to be sure we get our details straight today and stick to them from now on.'

'Why wouldn't we stick to them? We're just after the truth, aren't we?'

'Of course. And I appreciate your wanting to support your partner; we all want to help Sarah as much as we can. But beware of giving testimony that's not supported by the evidence. That makes us all look dodgy.'

'Dodgy?' Jason was becoming very angry, his back was up and he was breathing fast. 'I'll tell you what looks dodgy to me – it's holding this freaky dress rehearsal before the hearing, like we've all got to make up some phony excuses for why we behaved as we did. What the hell? We just did our jobs.'

'Excuse me, guys,' Sarah said, getting up suddenly, 'but I need a bathroom break right now.' She pushed her chair back fast so the legs shrieked on the tile floor, walked out quickly and left them sitting there, glaring at each other.

She took her time about it, freshened her makeup and drank some water. When she came back fifteen minutes later the room was empty. She sat reading through her notes, listening to the humming silence. She was about ready to give it up and go home when Delaney walked back in and sat down.

'Jason's gone on to his deposition. Just as well, I guess – give him a chance to get over himself.' Sarah sat silent, with no intention of rising to that bait, and presently he went on. 'I just have a couple more things to talk to you about and then you can get back to your . . .' He raised his eyes from his notes and looked at her straight, the first time today he had met her eyes. 'How's it going for you, after the shooting? Any trouble sleeping?'

'I'm all right,' Sarah said. 'I'll be better once I get back to work.'

'I know. I'm sorry it takes so long. Another week or two should clear it up.'

At the thought of two more weeks' idleness, Sarah shivered. Delaney looked at her closely and said, 'You're sure you're all right? We have a psychiatrist on call, remember, and it might be a good idea—'

'I'll think about it. There's something I would like to ask you.'

'Go ahead.'

'Have you talked to DeShawn yet?'

'Sarah, now, you know the rules—'

'He's the center of the whole case, the one with the money. Have you heard what he has to say?'

'No. That crazy knifeman put a lot of new hurt on him, so he's had to have more surgery. I'm waiting again for a go-ahead from doctors.'

'What about Jason's collar? Wheelchair man? He give you anything yet?'

Delaney shook his head. 'He's taking a long time to detox; got the shakes and sweats and he's babbling a lot.'

'Any chance he's faking?'

'The docs say not. He's been taking drugs and booze together, he's got DTs and they think he's got pneumonia. Now I've already told you more than I'm supposed to, so forget it, go on home and try to get some fun out of this. How's your mother coming on the booklist?'

'We got sidetracked onto flower beds. How'd you know about Mom and the novels?'

'Dietz told me your mother thinks paid leave is one of the department's better ideas.'

Sarah shuddered again. 'This leave is giving me new insight into one possible cause of depression. Maybe people shouldn't retire. It's very disorienting to have your routine yanked away.'

'Be patient,' Delaney said. 'Read some good books and keep your spirits up. I need you back here as soon as possible.'

Buoyed by that thought, she drove home. Her body was beginning to send messages indicating that one power bar is not, after all, a steak. She was in the kitchen, munching on a cracker and cutting up an apple, when the phone rang.

'Are you home?' Jason said.

'No, Jason, I'm out. But my amazingly lifelike answering service will be happy to take your message.'

'OK, Smart Ass. I meant have you got time to talk?'

'Yes. You're just in time to split an apple.' She hung up and immediately wished she hadn't mentioned the apple. Her stomach was lobbying for calories in a hurry, she wanted to eat the whole thing right away. But Jason was at her door in three minutes, he must have been just around the corner.

He came in carrying a bag of peanuts in the shell. 'I went by that corner fruit stand on Speedway and they were selling these. I couldn't resist. You got a bowl?' They sat at the round table tossing down fresh-shelled peanuts and juicy apple slices, and for a few minutes were all munchy noises and small talk – he had just been to look at the new water running in the Santa Cruz river.

'Call it effluent if it makes you feel better,' he said, 'I still think it's sewage. Who wants to go wading in *that*?'

Then he abruptly dropped all pretense at pleasantries and said, 'I really came to thank you for demanding a wiz this afternoon when you did. I think you saved my career.'

'You're welcome. What are friends for if they can't take a pee when you need them to?'

'And boy did I need you to. I was awesomely close to taking a punch at my boss.'

'It's too bad the way he gets under your skin. I'm sure he didn't mean—'

'Oh, bullshit, Sarah, he meant exactly what he said. For some reason he thinks we're not being exactly straight about what happened in that ICU.' He was suddenly angry all over again. 'And that's such a damn outrage! Think about it: with no warning at all, the three of us walked into a shitstorm in that hall. But we all kept our heads and handled it as best we could with a minimum of casualties, and now instead of an attaboy for avoiding a massacre we're taking crap about not remembering all the *details* exactly? Why doesn't this make you as mad as it does me? I was just about to tell him where he could put his *details* when you walked out.'

'What happened after I left?'

'His phone rang.' Jason laughed, forgetting his anger. 'Isn't that typical Delaney? He'd like to eat your liver but he doesn't have time, his phone is ringing!'

'So I suppose he stepped out—'

'Sure. Said, "I have to take this," and left for ten minutes. When he came back, he said, very stiff, "Well, I guess you need to get going to that deposition, eh?" It was way early but I flung him a yessir and rode outta Dodge at high speed.'

He laughed again and Sarah joined him. She saw no reason to tell him what she had once learned from his secretary after an outburst of her own – that Delaney had a button on his phone which, when pushed, elicited an 'emergency' phone call from her, that he would use as an excuse to escape the scene until tempers could cool a few degrees.

Instead, she said, 'I just remembered there's something I want to ask you. What happened to the car keys you found in your prisoner's pants? Did you follow through on that or—?

'Oh, yes, didn't I tell you? Guess I never got a chance. That car was registered to a rental agency.'

'So now you've got the name of the renter, right? Wheelchair man?'

'We wish. When I walked in with the keys and asked who rented that car, the two people at the agency started out all brisk and efficient and soon morphed into a blizzard of record searching and lot scrutiny. After a quarter of an hour they admitted that I had the car they were looking for, that was missing from the lot. But the original keys were where they belonged in the rack, and there were no contracts missing. Long story short: Delaney is now close friends with the regional manager, who's on his way here from Denver with a temp staff to take over till we unsnarl this mess.'

'Damn. It's like the handy chop shop, isn't it? I hate the way this keeps growing.'

'Me too.' Then Jason's hands went still on the table and he said softly, 'You know, I didn't realize until today that you saved my life in that hospital.'

'Oh, well—'

'Isn't it amazing? We were together the whole time, working in close cooperation, I thought, and yet we saw two different events. I thought I was pretty cool the way I deployed that taser—'

'You were. We're always testing ourselves on that damn thing, but this is the first time I've seen it used effectively, and I must say it's an awesome weapon in skillful hands.'

'Thank you. I think so too. But I'd still have been dead meat if you hadn't blown away the second man.'

'The second man that you couldn't have known was there. Don't give up any credit for your part. I just happened to be there at the right time.'

'But the point is until I heard your side I was sure I was the hero of this story, and I was kind of wondering, myself, why you didn't try the taser on the second bad guy. Now I realize that if you hadn't played it the way you did, he would have planted that screwy knife in my nice soft back, and right now the personnel department might be scanning their brains to find flowery adjectives for my obit.'

'Oh, hey, dismal thought. Let's not go there.'

'OK, then, let's go here: you saved my life and got rewarded with a furlough. Some people might find that a suitable gift, but I bet it works for you about like a javelina in a huddle. So is there anything I could do for you to brighten up this stupid hiatus?'

'Oh, no, now, Jason,' Sarah said, brightening perceptibly, 'just put that thought right out of your head.'

'Which thought?'

'The one about how if you nosed around – and I know I'm not supposed to discuss the case but, as you say, that's so unfair after we did that terrific job in the hospital, and now we're being treated as if we did something wrong, which isn't a bit like our boss, who's usually a straight-ahead guy, so something new must have been added to the mix this week, and I'm stuck here at home . . . but I know how much you dislike idle gossip and snooping . . .'

'Still, I am a detective,' Jason said, 'which implies a certain aptitude for poking around in corners, even if only to try to find an end to this sentence.'

'I bet you'd find more than that if you really turned yourself loose,' Sarah said, brightening some more, 'because for a handsome young man sometimes you can look a lot like Beelzebub.'

'Do you really think so?' Jason was beginning to beam like a lamp. 'And have you spotted a corner you think might reward my satanic gifts?'

'A couple of them, actually. Is your chair comfortable? Are you sure you don't want any more peanuts? All right then . . . remember I told you about how the Fairweather Farms case started, with the company van buried in its own garage door?'

'Yes, of course.'

'Now I think that besides delivering clients to their medical appointments, that van was delivering illegal drugs, mostly opioids and coke, to those same clients and some of their friends.'

'Oh, fun.'

'Yeah. I expect to prove it as soon as I can get back to work. Just lately I've been getting hints that maybe the regular driver, DeShawn, has a little pot-supplying enterprise of his own on the side. I think he's got a little smoking club going with fellow employees, and it might be useful to know who's in it.'

'Such a busy fellow. You want me to sniff around that for you?'

'In the dark of the moon. Yes.'

'Why do you care? Pot is available everywhere now – legal even for fun if our bone-headed federal government would wake up and join the twenty-first century. If you're going to prove opioids, why do you need pot?'

'I just want to know who values DeShawn and for what. And I think you should start by talking to an aide named Tammy. She seems a little evasive; I've never managed to talk to her myself.'

Denny came home from school just as Jason was leaving. Sarah introduced them on the front step and they stood a few minutes in the carport, quickly getting acquainted. Jason was perfect with her, treating her as an equal when he asked her opinion of her advanced placement classes, and they traded critiques of the latest Spiderman movie. He shook her hand when he said goodbye, and she watched him out of sight.

'Wow,' she said, as they walked together into the kitchen, 'no wonder you don't want to take time off from work.'

Sarah laughed. 'Jason's a cute guy, all right, but – oh God, I just remembered what a mess I left out there on the patio.

As soon as you change clothes, will you help me . . . let me show you.' She tore out the door with Denny at her heels.

Aggie was dozing in the shade on the big chaise. The tools were all put away; the shed was locked. The hose rack was back on the side of the house, not quite so far under the bougainvillea. The pile of gravel she had raked out of the space by the door was put away, in two cardboard boxes against the shed. The bare space where she had cleared the gravel was damp, and the top layer turned.

'You promised me you wouldn't do this!' Aghast, Sarah leaned over her mother. 'How did you manage to do all this by yourself?'

'I didn't,' Aggie said, sitting up. 'I was out here, dithering around, trying to put away the tools – do you know,' she turned indignant eyes on her daughter, 'I'm almost too wimpy now to even *carry* a shovel? How did I ever think I was going to dig up all these flowerbeds? Why don't you stop me when I get these crazy pipe dreams?'

'I don't understand,' Sarah said. 'How'd you get all this . . .'

'I just told you, I didn't. Stanley waved over the bushes and started in about what a nice day it was, and I said I guessed it was but I'd got myself into a heck of a mess, and he said why don't you let me help you with that? And oh, Sarah, I tell you, he may not be much for conversation but that man, when it comes to work, I never saw anything like him.'

She told the rest of the story in the kitchen, where she perched on a stool and played pit boss, reminding Sarah where to find pasta, sauce, and salad makings.

'What would you say,' Aggie asked between directions, 'if we split that bulb order with the Pettigrews? Stanley could help us do the kitchen-side plot and the bed in front of the carport, and take the rest of the bulbs over to their place, which really needs a little sprucing up.'

She was pretty sure, she said, that she could make that deal with Stanley.

'Aren't you the canny trader?' Sarah said. 'Where do I sign?'

TEN

'**N**ewsflash, guys,' Sarah said as she sat down to breakfast Wednesday morning. 'I've made a resolution.'

'Oh, drat,' Denny said, 'I suppose this means we'll all have to improve in some way.'

'Not you, just me. I thought about it and realized Mom is right. I should be making use of this paid leave to do some of the things I never have time for.'

'Good for you,' Will said. 'What's first – Aggie's booklist?'

'Yes. As soon as she shows up in here today, I'm going to call her bluff about this all-time best list she claims to carry in her head. She's sure she can come up with at least fifty great books if she takes time to think about it.'

'Wow. Fifty, really?'

'That's what she said. I think they'll be mostly novels and memoirs, but still . . . here and there a biography, maybe even a history – she reads pretty good stuff.'

'Well, that should keep you entertained for the summer,' Will said. 'What other wonderful things are you going to do in the next two weeks?'

'Remodel the kitchen. The three of us have faithfully added to the savings account every month since we moved in. So now the money goal is in sight and it's about time to start planning the makeover.'

'Already?' Will began making his evasive moves, checking his watch, patting his wallet. 'I'm glad that part's up to you and your mother.'

'And me, me, me,' Denny said, bouncing in her chair. 'I know I didn't put in any of the money, but you said I could be on the planning committee, Aunt Sarah.'

'Absolutely. You do your share of kitchen chores and then

some, so you have every right to say what you want in the kitchen. Not that we'll all get everything we want, but we should all be thinking about what we'd like to have in this big sunny family room we're hoping to create.'

'We are?' Will said. 'Big sunny spaces get pricey – have you thought about that?'

'Well, see, that's what we need you for, Will. You have the know-how for the planning. I don't know what materials are called or how to talk to a builder.'

'Oh, and I do? I'm just a fix-it man.'

'That's close enough. More than I know.'

'Ah,' Will sighed, 'the things I do for love.' He looked at his watch again. 'Time to go.' He got up. 'You ready to go, Denny? Got your lunch money? Got your books?'

'Um, well, I am brilliantly prepared except for those two things. Plus my homework.' She giggled and flew around the house filling her backpack, and in five minutes was out the door, trotting toward the bus stop, waving to friends. The two adults watched her indulgently. She had been managing much more ominous problems than the contents of her backpack when Sarah rescued her from her drug-addicted mother. It was a pleasure, now, to see how she blossomed with a little support.

When they were both gone, Sarah cleared the table quickly, eager to start her day. It would be an hour, at least, before Aggie came in from her casita, and Sarah wanted to use the interim for some planning of her own. She took her laptop to the desk in her bedroom and set up two lists, titled KITCHEN and BOOKS. She made no entry in either list, but set each up in a folder, ready to share with Aggie.

Now for the real deal. The actual resolution she had made yesterday concerned her work on the Fairweather Farms case. *They can tell me not to meddle in the work,* she had decided, *but they can't tell me not to think about it.*

And the items I need to think about are all here in this list.

She pulled up the case list she had started ten days ago. It was longer now. She had added the names of all the employees she'd met at Fairweather Farms, as well as the two she hadn't: DeShawn Williams, who was still recuperating, and Enrique Lopez, who was dead. Now she had some other items to add, and she wanted to think about them as she typed them in.

24. Gray DodgeXMZ? How disappear so fast?
25. Do we have a new chop shop that nobody knows about? Talk to drivers of chase cars.
26. Why DeShawn target? If he's in the game, why shoot him?
27. Were WKman &WCman the Monday shooters?

Number twenty-four made her so yearn to hit the streets that she could hardly stay in her chair. Instead, she moved to number twenty-five and sat thinking, watched a minute scroll by on her desk clock. Finally she told herself *just put it down any damn way.*

Quickly, she typed, *DeShawn is usual driver, money was in DeShawn's jacket, ergo, DeShawn is middleman in drug deal. If hit-run was an accident, his gang should know why he couldn't deliver the goods, so why punish him now? If hit-run not an accident, somebody was already after him before he missed the Friday run. Why?*

Thinking about DeShawn made her feel very deep in the weeds. Afraid of getting too discouraged to type, she set her jaw and looked at number twenty-seven. Quickly again, before discouragement stopped her, she typed the question she hated most because it seemed fantastic yet had to be asked: *Were WCMan and WKMan the shooters who chased after the van on Monday? The gardeners said those shooters spoke Spanish. The men in the ICU never spoke, but they didn't both appear Hispanic. Is it possible we've got two teams of bad guys chasing the same money?*

That fantasy seemed to turn her loose, and she typed in several more questions quickly:

28. If not, who? If so, why Spanglish?
29. What's up with Amanda's attitude?
30. Car keys from WCman – where was he headed?

31. What's Henry's problem?
32. Who is DeShawn's buddy @work?
33. Why is Delaney anxious?

She was staring at the next blank line on the page when her mother knocked discreetly on her open door.

'Ah, there you are,' Sarah said, switching to the BOOKS page. 'I've got something for you.' She made two copies and handed one to her mother.

Aggie lit up with delight. 'Wonderful! We can start this morning, but we'll have to keep an eye on the clock. This is our day for early lunch, remember? This afternoon's my appointment with the podiatrist.'

'Oh, my bad, I forgot! Remind me, what time?'

'Two o'clock. But it's way out east, in that medical center on Palo Verde Street . . .'

Sarah saved all her lists and closed her computer. She didn't think about her own list again until late afternoon, when her phone rang as she was helping her mother into the house. Aggie's right foot was encased in a surgical shoe, the bone spur was gone from her right second toe and she was foggy from a pain pill. Sarah let her phone call go to messages while she got her mother seated at the table and helped Denny dish up the dinner she had cooked. Will was out of the house, working late; the three women finished their meal quickly and split, Denny to homework, Aggie to bed in her casita.

Sarah called the number on the message and reached Jason's cell.

'Hey, I went by the hospital to check on Judy,' he said, 'and guess what? She's on paid leave too. Looks like she was hurt worse than we realized in that mess.'

'Oh? What, the wheelchair—'

'The nurses on the floor told me she was OK from that first knock-down, but the second bozo, the one you shot, kicked her really hard to get her out of the way and her hip hit the floor in a bad way. She thinks she cracked a bone, has very sore hips, hasn't been able to work since.'

'What a shame – such a nice, helpful person. But my bad guy really did her dirt, huh?'

'And she knows how to make it run downhill, apparently. She's put in a hefty work comp claim and the hospital is already talking to the city about shifting the insurance claim onto the police department.'

'*What?*'

'Yeah. They're saying it's our fault, we never should have been conducting police business in a hospital.'

'That is such a crock,' Sarah said. 'If we hadn't been there at that lucky moment they'd have been calling us a few hours later to help find a missing patient.'

'And when we found him he'd probably have been dead,' Jason said. 'Those lads weren't playing beanbag.'

'For sure. Anyway, this answers our question about Delaney, doesn't it?'

There was some breathing on the line and then Jason said, 'Which question was that and when did we ask it?'

'We've been wondering why he's so tense about my hearing, remember? I said it was so unlike Delaney, grilling us about details when he's usually ready to go to bat for the team, but now we see why, don't we? You can get over being so mad—'

'I might not get over that,' Jason said. 'Delaney owes me a few tantrums for being such a stiff-necked nitpicker all the time.'

'Jason,' Sarah said, 'I've had a long day and so have you, so let's give it a rest. Thank you for calling to tell me about Judy, and I wish us both a better day tomorrow.'

'Easy for you to say,' Jason said, 'there in your hammock.'

'You can put *War and Peace* on the list if you want to,' Sarah said the next morning. 'But I don't want to start with a door-stopper like that. Find me something easy to limber up on.' Gratified to find her library card still current, she had been abashed to see she hadn't checked out a book in the three years she'd lived on Bentley Street.

'Well, you've been going on a high lope ever since we moved into this house,' Aggie said. 'But you've got a little breather here and you should take the time to enjoy yourself. How about an amusing historical fiction called *News of the World*, that should warm you up.'

'OK, I see it, I'll put a hold on that.' Sarah had brought her laptop to the round table in the bay window where most family life centered. She was bouncing between the booklist and her library account.

'Now wait, while you're in there – have you read all the Jane Austen novels? How about *Emma*? That's the best one, I think.'

Aggie was having fun, sharing her major source of pleasure. She had a pile of book reviews on the table in front of her and a stack of handwritten notes she'd been compiling for years. Always an active reader, she'd become a voracious one now that age and illness had rendered her mostly chair-bound.

'Let's think about John Updike,' she said. 'Have you read all the *Rabbit* stories?'

'The what?'

'Right, we'll start with *Rabbit Run*.'

Sirens had begun to scream in the distance. Sarah noticed them first but didn't interrupt Aggie's happy flow until her cell phone dinged.

'It's a robbery,' Will said, 'at the Chase bank downtown. No details yet but we know there was shooting. Talk to you later.' He rang off without a goodbye, then called back in half an hour to tell her, 'A big gun battle, six injuries and two fatalities. One bank teller and one TPD patrolman – a ten-year veteran named Ed Nelson. You know him?'

'Long time ago. We were on the same shift on the East Side for a while. I know he had a wife, and I think some children . . .'

'Two,' Will said. 'Middle school.'

'Damn.'

'Yes. Gotta go.' They both felt it like a death in the family. It deepened the frustration of being on leave. Cops at work today would stop at a desk, or roll down a window in a patrol car, and ask each other quietly, 'You hear about Ed Nelson?' Sharing the grief and the unspoken dread. *Next time it could be me.*

Sarah put down the phone and turned a stricken face to her mother, who said, 'Bad, huh?'

'Awful.' Sarah told her as much as she knew. Aggie picked up her pile of book lore and said, 'We'll do this another day.'

'Come back for lunch,' Sarah called after her retreating back, 'at twelve o'clock, OK?'

Aggie did come back for lunch, and found her daughter transformed – grinning at the big sandwiches she was composing.

'Delaney called a half hour ago and said, "You heard about the shooting?" Then he told me they're bending a few rules at South Stone today.' She laughed, breathlessly. 'It seems he called Moretti and said, "I need all hands on deck," and Moretti said, "Whaddya say I write a memo that says I scanned the record and I find nothing to criticize?"'

'Heavenly days,' Aggie said. 'Can he do that?'

'Yes, when they're up to their eyebrows in work like this. He says they're interviewing everybody they can get to stop crying . . .'

'And this is what you're panting to get back to? I suppose,' Aggie said, 'he wants you back this instant.'

'He probably does, but he said tomorrow morning would be fine. I need to do some laundry.'

'Tell you what,' Delaney said, Friday morning, 'we talked to the most severely injured victims from the robbery yesterday, and today I'll get the detectives going on the follow-up from what they told us. It will take a day or two for the forensic evidence to start coming in anyway, so I'll help the three rookie detectives do the mop-up interviews while we wait.

'Can you pick up where we left off on the Fairweather Farms case by yourself if I give you the master file?'

'Sure,' Sarah said. 'I've still got my list.'

Delaney grew one of his bleak almost-smiles and said, 'Always good to have one of those.' The big desk in front of him was paved with lists, all covered with check marks and scribbled notations. 'The file number's 46539. I think you're familiar enough so you can handle most of this on your own, but of course, any questions, you can call me.'

If I'm drowning in a cesspool and can't reach a rope. Gotcha.

It took a few minutes to settle back into her workspace.

Somebody had used her chair, lowered it a couple of inches. She put it back where it belonged, telling herself not to get angry, it was the department's chair – but it felt like an insult. *Not bad enough to get put on leave, I have to put up with some fathead who comes along and squats in my space.* There were strange pens on her desk, too, and a wrapped piece of restaurant candy – she made a disgusted noise and threw it all in the trash.

She pulled up #46539 on her desktop monitor. It was already a big file – fifty-nine pages, with links to several other files. She paged through it for a few minutes, scrolling quickly to be sure she hadn't forgotten any details. When she came to the page where they found the money in the jacket, she slowed and read to the end of the incident. Grinned at the pipe bomb caper, grew thoughtful over Ollie's remark about the small amount of money.

She stared into the middle distance for a while then, reliving the crazy day at the senior living facility. Suddenly her eyes focused on a fat envelope in her in-tray, addressed to her in Jason's handwriting. The note inside read, *These are the keys I took out of wheelchair man's undies, minus the car key. The ABC rental agency is the one on Roger Street. I'm assigned to victims from the bank heist, and I believe Delaney gave you the Fairweather Farms case. I did not have time to find the doors that these keys unlock – JP.*

A steel ring held two keys, each stamped *Weiser*.

Front and back door. Wheelchair man's keys. Good a place as any to start.

The regional manager at ABC auto rental was a crisp-voiced man named Dunbar, who said he could see her any time. Sarah noted the VIN of the missing car and the address of the agency and was at the lot in half an hour. Fifty spaces for cars on a lot with hedges on all sides, on a narrow old street near Auto Mall Drive, two desk people in a small office with a sign that wrapped around the building.

Dunbar was a fit man in his forties, in shirt sleeves, sweating out his introduction to desert weather. He offered bottled water and she accepted. They sat knee-to-knee on two stools in his tiny back office.

'We have systems in place to prevent this happening, of course,' he said. 'Business has been slow and the staff got complacent, ran the revenue for the eighteen cars they had contracts for and skipped a couple of walkarounds. The keys were all where they belonged on the rack, and it's hot out there, isn't it? So they were very surprised when your detective turned up with another identical key, and the Nissan that turned out not to be here.'

'Plus these two other keys that must be house keys. Did you find the place?'

'No. I was busy, and I figured the detective would do that.'

'He was started on the search when the gunfight broke out at the bank. All our detectives are working on that now, so I came back off leave to handle this job.' *No need to tell him about administrative leave.*

Sarah took a walk across the hot asphalt to look at the Nissan, all cleaned up now and back in its slot. It was the pale sage that was 'this year's hot color,' Dunbar said, with racing stripes and Texas plates. 'A repo from Houston,' he said. 'ABC is a relatively new chain, small and opportunistic. The guy who owns it is a genius at cutting costs while keeping quality high. The chain is growing fast, and has a great future if we can get smart enough to stay out of kerfuffles like this one.'

'Obviously somebody copied the key,' he said, 'and I had no way of knowing how many more they might have copied, so I arranged for a new shipment of cars before I left Denver. Hired an off-duty cop to guard this lot for three nights till I got my new inventory in place, and sent the existing stock back with the same drivers.'

'Must have been a busy time around here,' Sarah said.

'You bet. Pricey too.'

'Did your night guards see any lurkers?'

'No. I'm beginning to think the thieves aren't interested in the car business, they just wanted one car for some reason. But I didn't *know* that, so . . . this quick change-out wasn't cheap, but better than taking a chance and maybe losing more cars. We have to be concerned about our underground image, too – you don't want to let the word go around that ABC is an easy mark.'

'You think your staff's involved?'

'No. My manager's been with me five years – she moved here to open this place for me. I had to lay her off to satisfy the home office, but I'm paying her salary out of my own pocket because I don't want to lose her. She's got two kids sick with flu so she was delegating to the part-timers she was training, and they failed her.'

'Who's around to look at?'

'Well, we use a cleaning service. They work at night, mostly use college kids but hire a lot of part-timers; probably don't check references much.'

Sarah took names and addresses for the cleaning service and a supplier that serviced the coffee services and coke machine. 'These searches don't often yield much but we can try. I'll let you know if I find any addresses at the squat these extra keys might let us into . . . when and if I find it.'

Back at the station, typing the data from ABC into the file, she noticed a note on her desk pad that said, *Ricky's clothes* in her own handwriting. *When did I put that there?*

She called the lab, got through to Lois in fingerprints, and asked about Ricky's clothing.

'I'm done with them, you can get them any time,' Lois said. 'It isn't going to help you much. This guy lived poor. Ragged boxer shorts, a worn-out wallet with his expired driver's license and twenty-three dollars. One credit card with a thousand-dollar limit and a few family pictures.'

'I'll stop in and pick it up this afternoon. I expect you need all your space now, for the new stuff.'

'Yeah, I'm buried in here. Tried to fix a paper cut this morning and couldn't find my band-aids.'

Sarah put down the phone and pondered. *Doesn't sound like Ricky's stuff will yield much.* She took a deep breath and decided, *DeShawn Williams, you've rested long enough.* She called the intake phone at the prison hospital, learned that DeShawn was still a patient and that his status had been upgraded from critical to serious to post-op, and asked to be put through to the guard on his floor.

'Oh, sure he can have a visitor,' a jaunty young male voice

assured her. 'He's been on solid foods since yesterday. He'd be out in the ward by now if he didn't have that hold Delaney put on him. We can't keep him in here much longer, though – we're short of beds after that shoot-up at the bank.'

'I hear you. Don't let him get moved anywhere till I get down there, please.' She gave him her badge number, described the workload at the station, and asked for his help.

'You're preaching to the choir,' he said. 'We got a big rush right after the sirens stopped screaming. I'll do all I can. But you'll be here soon, right?'

'Give me an hour.' She printed out the pages in the file that pertained to DeShawn, read through them quickly, put them in a folder and stuffed that in the day pack she was taking along.

The desert southeast of the city looked lush after a better than average rain year, but the end of the monsoon had been disappointing and she thought as she drove past tall stands of desert broom and tamarisk, *If this dries up now we'll be sitting ducks for a wildfire. The desert angst. Always too much or too little, we're never quite satisfied.*

DeShawn was sitting up in bed, reading a sports magazine. All his bubbling and hissing attachments were gone – there was just one IV tube hanging from a bag, feeding him whatever boosters the county medics thought he needed, through a needle in his arm.

The scrapes she had noticed on his face earlier had blossomed into a beautiful shiner around his left eye. Otherwise, he seemed surprisingly fit for a man who'd been through so much trauma – in fact, he looked younger than she remembered. Then she realized his caretakers had shaved off his elaborate facial hair, and his hyper-sexy look was gone with it. Now he just looked like the most appealing young male athlete she was going to see today.

She had already put in her request for some extra nursing in the recovery ward where he'd have 24/7 supervision. Not a luxurious recovery, but the best she could get for him here.

'How do you feel?' Sarah asked him – not the way you usually start a prisoner interview, but the man was in a hospital gown.

'Thirsty,' he said, 'all the time.' He was drinking from a tall glass of ice water on the tray table that covered him. 'And hungry about five times a day. But they tell me I'll catch up in a day or two.'

Sarah gave him her bona fides, showed him her badge. Drew up a chair to the side of the bed where his ankle chain showed beneath the cover, clipped to the bedrail. Took out her tablet, entered the date and time.

'Let's get some facts agreed on first,' she said, and they began to go over his place and date of birth, parents, schooling – all review, the first part, but it got the silent ones talking. She knew most of his duties at his current job, they didn't spend much time on that – what about the one before that? She watched his face as he answered. There wasn't a tremor as he recited the name of the hotel in California, the source of the reference he'd given Letitia.

'I called there,' Sarah said. 'The person on the desk and the manager she switched me to never heard of you.'

'Not surprising,' he said. 'I heard it changed hands. Happens all the time with those chains, that's why I got my manager to write that letter I carry. I asked that nice girl in the office where I work now, what's her name, Amanda? I asked her if she could write me one like that for the Fairweather and get Letitia to sign it . . .'

'You were thinking about leaving?'

'Well, no, I hope not. I'm really happy there, but you never know.' He drank some more water and sighed. 'I mean, look at me now. I certainly didn't plan this.'

His story agreed with Letitia's as to how he got his job at Fairweather Farms, and he professed to be very satisfied with the place and his duties there. About the accident that put him into St. Mary's, he said he remembered almost nothing – a bright light, noise and then terrible pain.

'You sure it was an accident? Not somebody out to get you?'

'Where'd you get that idea?' He chuckled. 'I haven't been in this town long enough for anybody to work up a grudge.'

'So you think it was just some crazy drunk?'

'Sure. And a lot of first responders did their jobs right or I wouldn't be here,' he said. 'I'm already walking, they tell you that? Every time anybody can spare time to unchain me and bring the walker, I walk as long as they'll let me. I'm a big nuisance to these folks here, but they've sure been kind to me.'

Sarah listened to his story, thinking, *Sweet as honey. Typical jailhouse manipulative persona.* She asked him, 'How did your drug dealer find you, DeShawn? Or did you bring that connection with you when you got the job?'

He sat still and straight against the pillows with his good-boy face full of innocence and said, 'I don't know what you're talking about.'

'Oh, sure you do. Let me tell you how much we already know about it.' She told him about the chase, the van in the garage door, and then about finding the thumb drive and the money in the jacket. 'So there's no use tap-dancing around this – we've got all we need to hold you for dealing. But much worse than that is Ricky's murder, and the chief is hot to go after you for aiding and abetting in a homicide, too.'

'Oh, whoa, wait now . . .'

'Why not? You set up this drug ring, so you're just as responsible for Ricky's death as if you shot him yourself. Lawyers can make that connection; it's what they get paid all those big dollars for. But if you were to help us out with the names of the buyers and sellers in this deal, so we could put away some of these outlaws . . . well, that might make all the difference in the world, you see? But we need to see that you're ready to work with us, DeShawn.'

'I still don't understand what you expect to get from me. I mean, I got hit in traffic on Sunday night and for days I was out, blotto, just a piece of meat getting experimented on by interns – you ever see who gets stuck with the duty on Saturday night in those emergency rooms? Looks like the deli counter at the Safeway store.'

'These are the same folks whose kindness you were just extolling to me?'

'I mean, I just don't get – what does that mean, estrolling? Sounds like the Mexican word for walking around.'

I bet he can play this artful dodging game all day long.

Let's cut to the chase. 'Who puts the money in your jacket, DeShawn?'

'Boy, I wish I knew,' he said, with a little soft cackle. 'I'd try to get to know him better.'

'What do you mean? You're finding money in your jacket every so often and you don't know who puts it there?' She got ready to poke holes in that ridiculous story.

Which turned out not to be the one he was telling. 'Detective,' he said, leaning forward off the pillows to look earnestly into her eyes, 'I been working at that old folks' home going on four months now' – *his speech gets folksier when he presses his sincere button* – 'and this is the first I heard about cash in that fancy jacket she give me – hell,' he waved his one loose arm dismissively – 'up until now I didn't even know the damn thing *had* an inside pocket.'

'So your story is that this one time, when the bus got wrecked and Ricky got shot, is the first time anybody ever put money in your jacket?'

'That's my story because it's what happened.' Sincerity shone out of his undamaged brown eye on the right, and even glimmered a little out of the one with the raccoon surround on the left.

'Well, DeShawn, that's really hard to believe.'

'Ain't it, though? And to think I slept through the whole thing. I mean, it almost makes you think about the tooth fairy, don't it?'

Oh no, now, you're not going to ruin the tooth fairy for me too. Sarah turned off her tablet and stood up. 'All right, DeShawn,' she said. 'You've had a rough time lately, getting wrecked in traffic and beat up in bed, so I guess you figure it's time you had a little fun mocking the cops. But think about this while you convalesce in the ward out there: I'm your only ticket out of here. Homicide means it's this cold cell or another one like it for the rest of your life. All my colleagues are busy with that massacre at the bank downtown. Nobody but me gives a damn right now how you got that money. And you won't give me anything to work with, so you're going to take the fall for being part of the gang that shot up the Fairweather Farms van and murdered Enrique.'

'Who?'

'Ricky Lopez. The nice man everybody loved who was driving the van you should have been driving.'

'How could I when I was in the hospital after I got T-boned in traffic? How come I can't get any sympathy out of you?'

'Because I'm the hard-hearted detective who thinks you lie like a snake. So here's my card.' She put it on his tray table, beside the water glass. 'When you get ready to do yourself some good, you can call me.'

The last she saw of him as she walked out of this spartan recovery room that was so much better than what he was going to get next from Pima County, he was leaning toward her in the bed wearing his most appealing expression.

Think hard, Romeo, she thought as she walked away. *It isn't always as simple as making somebody fall in love with you.*

Driving back toward the station, she asked herself, *Why does this bozo annoy you so much?* She shifted restlessly in her seat several times, trying to get comfortable, until her tireless inner critic, the part of herself she called the Hall Monitor, told her, *He's one of those people who think they can always beguile their way out of anything, and as usual you have to prove him wrong.* She knew why she had this twitch: her sister and her ex-husband had both been greatly loved beguilers who had left her feeling short-changed and resentful.

But you promised me you were going to get over that, the Hall Monitor said, and the good Sarah, the dependable sidekick who believed in reasonable answers, said *I am over it, mostly. Almost entirely. And to prove it I'm going to show you I can do a fair and balanced assessment of DeShawn Williams.*

Probably ought to start with the people who were most recently beguiled. She turned off the highway at Grant Road and followed Silverbell toward Fairweather Farms.

ELEVEN

T he garage door had been replaced and a new van, a duplicate of the one that had been wrecked, was unloading a half dozen passengers under the porte-cochère. Henry stood by it with his arms out, helping an elderly woman down the steps. Maybe not as zealously attentive as Ricky had been, certainly not as sexy as DeShawn would be, but he was doing a nice, professional job, and everybody looked pleased. Including Henry, which was a nice change of pace, Sarah thought, nodding as she passed him. She went inside to find another brown-clad attendant at the maître d's stand in the hall.

'So, is Henry driving the van now?' she asked as she showed her badge to the attendant, whose pocket read, *Anna*.

'Yes. All but the weekends when the college boy comes for the relief.'

'What about all that yard work?'

'There's a new man named Francisco on the maintenance crew with Jacob.'

'Henry's got the driving job for good? DeShawn's not coming back?'

'Not likely.' Anna lowered her eyes discreetly to the calendar on the dais in front of her. 'Help you with anything else?'

'I'm hoping to have a word with Letitia, is she in her office?'

'Leading some folks on a tour right now,' the woman said, 'but Amanda's in her office, will she do?'

'Well, I can start with her,' Sarah said, and walked the dim quiet hall, past Letitia's closed door, to find Amanda. It was twenty minutes past eleven, which in this venue meant almost lunchtime, and most of the clientele were in their rooms, getting ready. Behind the door marked *Supplies*, a busy tapping sound was accompanied by the whir and squeak of a printer duplicating a page. The door was ajar, so Sarah tapped lightly and pushed it open.

Amanda was typing, keeping a brisk rhythm, a little frown of concentration creasing the space between her eyebrows. She did not pause as she looked up, just said, 'Hang on a minute,' and typed on to the end of the page. Even then she didn't offer a greeting, just stopped moving her fingers and raised her eyebrows as she said, 'Help you?'

'I have a few questions,' Sarah said, 'about DeShawn Williams.' She found the folding chair, turned it to face Amanda and sat down, pulling her tablet out of her day pack.

'I'm raging busy,' Amanda said. 'Can it wait a day or two?'

'Afraid not,' Sarah said. 'But I won't take much of your time.' Ignoring Amanda's sigh, she opened a page on her tablet. 'When DeShawn came to work here, what was he driving?'

'I don't— Why do you need to know that?'

'Amanda, I'm a homicide detective. I don't have to tell you why I ask the questions I ask. DeShawn came here in his own car, didn't he?'

'Yes.'

'What was it?' His elaborate haircut and beard had given her a conviction, *DeShawn is concerned about his image; he will drive the best he can afford.*

Amanda treated Sarah to her coldest stare and said, 'He had an old beat-up Volks with replacement doors that didn't match. But I don't suppose there's enough left of that car to drive now.'

'Ah. So he must not have been flush with cash when he got the job. And Fairweather Farms gives a free meal every work day but they don't have a housing allowance, do they? So even if some of these people tip him fairly well, DeShawn is just about breaking even, not much over, right?'

'Nobody here is getting rich. Did you really think we were?'

'No. Does he have another job, do you know? Moonlight for Uber on his days off, anything like that?'

'I wouldn't know. Why is everybody always asking about DeShawn?'

'Who else is asking?'

'Oh, I don't know, it seems like . . . that cute black detective, is his name Pete?'

'His last name is Peete, with three E's. Who else?'

'Some guy in a sage-green Nissan drove up to me as I was getting out of the van a few days ago. I guess he could tell I worked here because I had my arms full of brochures . . . he just slewed to a stop alongside me and started asking questions about DeShawn Williams, did he work here, was he on duty now, all like that. Uppity, like I should feel thrilled to be answering his rude questions.'

'Would you recognize him if I showed you a picture? Could you pick him out of a line-up?'

'Sure. A blond guy with dreadlocks? How often do you see that? Plus, that look on his face like he thinks he's the studliest man on two feet.'

Oh, yes. I remember that well.

Amanda wasn't going to come down to Miracle Mile to look at any photo lineup, though – she didn't have time for that. Sarah explained a few things about how inconvenient subpoenas could get, and they were soon on their way to the crime lab. And once there, despite being thoroughly pissed off about this interruption to her routine, Amanda could not resist the opportunity to show off her eyesight and memory, and picked weird knifeman out of the pack in two minutes flat. She seemed only marginally interested to learn that she had just identified one of the would-be kidnappers of DeShawn Williams.

'Amanda,' Sarah said, as she drove her reluctant witness back to Fairweather Farms, 'why do you suppose that man and his partner tried to take DeShawn out of the hospital?'

'I have no idea.' She drew herself together in a tight ball of anger and said, 'I should think *by now* the police would know.' She flounced into her office and closed the door firmly behind her.

Anna was tidying her reception desk, getting ready for the end of her shift, but she smiled a welcome and said Letitia was back in her office. 'You want me to ring her?'

Sarah said, 'I'd really rather talk to Henry first – do you think you could find him?' And Anna, who seemed to have

what in the innkeeping trade is called a front-of-house personality, smiled contentedly and said, 'Oh, yes, I can always do
that.'

She pressed a button on the side of her dais and spoke his
name into a public address system. The message boomed softly
around the building. 'Henry, come to reception, Henry . . .'

'Be just a minute,' she said. When it proved to be more
than a minute, she said, 'Well, after a run, he has to put the
bus away in the garage.' Then, as the wait went on, she added,
'Sometimes after he gets the bus put away he stops over in
the maintenance shop for a few minutes to have a smoke.' She
shook her head, looking sad. 'So bad for the lungs. And so
far from the lobby.'

Henry finally came stomping in from the back of the
building, looking busy. He got his grumpy face back when
he saw he'd been called away from his illicit break to talk
to the detective.

Sarah settled across from him in the employee breakroom
and asked, 'How well do you know DeShawn Williams?'

'About as well as I want to,' he said.

'You don't like him?'

'He's not a rising favorite.'

'Could you point out a specific flaw in his character you
find objectionable?'

'It's a lot fancier the way you say it,' Henry said, 'but he's
a lying, cheating sonofabitch that ought to have his cock fed
to him out of a meat-grinder.'

'Dear me,' Sarah said. 'Does he know you disapprove of
him so wholeheartedly?'

'Poke fun at it if you want to,' Henry said, 'but I don't think
it's cute when a guy smooths his path through life by patting
every female fanny he comes across.'

'DeShawn is nicer to the women than the men?'

'By a country mile.'

'Consistently?'

'Every day since he came to work here in May. I can't
speak for before that.'

'Do the women seem to enjoy his attention?'

'Like a cat goes for catnip.'

'Well, I suppose that must be annoying to work around. What else do you know about him?'

'He doesn't respect the vehicles he drives. Pays no attention to the maintenance schedule, never checks the tire pressure.'

'Can you tell me anything about personal stuff? Like where he lives or what he drinks, or does he have any hobbies?'

'Why would I know any of that? I don't hang with the little slimeball. Why don't you ask Amanda in the office there? She knows all the private stuff about everybody, phone numbers, addresses. Probably knows more than that about DeShawn; I've seen him sneaking into her office every so often when he thinks nobody's looking.'

'Who's that you're talking about now, Mr Gossip Man?' Anna said, walking into the breakroom and sitting down next to Henry at the table. Anna, it turned out, was Henry's wife. Their relationship seemed to float on a solid cushion of raillery and sniping.

'Never mind who I'm talking about,' Henry said, 'you don't even belong in this conversation I'm having with my detective friend here.'

'No? Then gimme the car keys and I'll go get the groceries while I wait for you to get off work, if that's what you call this tattle-tale session you're having.' Underneath all the chafing there was evidently a plan for the afternoon – he dug out a set of keys and handed them to her, she grabbed them and said, 'Four o'clock right here. Don't be late or the ice cream will melt.'

'I'll be ready. I told everybody, don't ask me for any extras at quitting time tonight.' He watched her out the door and then told Sarah, 'Big birthday party tonight. The grandson is five; he's just started kindergarten. We're giving him a new backpack.' He smiled ironically. 'We start 'em out right in this country, don't we? Load 'em up with burdens right from the git-go.'

It was a curmudgeonly remark but a surprising burst of friendliness from a normally taciturn man, and Sarah, wondering why his attitude had changed, asked him, 'Do you like driving the van, Henry?'

'You bet. Best job in the place. You get to know all the

clients, help them out with little things, and every so often they show a little gratitude.' He held his right hand up and rubbed the fingers with the thumb.

'Why didn't you try to get the job before, when the first driver left?'

'I did. But I don't have a commercial license and pushy DeShawn came along and did have one, so he grabbed the job. But now that he turns out to be a rotten drug-dealing crook like I always suspected he was, he's gone and they're not so picky about the license.'

'Oh, but doesn't the law require—'

'Sure, but Letitia's willing to list me "in training" while I study to get the license. The company's going to pay the fees, too – that was the other problem. They don't usually do that, but Letitia went to bat for me, told them what a good long-term employee I been.'

'Well, good luck with the test.'

'Thanks. The driving's no sweat – I'm a good driver. But the written test is a bear.' He scrubbed his chin with a nervous hand. 'I'll get it. It just takes time.'

Anna's replacement at the reception desk was named Dorothy; she had the same accommodating personality that Anna did, and was glad to call Letitia to ask if Sarah 'might have a word.' In two seconds Letitia was standing in her open door, calling, 'Come on in here, Detective, I'm glad to see you!'

Letitia was in a good mood, pleased with herself – she wanted to show off to Sarah how fast she'd been able to put everything to rights. 'Did you notice the garage door is fixed? And I got a whole new van – they totaled the other one. But listen, I want to hear all about that shooting in the hospital, wasn't that just awful? I don't see how you stand your job, honestly.'

'Could we have the door closed for a few minutes, Letitia?'

'Of course! I've got questions too.'

'You can ask,' Sarah said. 'I may not answer. My questions first.'

'Of course.' She told Dorothy to take messages and sat erect behind her desk, hands folded like a good girl in school.

'You know DeShawn is under arrest?'

'Yes. I couldn't be more deeply shocked. I would have bet real money on him. If he'd asked me, I'd have written him one of those letters like the one from California he showed me. DeShawn is about as close as I've ever come to having a perfect employee.'

'How well did you check out that reference he showed you?'

'Well. I checked on the license, it was valid. And I called the hotel on the letterhead, got a clerk on the desk, asked to speak to the manager and was told he was in a meeting. She said I could leave a message so I did. He called me back the next day while I was taking two couples on a tour. I had to have a driver; I wasn't getting applications from anyone with a chauffer's license. The van has to run every day, it's part of the service people are paying for. So I put DeShawn in the driver's seat, making it clear it was tentative till I got confirmation on the letter. That manager and I played phone tag for another couple of days, it got to be a joke between us – and by then all my clients were telling me how much they liked the new driver, so . . .' Letitia looked out the window with her fingers over her mouth. 'I was busy. I let it go.'

'And you've never been sorry?'

'Not until now. I told you, he pleased everybody.'

'Did you know he was running a small drug business out of your company van?'

'No! My God, no. Do you really think I would put up with that? That's a disaster for us – our whole franchise is at stake. And DeShawn, of all people – he's always been so reliable. I trusted him completely.'

Now that I've talked to him, I can believe that. Sarah tapped her cheek, thinking. 'Who was he friendly with, on the staff?'

'Everybody. DeShawn is friendly with everybody.'

'Henry seemed to suggest he was extra close to Amanda.'

'Oh, I doubt that. Amanda's pretty standoffish.'

'That was my impression, too. Is that why she uses a Mail Boxes address with your company?'

'Oh, you noticed that? So did I, but the Phoenix folks didn't.

I was curious, of course, so I asked her, and she said it's on account of her ex-husband.'

'Oh? She didn't mention him to me.'

'And she never will, unless she has to. She only told me in order to explain her address.'

'What, she's a battered wife?'

'Yes. She didn't give me details, thank goodness. Just said she had to flee and left a lot of good stuff behind. Worth it, she said, to be free. So we list the address she gave us and like many of my employees now she has a cell phone only.'

'Your company's OK with this?'

'Hey, it's the way the world is going – the economy's to blame and what are we supposed to do about that? I tell them how hard she works and they cut me a little slack.' She gave me a grim little half-smile. 'I also work very hard, and some-times I insist on a little payback.'

'And you really don't know where she lives?'

'Don't know and don't want to know. She always answers her phone when I call, which I hardly ever do. We have a good work schedule and stick to it. She could live under a rock for all I care.'

Under a rock might be good enough for you, Letitia, but I'm a homicide detective. The fact that Amanda wanted her address unknown was reason enough for Sarah to want to know it. It didn't come ahead of everything else on her list, though, and her watch said four o'clock. *I'll go back to my office and put it on the list.*

Several other detectives were settling into the workspace, unloading day packs, checking their phones for messages. Sarah was a little embarrassed about how good it felt to be back, even before she heard a familiar voice say, 'Hey, she's back! Hi, Sarah,' and Ollie Greenaway stuck his cheery grin into her cubicle.

Ollie was a twenty-year veteran who spent all his summer spare time keeping his three kids happy at their lake house. By September he was tanned caramel all over, including his buzz cut.

'Ollie, how's it going? You working the bank heist?'

'Yeah, we all are, there's plenty of sad stories to go around.' He shook his head and looked grave. 'You didn't get assigned to any of them yet, huh?'

'Nope. I'm back at Fairweather Farms. That shooting didn't solve itself while I was gone.'

'Didn't get any simpler, either, I hear. Is this gonna change your attitude toward hospital visits?'

'Yeah, you know, up until now I've just been worried about catching what everybody's got in there. From now on I'll be watching for weapons, too.'

'Good plan.' He turned on his desktop, pulled up the case report for the Chase Bank, and sighed. 'Be glad you've still got that senior living place to work on. This bank job is hard.'

'Complicated, you mean, or—?'

'No, just – the people are so *traumatized*. They just keep bursting into tears! They all say they expected to die, every minute those men were in the bank. *Would* have died, they feel certain, if those two bank guards hadn't called for backup right away.'

'But then one of those guards got shot, is that what—?'

'They both got shot – only one died. But it was other things too – do you know Laura Snively? Nice, dignified middle-aged lady, polite to everybody. When she didn't open the safe fast enough to suit them they pulled her skirt off. Made her stand there in her half-slip and fumble with that combination – shaking, you know, and tears running off her chin, with a roll of fat showing over the top of the slip.'

'Horrible,' Sarah said. 'But still, only two fatalities, that was lucky.'

'Because street cops just swarmed the place – I think they must have set a new land speed record. It's the one upside to the whole mess – Moretti's going to be giving out a lot of commendations.'

'Well, that'll make everybody happy.'

'It'll make *us* happy. But the victims are going to take some time to heal, I think. They've all got this spooky feeling that the world has grown more dangerous – and I begin to think they're right. These bad guys that came after the bank money seem to enjoy inflicting pain.'

'Shee. So much violence and once again nobody got much money, did they?'

'Hardly any! Rotten shame – they killed Ed Nelson for nothing. Our guys got there so fast – the baddies were just starting to bag the money when cops came running in all the doors. So . . . they may have kept whatever they had in their hands, but they dropped the bags and shot their way out. Is that your phone? Talk to you later.'

'Sarah,' Delaney said when she answered, 'come on in my office, will you?'

He looked drained, and his voice sounded as if it was being dragged through a gravel pit. Sarah said, 'Ollie tells me the bank robbery is hard work.'

'It's the pits. The people are so distressed. The bank manager told me, "They made me feel like a piece of meat." With tears running down his face! And this is Elliot Newburger, the darling of the after-dinner speakers list, always on the committee to fix everything. I would have said his ego couldn't be damaged if you dropped him down a well.'

'Well, nobody seems to know this gang of thieves,' Sarah said. 'Maybe we'll get lucky, and they're just passing through town.'

As she hoped, the blithe wrongheadedness of the remark struck him funny. He vented a hearty laugh and began to look a little less likely to throw himself off a high place.

'Right, let's hurry them along to Salt Lake City, shall we? Listen, I called you in to ask you about Bogey. You worked with him when we first got the Fairweather case, didn't you?'

'Yes, you sent him along with me, remember?'

'Yeah, well, what about him? Did he seem to know his stuff – was he any use to you?'

'Oh, he was polite and did whatever I asked.' She tried to remember anything memorable about Bogey. 'Drives well. Let me think – he got very interested in the ammo, did I tell you that?'

'Yes, but I never understood why. The bullets were all the same, .223 all the way. What you'd expect with the guns they were carrying. So nothing to get excited about. We indulged his request to go along with Banjo to inspect the van, but nothing came of it.'

'Except he found the thumb drive,' Sarah said.

'Well, yes. But that was just a happy accident. We don't usually give points for those.'

'Are we totting up points, now? You're on his case, huh?'

'No, I'm really not. I mean, he's amiable enough, I like him. But I took him along on a couple of interviews and he was next to useless. Couldn't think of any questions to ask, didn't seem to get the significance of the answers I got. Is he shy? Shy people don't apply for the detective division, do they?'

'You kidding? Everybody in here's got fangs and claws.'

'Well, there you go. But my impression of Bogey is he may be hell on wheels in a bar fight, but I suspect he's a case of, what's the name of that law? Says you'll keep advancing a bright guy till you push him past the threshold of his maximum usefulness.'

'It's not Murphy – that's the one about everything going wrong that possibly can. But I know what you mean, and I'm sure – is it the Peter Principle? Listen, do you want to give Bogey to me for a few days, see if I can light his fire? I could use some help snooping.'

'Yes, I was going to suggest that, Sarah. He's a nice guy but he isn't producing much where he is, so if you can help him find a niche, so we don't have to send him back to the ranks . . . that's usually not too successful.'

'I've got plenty of work, I can keep him busy. If I make him into a good spy, will you help me set up a session in the box for Wheelchair man?'

'Who? Oh, you mean the guy Jason tased in the ICU?'

'Yes. Have we got a name for him yet?'

'Yeah, he's carrying a Mexican driver's license, says his name is . . . where is it? Right here someplace . . . here: Eduardo Flores.' He spelled it and shrugged. 'Not necessarily the one he was born with, of course.'

'Is he compos mentis yet?'

'Well, they tell me he's sobering up, and his fever's gone down, so he can talk. What do you want to interrogate him about – you think he's got something to do with that car chase at the senior living place?'

'The DeShawn he was trying to boost out of St. Mary's is the usual driver of the Fairweather van, so Eduardo's in the mix some way.'

'You think he's one of the shooters that killed the replacement driver?'

'He doesn't fit the description, but I'll be glad to consider him if we can match a fingerprint, or . . . you know, it would just be swell if we could get him to say why he wanted to grab DeShawn out of the hospital. He can't deny that's what he was doing there – we saw him getting ready to do it.'

'Right. And I suppose you'll want Jason in there in the box to help you with the questions, won't you? And while I'm setting that up you can try to get Bogey up and running, right?'

'Sure. I'll look around in the closets at home, see if I can find that old cattle prod Ma used to use on us down on the ranch.'

'How can you tell such awful lies about that nice lady?'

'Listen, Aggie used to be fierce – still is, some days.'

'Delaney told me to report to you,' Bogey said, walking into her workspace the next morning. He had changed a little, she thought, in the scant two weeks since she had first seen him in Delaney's office. His appearance then had triggered a memory of a word she couldn't quite spell or define, and on a busy morning with plenty else to think about, the word had kept bothering her, like an itch she couldn't scratch. Finally she pulled up the dictionary app on her phone and found it: 'insouciant' and read the definition – 'carefree, nonchalant.' *The perfect word,* she had thought that morning, *for the way this new guy walks around.*

In the bizarre crime scene they were soon working together, he had behaved with as much care as she did. But that first impression remained – even more than most cops, Bogey moved like a man who knew how to take care of himself.

Watching him approach her desk this morning, it seemed to her that his confidence had ebbed a little. *Delaney must have been hard on him.*

'Have a seat,' she said, and after a few pleasantries she described the search she wanted him to try today. 'You can have all day for this, even tomorrow if you think you're making progress, but if you don't find anything promising by tomorrow night we'll have to turn it over to the stolen car guys. The terrain will be familiar for you, it's where we worked together before.'

'The senior living place, with the van in the garage door? I sure as hell remember that.'

'Right. You remember the story – the van being chased by a pickup that took off as soon as the patrol cars showed up? And how the chase got reversed then, the pickup running away with our guys after them? The riddle that bothers me is how fast that pickup disappeared.'

He frowned. 'We never actually saw the pickup, did we?'

'You and I? No. But the two patrol cars were in close pursuit from the minute it pulled out of the Fairweather Farms yard. Yet they lost it, within a few blocks. They had it in sight and were gaining on it until it turned off on Camino Del Cerro. Right there at the light, they had some kind of traffic pile-up for a minute, and by the time they got free to follow it again it was out of sight and they never found it again.'

She handed him the copy of the incident report she had printed out. 'This has all the details, including badge numbers of the officers in the pursuit vehicles that day. I want you to find them, get them to show you exactly where they were when they last saw the Dodge, and which blocks they drove around before they abandoned the search.'

He raised a quizzical face from his notetaking and said, 'And then – what?'

'Take a city map, draw a circle around the place where they lost him – say twenty blocks. Within that grid, drive it, walk it, make it your own. Mark any place you see where they might have hidden that Dodge pickup in under five minutes. When you think you've exhausted the possibilities, bring the picture to me, and we'll decide whether to investigate further.'

His no-color eyes met hers briefly and went back to the incident report he was holding in his left hand. 'Wasn't there something about a partial plate number?'

'Yes, it's on that report somewhere. But in the very unlikely event that you find that Dodge pickup, those plates are even more unlikely to be still on it.'

'Why am I searching if you don't expect me to find anything?'

'Because if you get a strong hunch about where that Dodge went to ground, we might be close to finding somebody who knows what's going on at Fairweather Farms.' She didn't say, but thought he knew that this was a test.

TWELVE

Wheelchair man, newly recovered from alcoholism, chlamydia, and an overdose of Oxycontin, perversely looked fresh as a daisy. He was younger than she'd thought, and the brown eyes that had been so bloodshot when Jason tased him were clear now. The asthmatic rasp was gone from his breathing and his greasy brown pigtails had been combed out and shampooed into a nice shoulder-length bob. The chains that held him securely in his seat in the box, the no-frills interrogation room at North Stone, almost looked like child abuse.

'What's happened to this guy?' Sarah said, peering through the observation window. 'He looks like Prince Valiant.'

'I'm resentful too,' Delaney said. 'What can I tell you? He's nineteen and he's just had two weeks of the best medical treatment money can't buy.'

'Has he got a record?' Sarah asked.

'He's a US citizen,' Delaney said. 'Born in Douglas, Arizona. But his father's Mexican, and so are the grandmother and aunt who mostly raised him. So he spent most of his childhood in Mexico but went to school for a few years in Arizona. Speaks both languages but doesn't claim to be very fluent in either. I'm trying to figure out if he knows more than he lets on. He's waived his right to an attorney.'

'Hard to believe he's the same guy I barely got the cuffs on in the ICU,' Jason said, taking his turn at the window. 'I wonder if he still wants to eat me.'

'The way you look today, I could hardly blame him,' Sarah said. Jason was resplendent in a three-piece charcoal suit. 'Why are you so spiffed up?'

'I've got a dream date, right after work,' he said. 'I'm taking a classy young woman to the Bach concert at Saint Andrews.

Going to upgrade my public image.' He did a little ballet twirl
and then, seeing Delaney start to look disgusted, drew himself
up into Mountain position and asked, 'What do we want to
learn from the loathsome little man-eater today?'

Sarah said, 'I want him to tell me why he tried to swipe
DeShawn Williams out of the hospital.'

'Come on, you know the answer to that. He wants to chop
him up and scatter the pieces in the desert. You think he's
going to share his motives with you?'

'Not if he can help it. But sometimes if you talk a while,
little pieces of truth just sort of pop out.' She asked Delaney,
'Anything you want us to ask?'

'I'm looking to make a deal. This kid has warrants up the
yazoo. He and the partner you killed have a string of break-ins
and home invasions in every town and village between here and
Agua Prieta. They've been careful about prints but he doesn't
seem to realize how many places have automatic cameras – and
they were quite a striking couple so we have enough to keep
him incarcerated till he grows up.

'So while you beat up on him about the car he stole from
ABC Rental, I'll be listening to find out if he knows anything
useful about the drug business in Tucson. If he can help us
enough, we might be able to winkle out a sentence in the state
system for him. Otherwise he goes to the feds, and that'll be
the end of this pretty boy.'

'Don't feel bad,' Jason said. 'He's all shined up today, but
just underneath that top layer is a paranoid drug addict. What
could he have that you want?'

'What I always want,' Delaney said. 'The truth.' The air
around the interview room was developing an electric crackle
– truth was a tough nut to crack, when Jason and his supervisor
searched for it in the same room.

But it was today's job, so Sarah and Jason walked into the
room with the spit-shined felony suspect, and Delaney hooked
himself up to the watching and listening apparatus outside.

Sarah started, telling the suspect their names, asking him,
'I understand you're bilingual. Are you comfortable speaking
English, Eduardo?'

'Oh, yes,' he said, but then shrugged. 'Not perfect.'

'Well, ours isn't perfect either – don't worry about that. But you know enough plain words to answer the usual questions, do you? OK, let's get the boring stuff out of the way first.' Her tone was matter-of-fact, not chummy but not threatening either. 'Where do you live, Eduardo?'

'Mmm . . . kind of between places right now,' he said, looking at his shoes.

'Been travelling, have you? But when you're at home, Eduardo, where would that be?'

'Mmm, most times, I stay with my nana in Agua Prieta.'

'What's your nana's name?'

'Mmm, Rosa.' It wasn't exactly a stammer. More like a little hum to help him think. He seemed to be asking himself if he should trust Sarah with this precious information.

'What's Rosa's last name?'

'Ahhh, Rodriguez?' As if he might be wrong.

'How do you spell that?'

'Mmm spell? Don't know.'

It went on like that – simple questions giving rise to short answers that evidently had to be considered carefully. His English accent was street American, though, on the words he knew. So presently she asked him if he'd learnt English in school.

'Oh, yes.'

'In Agua Prieta? Or . . . .?'

'In Douglas,' he said with a little nod. 'When I was young?'

The detectives both smiled at his suggestion that he was no longer young. Their smiles perked him up a little; he volunteered a bit of information.

'I live with my *Tia* Luz there.'

'So you could go to school in Douglas?'

'*Si.* Yes.'

There were many arrangements like that in border towns, hard-up Mexican parents and grandparents sent their kids to uncles and cousins who were US citizens in sister towns north of the border, so they could get an education, become bilingual, and have a shot at a cross-border career later on. People on the US side grumbled about the burden on their school systems. Mexicans saw it as payback for the millions in payroll taxes undocumented Mexicans left unclaimed when they went north to work. Sarah thought they were both right.

'How many years did you go to that school?'

'Mmm three years? A little over – till *Tia* Luz got a boyfriend.'

'Ah, the boyfriend wanted you gone?'

'Yes.' A dark look – shamed, Sarah thought.

'The boyfriend was bad news?'

An angry nod. 'He tied me up and beat me.'

'Did you go back to Agua Prieta then?'

'After I got away. Yes.' Getting away, his look said, took a while.

'Did you go to school there?'

'No. No money there.'

'So what did you do there?'

'Yes, well, *eso es*' – he shrugged and turn his hands over, one cuffed and one free, side by side on the little table – 'the problem.' He pronounced it about halfway to Spanish, PRO-blem. 'In Agua Prieta, *no es* . . . very much.'

'Did you go back to your nana?'

'Yes. My nana says, "Always be rice and beans for you here, Hijo." But she lives on little bits her daughters send . . . two girls . . . mmm, clean rooms in Tucson. So I can't be a burden, I look for work. Pick fruit, till grown-ups, mmm' – he made shooing motions – 'chase?'

'They chased you out of the fields?'

'Yes. But at racetrack—' He made shoveling motions.

'You cleaned stalls?'

'Yes. And walk horses. Also learn to run . . . mmm?' He had to think about it. 'AY-rands?'

'You ran errands for the jockeys?'

'No.' He shook his head. 'Run AY-rands for girls at *casa de* . . .' he made a crude gesture with his hands.

'The girls at the whorehouse?'

'Yes. Very nice women, give tips.'

'So you did a little of everything for not much money, is that right?'

'My nana kept a bed for me. But I'm hungry some days, until I meet Russ.'

'Is that – um – Russell Sexton?'

'Yes. My friend,' he said proudly.

Sandy hadn't matched any fingerprints yet, but Sarah had the torn slip of notebook paper she'd found in the shoe of the man she killed with the name, 'Russell Sexton,' in bold handwritten letters, that she hoped the shoe's wearer had written. 'How long ago was that?'

'Mmm, almost . . . one year,' he said. So she was right about the name. She waited, nodding encouragement, and finally he said, 'Meet him at work.'

'What kind of work?'

'Mmm. *Pues*, we, mmm, help this man to build a shed? Carried some sticks? Mmm . . . boards?' A shrug, a little wave-off with his free hand, and then he added, 'Russ got a truck?' There was a lot about getting the truck that couldn't be explained, evidently, but after some more shrugging he thrust his hand out, palm upward, in a gesture that seemed to mean, *Here's the deal*, and added, 'He said he could help me. So we can, mmm, work together.' Another nod and then, proudly, 'Worked out very well.'

The gesture and statement seemed uncharacteristic and Sarah felt certain they were copied from Russell Sexton. She asked him, 'What was good about working with Russell?'

'Hmm? Mmm . . . Russ makes things . . . mmm . . . fun.' Eduardo was warming up; words were coming back to him. '*Antes* – before? Yes. I tried marijuana before? Makes me dizzy! Hmm . . . but Russ knows how.'

'Russ knows how to find the good stuff?'

'Yes. Also where other fun stuff is, so I learn about rum? And good things to eat and who, mmm, has handy stuff to sell?'

'Handy stuff? Like what?'

'Like bed for me. And good chair for me, almost free – at yard sale.'

'So you did whatever Russ said, is that it?'

'Sure, because Russ knows how to make the money go.' He spread his hands.

'Makes the money go around, you mean? So you have enough?'

'Exacto.' He laughed. 'That's how he says, eggs-acto!'

'Russ is fun, huh?'

'Yes. And plus Russ is best at finding jobs. Knows to sit around in bars where men . . . you know . . . bullshit? Yes. So then we learn how to deliver *las drogas*, fun stuff.' He sat, nodding, pleased that he had remembered enough words to tell the story.

'Did you get to use some of that fun stuff?

'Some time. Yes.'

'So you met Russ and did some jobs and started eating better and having fun, is that the story? And how long have you been working for the gang, outfit, whatever, that's selling drugs off the Fairweather Farms van?'

'We mmm not work for them. Mmm, we do one job, one time. But . . . just free . . . um, *como se dice*?'

'Freelance?'

'*Si*, exacto. One job, one pay, correcto? Freelance. *Independent*.' He came down strong on the last word, he was proud of that one.

'All right,' Sarah said, 'so you agreed to independently grab DeShawn Williams out of his bed in St. Mary's Hospital. Why?'

'So he be out.'

'Well, sure. But who wants him out and why?'

'*No se* who wants. Russ says friends. Friends want to help him, mmm, free him out of jail.'

'Do you believe that?'

'Sure I believe. I do same for Russ if he's in jail, and he does for me also. He said "he doos for me." Watching Eduardo inch his way through his second language to describe his life of crime was weirdly unsettling. He seemed like a child who'd been carefully reared by vicious criminals. Yet his account of his nana in Agua Prieta seemed tender and sweet and the truest part of his story.

It was hard to believe he was as gullible as he seemed, Sarah thought, but he'd have to be a brilliant actor to be playing her for a fool. He didn't seem that bright. Thinking she would like to watch for a while, maybe make up her mind about Eduardo, Sarah asked Jason, 'Are you ready to talk about the ABC Rental job now?'

'Sure.' Jason put some notes on the desk, cleared his throat, and began to tell Eduardo a short version of the story he had told Sarah earlier, about walking into ABC Rental with the keys to a two-year-old Nissan, and being greeted by a crew that was not aware, till that moment, that anything was missing.

'But after they got done praising me for bringing back the car, they still wanted to know, how did somebody do this?' Jason said. 'Because the original keys were in the rack where they belonged. And now the car was back and they had two sets of keys. But there weren't any signs of forced entry.'

Jason sat still a minute, watching the pale young man with the noble face. Eduardo was paying rapt attention, trying to follow the story. His face was intent but not hostile; he didn't appear to remember that Jason was the man who had shot him with a taser and tied him up. After a short wait elicited nothing but a quizzical look, Jason leaned forward and asked him gently, 'So how *did* you get in there?'

'Mmm. *No se*. Russ gets in. Russ is, mmm, *inteligente*?' His Spanish pronunciation was better than his English; he got the silky sibilant of 'hen-tay' just right.

Jason said, 'Smart?'

'*Si*, smart.'

'Also, it helps to have these, doesn't it?' Sarah said. She had been silent, trying to give him the benefit of the doubt about how much he knew or understood, but now she was annoyed by his claim that he didn't know how to go through a lock. She held up the ring of burglary tools and shook it so it gave off a nice jingle before she dropped it on the desk in front of her. 'Russell's tools got the two of you in, right? So then you must have taken the Nissan keys to a twenty-four-hour copy shop and got them copied, and returned the originals to the rack before you took the car.'

'*Los amigos*,' Eduardo said, staring at Sarah in surprise.

'What?'

'What Russ, mmm, names.' He pointed at the tools.

'What is he saying?' Sarah asked Jason softly.

Jason said, 'I think he's telling us Russell called these tools "*los amigos*".'

'*Si!* Yes, yes!' Eduardo was excited, bouncing on his little hard seat. 'How'd you get them? Russ never loses *los amigos*.' Alarmed, he demanded of the two detectives, 'Where is Russ? Why he's not here?'

Nonplussed, both detectives stared back at him for a few seconds, until he demanded, louder, '*Donde esta . . .*' He shook his head. 'Where is Russ?'

Sarah had a sudden dismal insight. Eduardo had been on the floor, she realized, almost but not quite immobilized, fighting as hard as he could to keep Jason from putting cuffs on his hands and feet. He had probably not seen his partner get shot. He was high and very sick when he got hauled out of St. Mary's. The patrolmen who took him to the prison hospital would not have bothered to explain much. Most of the events in St. Mary's had probably flown right over his head.

'Eduardo,' she said, aghast, 'hasn't anybody told you that Russell Sexton is dead?'

'What?' He began to yank on the stout line that fastened his right hand to the metal upright under the tiny table in front of him. 'Where is he?' he yelled. 'I need to see!'

He began tugging on the line that tied his right hand. It didn't yield to him, of course – the equipment in the box was there to hold him in place, and it did. The tightly woven nylon line held his right hand, with about four inches of slack, to the table, and the steel chain fastened his feet within twelve inches of where it was clipped to the floor.

And as the truth of that confinement came home to him, Eduardo Flores went spectacularly nuts.

He yanked and yanked on the heavy line, quickly chafing the skin off his wrist. As the bare spots began to burn, he assumed a half-standing position and pulled harder till he drew blood. He flailed his feet around and around the small space the chain allowed them, in the soft canvas shoes that were furnished in the hospital. Soon he had reduced the shoes to shreds and proceeded to tatter his feet.

Sarah said, 'Wait.' And then, 'Stop, now.' When she saw he was beyond listening, she got out of her seat and headed for the door. Jason was right behind her and Delaney met them there. He had already called for help. The two uniforms that were always on call were coming fast along the hall and the medical team was pounding up the stairs.

'I feel rotten about it,' Sarah said later, in Delaney's office. 'If I'd known—'

'But you didn't,' Delaney said. 'And I didn't. Even today, after I got his records – they're so sparse. Nothing to indicate . . . I didn't realize how disadvantaged . . . my God. He's a United States citizen but he's not just illiterate, he can hardly talk. Mute in two languages, how's that for neglect?' He picked up three or four of the notes that littered his desk and bashed them onto a spindle as if punishing memos might right the scales of justice.

'I asked the lab to put a rush on the prints and DNA studies for the two of them. The guy you shot has several priors, probably more that were just listed under Russ's name – it's obvious that Russ was the leader. We're not finding anything on his name, but that doesn't mean anything – he's probably got several names.'

'Sure. He had it printed on a scrap of paper that he stuck in his shoe – he probably copied it off an ad for office supplies.'

'Or a diet plan. Anyway, they've got Eduardo tranquilized now, and I've found a psychiatrist at County who speaks Spanish. He's going to try to find time to talk to him tomorrow. Maybe with scraps of two languages we can find a way to get him out of that padded shirt. Having his hands tied behind him like that is going to drive him crazy all over again every time he wakes up.'

'Don't dare turn him loose, though – he'll eat a doctor's assistant,' Jason said. 'Jeez, to think I put the cuffs on that guy all by myself. Good thing he was high and tased, or I'd be hamburger.'

'Maybe you should get an award,' Sarah said. 'You're tougher than you thought.'

'Tougher than you thought, is that on the awards list?' Jason said. 'Where's the application form for that?'

Delaney swiveled his desk chair to the right and lifted his left shoulder, putting Jason out of his sight. He told Sarah, 'This still leaves us with a great big problem, you know.

We still don't know who sent those two after DeShawn. But we do know they didn't get him, so we have to suppose there'll be somebody else hired on the job tomorrow.'

'Attacking DeShawn Williams is getting to be, like, the favorite hobby of the Fairweather Farms Opioid Club,' Sarah said. 'What do you say I wrap DeShawn in a sturdy box and mail him to Detroit?'

'OK.' Delaney twirled his chair to face his two detectives evenly. 'You two – for some reason your brains are fried. What were you working on before you came here this morning? You can get back to that, or I'm putting you both on street patrol.'

'I was in the middle of an interview with a bank teller. I better go find her before she cries herself sick,' Jason said.

'Go,' Delaney said, and Jason strode out without another word.

'Now you,' Delaney said, 'What's next?'

'I have to look at my list,' Sarah said.

'You still working on that same list?'

'It's kind of a magical list,' Sarah said. 'The faster I cross things off it, the longer it grows.'

It was cool and quiet in the Pima County hospital ward. Lunch trays had just gone out, patients were digesting their macs and cheese, starting to snooze. There was only the hushed bustle of nurses' aides moving gently in Nike trainers, passing out meds, checking blood pressures. Even without privacy-curtains every bed seemed to maintain its own little dimly lit zone of suffering and recovery.

'It's just about my nap time,' DeShawn Williams said, when Sarah appeared at his bedside. 'Can't this wait?'

'Sure,' Sarah said. 'It can wait forever as far as I'm concerned. I'm sick and tired of trying to figure out who's trying to kill you, so if you don't want to tell me, I'll go have a beer at O'Shea's and read thrillers till whoever it is gets the job done. Then I can write up the report and cross you off my list.'

'God, you're a hard woman,' DeShawn said. 'What kinda folks raised you, made you so snarky?'

'The kind of folks that like to hear the truth, DeShawn,'

Sarah said. 'The kind that just can't stand to be played.' She had brought along two photos, the handsome one of Eduardo as he had looked this morning before he went off the rails in the interview room, and the grim one of Russell two Tuesdays ago, with his dreadlocks soaking up blood on the floor, after she'd shot him in the ICU. She laid the pictures across DeShawn's knees, asking, 'You recognize these two dudes?'

He glanced at them briefly and said, 'Nope.' He was propped up in bed, looking young and vulnerable in a skimpy hospital gown that opened in the back and left him feeling exposed even when he was covered up. Convalescence was returning him, Sarah thought, to the teenage attitudes he had just grown out of. They were keeping him clean-shaven in here, there was no trace now of the sexy beard and mustache that had set him apart as chick bait when she first glimpsed him in St. Mary's.

She squinted up at the ceiling fixture and said, 'Got enough light in here? Can you see them clearly?' She picked up the two photos and held them upright in front of him.

'I see them fine but I don't know them.'

His face showed absolute sincerity. *He's trying his guileless look on me again. If there's one thing I know he isn't, it's guileless.*

But staring at him, resisting the impulse to bash him in the head with her day pack, against her will she had an insight: *It's possible he really doesn't know them. Eduardo said they just took on this one job. Freelance, he called it – so proud of knowing the word.*

Maybe I should hit him with a big chunk of the truth.

'DeShawn,' she said, leaning toward him over the bedcovers, holding the photos up close to his face, 'Take a good look now. This is the team that came to grab you out of St. Mary's Hospital. Remember how much it hurt when they tore you out of your hook-ups? If we hadn't been there that day, these two men would have you now.'

DeShawn's face jerked and a small squeak of distress came out of him. Looking straight into her eyes, he leaned toward her and hissed, 'I don't fucking know them. Will you please, for fuck's sake' – she was leaning over him, holding the pictures, and he grabbed her upper arms – 'help me!'

She had only a couple of seconds to decide. He had her in a firm hold, but her hands were free – she could put him in a chokehold right now that would cut off his breathing and render him helpless in seconds. They were in a ward full of people and he was chained securely to the bed. She looked calmly into his eyes and said, 'Let go of me right now and we can talk.'

He let her go at once. His hands dropped onto the bedspread and then went up to cover his face. 'I'm sorry,' he whispered, through his fingers. 'Shit, I'm sorry.'

'Understood,' Sarah said. 'I'm going to sit down here now and give you time to—'

'Excuse me, ma'am,' a voice said at her elbow. 'Are you doing something to upset my favorite patient?' The large attendant she had noticed before in the ward, one she always called, in her mind, Big Nurse, was standing at her elbow. He was nothing like Ken Kesey's character, he was a big soft man with plump cheeks and a sensuous mouth, but right now he looked firmly determined to intervene.

'Oh, hey, bro,' DeShawn said. He took his hands down from his face and turned his beautiful brown eyes, dripping with honest-to-God tears, up to the attendant in scrubs who loomed beside Sarah. 'Listen, you're a pal to come to my rescue, but this good police detective here,' he smiled at Sarah as if they had never exchanged a cross word, 'is just trying to help me figure out a problem that I foolishly got myself into, you dig?'

'Oh. Well, then. If you're sure you're OK.'

'Absolutely OK,' DeShawn said. He grabbed a couple of tissues out of the box on his tray table and mopped his face. He hiccupped a couple of times, and drank some water while they watched. When he was rehydrated, he said politely, 'Detective Burke, may I introduce you to my new friend Etienne?'

Big Nurse performed a gallant bow and declared himself delighted to meet her. 'But is it possible this pretty lady is a police officer?'

Sarah managed a pleasant expression just short of a smile.

'Etienne's really something,' DeShawn said. 'He's from Louisiana, way down on the Bayou as they say, right?' They high-fived over that, and DeShawn went on, 'He's got a wonderful Creole last name too, but I'm not sophisticated enough to pronounce it.' That caused a lot of delighted chuckling that made Big Nurse bounce all over like Jell-O.

When it was clear to Etienne that DeShawn was not being threatened, he exchanged a complicated fist bump with his patient and moved away, but continued to monitor their conversation from afar, Sarah noticed.

'Jesus, DeShawn,' Sarah said, 'I wish we had a negotiator like you on our SWAT team – we'd never have to fire another shot.' She pulled a printed form out of her day pack. 'This is a document that says you waive the right to have an attorney present during this conversation. If you sign it and answer the questions I'm about to ask you, I promise to help you find a good public defender to help you get your case moving as soon as you're well enough to get out of here.'

'That's all I get? How about immunity for everything I tell you about?'

'That's specified on this form. Just for the stuff you tell me about. Your attorney has to get you the rest of the favors – I'm just the poor hard-working detective who's trying to get you out of here before every two-bit hoodlum in this valley has had a go at offing you. What did you do, DeShawn, to make somebody so freaking mad at you?'

'Nothing! Honest, lady, all I do is drive the damn bus!'

'You're a hard one to help, DeShawn, I swear. Sign the damn paper, will you? There now.' She dug out her recorder and looked around for an outlet.

'Oh no, no, no,' DeShawn said. 'Please no recording, I'll get killed for sure if you do that.' He was all loosened up now; he could cry on demand.

'All right, all right I *hear* you,' she said. 'Do you have to keep bubbling like that?'

'I'm sorry,' he said. 'It's just such a relief to have somebody to talk to.'

'I bet. Let's get back to the questions, can we? You all dried out now?'

'Yeah.' He blew his nose elaborately, taking two tissues to finish the job. 'Go ahead.'

'This isn't hard, just answer yes or no. When you drive the Fairweather Farms van, do you deliver the clients to their medical appointments, therapy sessions, and so on?'

'Yes. Shopping too, and sometimes theater and ball games.'

'And while you do that, you deliver drug orders at some of the stops, is that right?'

'Um. Well . . . yes.'

'Are these drugs you deliver available in the drugstore?'

'No. Are you kidding? Of course not.' He couldn't seem to stick to just yes or no.

'These are illegal drugs that are not licensed and taxed for sale, is that correct?'

'I don't know much about licenses and taxes.'

'But you do know the drugs you deliver are illegal?

'Well . . . I'm no authority on what's legal or . . . yes, all right!' He was getting very nasal again. He cleared his throat, said excuse me, pulled out more tissue and went back to work on his nose.

Sarah waited patiently, grinding her teeth. When he stopped blowing his nose and laid his head tiredly back on the pillow, she asked him, 'Do you know who the buyers are?'

'No.'

'What, you just drop the order where you're told to drop it?'

'Yes.'

'And collect the money at the same place?'

'No, no, that's what I keep telling you – I don't touch the money.' He sat up and got quite agitated about the money, regaining enough strength to make sure she understood. 'They get paid some other way. That money you found in the jacket? That wasn't mine. I don't know who put it there. You understand? That wasn't part of the . . . what I agreed to.'

'OK. I believe you. But let's get down to that now,' she said. 'Who's they?'

'What?'

'You said, "They get paid some other way." In that sentence, who is "they'?'

'Oh. Well, I don't know any of their names. I mean, it's a gang, part of a cartel, I guess. Sort of a small-timey part. They call themselves "Los Verdes"?'

'The Greens?'

'Yeah, they all had matching caps, I guess, to start with. Just a little street gang in south Tucson, but they got started selling weed and a little crack. They're way past that now, they mostly move opioids and white powder cocaine. I hooked up with them soon after I got to town.'

'How'd you do that?'

'We-ell, I got my start with a street gang like them in California, and you know, once you been in the trade you can spot the signs pretty easy. Me and a couple of my buds ran some routes out of a nice area of hotels and boutique stores in a touristy part of LA.'

'Is that how you got the letter of recommendation from the Fairmont Hotel?'

'Yeah, I stole some stationery from the writing desk in the lobby. I'll plead guilty to that – you want to charge me? I didn't take none of the pens, though. That was somebody else.'

'I'll keep that in mind. If you were all set up with your routes in LA, why did you leave?'

'I got crosswise with one of our suppliers. It was over nothing, really, just a . . . I should have known better. But Chelsea was so hot, I couldn't resist, so . . .' He sighed. For a moment, DeShawn's face recaptured the smug expression he had shown in the ICU in St. Mary's. Even without the killer beard and sideburns, despite the shiner and the runny nose, he'd got back most of his Lothario look.

Sarah said, 'You got in a fight over a girl? Really?' She watched him, wondering if he was serious. 'That seems sort of . . . high school.'

'Yeah, well.' He shrugged. 'Shit happens. Jaime and I were both dating the same girl, but I knew it and he didn't. And he was a Blood, he came up in that south LA culture, so when he found out I was poaching on his turf he said he would cut off my balls and I knew he wasn't joking.'

'So you wrote the letter and vanished.'

'Ooh, vanished, you do know such nice words. But the Bloods are known to be without pity when their honor is challenged, so I *vanished* first and wrote the letter on the road.'

'How lucky, then, that you arrived in Tucson just in time
to fill a vacancy at Fairweather Farms.'

'Well, you know what they say, luck happens to the prepared
mind. I believe that, so I try to stay tuned up. I drove the airport
shuttle for a Holiday Inn in Fresno when I was first on my own
– I had to get a commercial license to get the job and I've
always kept it current. Driving the company vehicle is one of
the best ways to get established in a new company or town.'

'I didn't know that.'

'Most people don't. It looks like a job for deadheads, but
really it's the quickest way to learn the ropes in a new place.
Who's in charge of what and if anybody's holding a grudge?
And you make yourself handy to people with money to spend,
people who want things, so as time goes by you'll have some
studs asking you, who's got the action? And before long, that
can be you.'

'So is that how it worked here in Tucson? You got the job
driving the van and the drug deals came along after that?'

'That's right. I was almost completely broke when I got
here; I pulled out of my previous squat without waiting to
pack. So I had to get a gig right away in order to eat. And I
nailed that, all right, and then the deal with the Greens. But
since then' – his voice trailed off for a minute, and when he
resumed he seemed to feel sorry for himself again – 'since
then I been through some very hard times. And I feel totally
worn down ever since I got in that freaking accident.' He did
look tired, suddenly, and cold; he slid down in the bed and
pulled the cover up around his ears.

'I understand that,' Sarah said. 'Just stick with it for a few
more minutes. You've been doing a great job of telling the
truth here, DeShawn. If you can keep it up a little longer I'll
have enough to put away these people who keep trying to
murder you, won't that be good?' That was condescending
bullshit, she would later admit to herself. So maybe it was her
fault, what happened next. But the change came so suddenly
and silently that she didn't realize until too late that DeShawn
had lost his enthusiasm for telling the truth.

Or for much of anything else, she saw with dismay – he
was beginning to look like a TV ad for one of those night-time

cold cures. Tears ran freely down his cheeks and his nose was running again too; he pulled two tissues out of the box and went to work mopping. When he surfaced, he said, 'Listen, you know I'm really pretty sick. So I need to rest now and we can talk some more later on.'

'OK. Listen, just give me the names of the people you dealt with here, so I can—'

'I told you, they called themselves The Greens. God, I'm getting feverish.'

'Come on, DeShawn, you don't make deals with a whole gang, you must have had one or two guys you dealt with who had names. Just give me one name and I'll leave you alone till tomorrow.'

'Why do we have to do it all in one day?' His voice went shrill, he sounded like an ailing child. Face flushed, he wailed, 'I'm hot and cold and I'm getting a sore throat.'

Then Etienne was back at the bedside, along with another attendant who had a stethoscope hanging around his shoulders. He put the device in his ears and listened to DeShawn's heaving chest.

Etienne glowered at her, said, 'Excuse me,' and made little shooing motions. Sarah got out of her chair and stood in a space in the aisle between DeShawn's row of beds and the next. It was crowded and awkward; she felt blamed but could see no chance or reason to defend herself. She put a card firmly in Etienne's hand and said, 'Call my cell when your shift ends.'

She turned and made her way between the rows of beds to the door that led out to the exit. As she reached the door it opened but no one came through, so she walked through the opening and found Bogey standing on the other side, holding the door.

'Oh,' she said sharply, 'what are you doing here?' Already discomfited by the way DeShawn's health problems – or his exaggeration of them – had squeezed her out of their conversation, now to find Bogey where she least expected him felt annoying and wrong.

'I came to find you,' he said. 'I called the office and they said you'd be here.'

'Interviewing DeShawn Williams. The man who was supposed to be driving the van that got shot up.'

'Oh, yes. But he got hurt in traffic, was that it? How's he doing now?'

'Well, I thought he was doing quite well, but he appears to be having a setback just now. He seems very unstable, but – he's got a lot of injuries to heal, so I guess it's not surprising. What did you come to tell me? You didn't need to do that, by the way, you could have texted and saved yourself a trip.'

'Well, I know, but I thought what I found about the area might change the way you think about the case, so maybe I should show you.'

'Oh? Well, let's see, what time is it?' She felt as if this day of male histrionics had been very long already.

'Two-thirty,' Bogey said. 'Want to take a look at it now?'

'Sure, still plenty of time. Is your car outside? So's mine – meet me at the exit closest to town, or wait, let's rendezvous at the light on Grant Road and Silverbell, OK?'

After the cool in the ward, the heat in the prison parking lot felt like an assault. She had parked under the shade of a young desert willow some distance from the entrance, but the sun had shifted while she was inside and now her car stood in the open, giving off waves of reflected sunlight. She cursed herself for her choice of parking spots as she walked what felt like a mile across the blistering asphalt. Once inside the oven heat of her car, she started the motor, rolled down the windows and adjusted the A/C to blow some of the heat out. After a minute she closed up, turned the vent to blow air directly into her face and leaned back in the seat, taking deep breaths. When she was back to cool and calm, she pulled onto the highway.

THIRTEEN

Monday afternoon

Bogey was pulled up close to the metal pole that held the Grant/Silverbell sign. There was not much room in the intersection, so Sarah rolled down her window and called, 'Let's move up to the Goret Road intersection, there's more room there.' She pulled out ahead of him and parked in the pull-out at Goret Road, facing east with a view of the golf course. When he pulled in beside her she got out and transferred to his passenger seat.

'OK,' she said, 'show me what you've got.'

He plunked a thick, spiralbound book of sectional maps in her lap and said, 'Let's look at the map first and then drive it.' He had the page turned to the area they were sitting in. 'This book is five years old so Fairweather Farms doesn't show on this map, but I marked it with a Post-it dot.'

'I see it. You've got it just about right – the place is just about halfway between Camino Del Cerro and Sweetwater, on the right of the highway as we're facing it now.'

'Yes,' Bogey said. 'There are a few more buildings in the vicinity than when this was drawn, but the streets are the same. And as we drive northwest from here, the city is to your right. All turns to the left lead to open desert, with occasional clusters of housing. I know you know this from your days on patrol, but—'

'That's all right, you're showing me what you've learned about this incident. And actually, the half year I was assigned to this section of town I was on the night shift, so mostly all I saw was streetlights, bar signs and fast food places.'

'There's a lot more than that to see out here. Let's drive down the highway now and I'll show you what I mean.' He looked around and then pulled onto the highway. Traffic was light on Silverbell compared to the steady stream on Interstate

10, though they both followed the same route along the north-west edge of town, on either side of the dry bed of the Santa Cruz River. With few cars to worry about, Bogey drove slower than the posted speed limit so Sarah could look at both sides of the road.

'Looking forward,' he said, 'there are three stop lights on this section of the road – Sweetwater, Camino Del Cerro and Sunset. But the three patrol cars that answered the call for help at Fairweather Farms that day all came out on Camino Del Cerro, turned left on Silverbell and approached the senior living place at high speed.

'They all remember the incident clearly and their accounts agree. Tom Newsom drove car thirty-five and he told me it was his first call to this new place and he wasn't familiar with the entrance. They could all hear gunfire as they approached, and then yelling and more shots. So they had their sirens going and were ready for a fight but the way that road dips and turns, they really couldn't be sure what was going on until they were right on top of it.

'The other two cars agree; their destination was a sharp left turn off the highway as it rounded a bend. There were a lot of bushes on either side and they were going so fast they missed it. Tom was in front, and when he saw the gate flash past he called the other two cars and said he was past it and would come back. But he was just too late; the other two cars came blazing past it also, so they all had to risk their necks making instant u-eys on that narrow two-lane.

'But as it turned out that was not such bad luck, because as they all came roaring back north on Silverbell, the shooters who had been following the Fairweather Farms van got scared by the sirens and drove back out on the road, just ahead of the police, and took off north like scared rabbits.

'Tom was in the rear by then and he told the other two, "Go get 'em and I'll check out this farm here." None of them knew yet what kind of establishment they were heading for. He stopped at Fairweather Farms and I think you've heard from the employees there how he and his colleague helped them get the passenger off the van.

'Cars twelve and forty-eight followed the shooters back to

Camino Del Cerro. Here's where it gets interesting: those two cars had the Dodge pickup in sight all the way to the light on Camino Del Cerro. They were all going flat out and they were gaining on the Dodge.

'But the driver of the pickup didn't give a damn for traffic signals, of course, and when he turned right and ran the red light at Camino Del Cerro, he caught the front bumper of a Kia that was exiting off Camino Del Cerro onto Silverbell, and knocked him into the middle of the intersection.

'The Dodge grazed two other cars approaching from the east. The situation had the potential for serious injury, so car twelve, Henderson, stayed to sort out the traffic problems and car forty-eight, driven by Jack Bertram, got back on the chase. But the mess at the stoplight had cost him a couple of minutes, and in that time the Dodge with its load of shooters disappeared.

'Bertram assumed the Dodge had made it across this weird interstice where Camino Del Cerro goes over the railroad and turns into Ruthrauff' – he was driving it as he spoke – 'and once on Ruthrauff the shooters had about a dozen options every minute for where to turn and get lost.'

'That's right,' Sarah said, 'this section of Ruthrauff is all small streets lined with small businesses. To pass the time, one of those dismal nights driving patrol in this part of town, my colleagues and I tried to count the number of privately-owned businesses on this street between the railroad tracks and the Tucson Mall. I think we came up with 158.'

'Of course it's turned a couple of corners and become Wetmore Road by then.'

'Yes. And every little side street leading off Ruthrauff has more of the same. And yes, somewhere in here, without trying anything drastic like hiding the lug nuts in with the table silver, it might be possible somebody's got a small chop shop tucked in behind a hamburger joint. I hate to think how many search warrants it would take to find it.'

'Agreed. Let's go back out to Silverbell now.'

'Ah,' Sarah said. 'The next idea?'

'Yes. Hang on, now, here comes the bump over the tracks.'

But then he didn't go on out to Silverbell. As soon as he

got over the tracks, he turned sharp left and darted under a small sign that read *Christopher Columbus Regional Park*. They drove under low-hanging bushes into a narrow lane that led onto a large paved parking area. He parked against a concrete bumper that looked out across a softball diamond in a grassy pasture-like area.

'Ah, yes,' Sarah said. 'I haven't been in here in a long time. Isn't it pretty?'

'This part is. Some of the rest of this park is pretty run down. You can get through this little gap in the fence here and follow the track out to the rest of the park. You have to know what you're looking for to get much fun out of this section, but farther down – it's almost all weeds and mesquite – there are a lot of leftover ideas buried in the underbrush.

'Nature's taking some of it back now,' he said. 'Look at the hawks.' They watched a pair of red-tail hawks soar over a spot in the dusty green foliage between them and the highway. Something must be dead or dying out there in the mesquite.

'I guess it depends on what funding's available as time goes by. There used to be a sweet little lake, I remember, with picnic tables and benches. And reeds around it, and a lot of frogs. I wonder if the frogs have survived. Oh, and there was a nice grassy dog run. I had a dog once and I used to bring him here on my days off and watch him go mad with joy, rolling around in the turf with his friends.'

'Sounds nice. I didn't have time to find everything, but I saw one hiking trail and a railroad trestle. Not sure if those two go together.'

'Probably not. A lot of it is buried in weeds now but there are still some good birding spots. And down there where the park ends there's a fishing pond and a golf course – did you find all that?'

'Yes. Looking forward to trying some of it out.'

'The amazing thing about this recreation area is that it's surrounded on all sides by fast traffic, but once you're in here it's quiet. And secret, sort of. You can drive by it on Silverbell for years – I did – and never guess at all the fun stuff that's in here, in this small space between two highways. All you can see from the road is bushes.'

'Sure would make a fine place to hide a Dodge pickup for a while,' Bogey said.

'Yes, it would.' She looked at her watch. 'It's almost four o'clock and I've never had a coffee break. Or lunch, come to think of it. Let's go back out there on Ruthrauff and find a fast-food place so we can snack while we talk about this.'

In a cool booth, Sarah yearned briefly over an all-day breakfast menu but decided not to ruin her appetite for dinner and settled for pie. When it came, she downed it fast with two cups of coffee. While she ate, she listened. 'Go ahead,' she told Bogey, 'tell me where you think the pickup went.'

'Well, that's the trouble – there's too many good options. Ruthrauff is a conspiracy-lover's dream – on the map, anyway. All those little side streets? You want to stay all year and walk every one. In reality a lot of them are grubby and not at all romantic. Tire shops, paint stores, fake nail studios . . . no zither music. A ton of fast food places.'

'Do any of them look like chop shops?'

'No. But there are dozens that could be, in the back. Or underneath, or with the addition of a little piece of land they maybe own out in the desert.'

'You think it's possible somebody's got a little chop shop tucked in behind the walk-in cooler in a burger joint? That's very tantalizing – I almost want it to be true. But also a little crazy, I think. Wouldn't people notice the traffic?'

'Not if you stagger the hours. Hot cars mostly move at night, don't they?' He had a distracted, hard-working expression, as if it was up to him to figure out how to make it work. 'But I agree with what you seem to be thinking, that it's a lot easier to imagine the shooters darting into the park while the patrolmen were snarled in the traffic jam at the intersection. There's no place in the park to dispose of the pickup, but you could certainly hide it till it was convenient to haul it away.

'I know you told me to figure out how the pickup could disappear so fast, and I can certainly see how it could. But as for finding it – I think we've got so many possibilities we're kind of bogged down. Am I wrong? Do you see a way to sort this out?'

'No. I think that pickup got away from us by wrecking an

innocent bystander at the light, and we'll only find the Dodge if they're stupid enough to bring it out and commit another crime with it. I'm not holding my breath waiting for that.'

'So I'm sorry I failed in my mission—'

'You haven't. I asked you to explore one possibility. You did and now I can cross that one off my list.'

'Do you really have a list?'

'Sure. I always do when I'm the primary on a case. I can't possibly remember all the details.'

'But we all add stuff into the case report every day—'

'Well, yes, we do. But before a detail ever makes it into the case report, it often spends a long time being a thorn in a detective's side.'

'A what?'

'A nagging little nothing. A piddling snag. For instance, at Fairweather Farms, why is Amanda so hostile to me? She seems to get along fine with everybody else. It's just a small thing that may mean nothing – she's got a grudge about women in law enforcement maybe. But Letitia says she doesn't, so until I figure out why she doesn't want to talk to me, Amanda's attitude is on my list.'

'Wow. I'll have to think about that one. You know I'm glad to have this chance to work with you while I'm getting started – the guys all say you're the best one to ask while I'm learning the ropes. You know they call you Detective Do-Right?'

She waved him off. 'Don't pay any attention to that nonsense. The brotherhood likes to needle me because I'm a fussbudget about details.'

'Still, I hope you won't get tired of questions. I know I have a lot to learn.'

'I suppose,' Sarah said, picking her words carefully, 'there are some drawbacks to getting boosted into homicide so fast.'

'Everybody seems to think I've got an uncle with influence or something,' Bogey said, adopting the behavior she'd noticed whenever he suspected people were thinking about his rank. 'Honestly, Sarah, I just got the rating because I made that one lucky arrest.'

'I wouldn't write it off as lucky,' she said, 'bringing in five guys by yourself. Did I read the wrong report? The one I saw said they were all armed and dangerous.'

'They were all armed. I'm not persuaded they were very dangerous.' He did the shrug again, the one that suggested he should apologize for breathing nice clean air meant for somebody more deserving.

'Whatever else we do together,' Sarah said, 'I'm determined I'll get you to stop apologizing for getting promoted. A job in homicide is God knows not a nifty gift with a bow on it, but it's nothing to be ashamed of, either.'

'Yeah, well . . .' He did his other evasion trick, looking at his watch and patting his pockets.

'Tell you what,' she said, 'if I assure you your pockets are safe in here, why don't you just relax and tell me how you did it? Maybe that will set your mind at ease about the reward.'

She was encouraged by his response to the challenge – his eyes grew a spark, like, all *right*, and he sat up straighter and got ready.

'It was out on East Speedway, in that section that's all antique shops and paint and decorating places and there's a bar with off-track betting. Four young Hispanics, standard south Tucson street gang types, hanging around an ancient Cadillac Eldorado – the one with the killer fins, I couldn't believe there was one still running – it had a repaint job, hot pink – and they were parked on the side of that bar with the painted pony, what's the name?'

'The Spotted Pony?'

'Yeah, that one. They were all high, making a big show of smoking pot, and every so often they'd pop the caps on a couple more cans of beer – they had a cooler in the open trunk of the car.

'They had a buddy, all smiles, a PR-type guy a little better dressed than the rest, who came and went, talked to everybody. He'd pop into one of those sports bars for a while and then come back and share a joint.

'And you know, there wasn't anything seriously criminal in what they were doing, but all their moves were kind of provocative. I could have got in there and charged them with loitering, creating a public nuisance – they might have had enough pot in the car to call it suspicion of dealing. But I thought it was more interesting to wait and see what they were up to.

'It was all pretty juvie, ball caps reversed, jeans hung so low they showed their rumps every time they bent over for another beer – the whole thing was so schoolyard, and yet kind of ominous – they were set up, waiting for something. Or someone.

'So I circled the block a couple of times, left to answer a nuisance call and came back. They were all still there, showing off their little bits of Spanish to each other and speaking English to passers-by who stopped to admire the car. So I pulled into an alley up behind them where I had a view of them but they couldn't see me, called Dispatch and asked what's going on in this part of town today? "Pretty quiet today," the officer said, "everybody's in the bars with TV, waiting for the race to start." Turned out it was Kentucky Derby day.

'I had a hunch then, so I tuned in the race on my radio and waited. Pretty soon the race was run, there was the usual screaming and crying and talk about a Triple Crown, and then, along the sidewalk from the off-track betting bar came the better-dressed buddy, smiling brighter than ever with his arm around the shoulder of a new best pal. He was your typical race-day gullible Tucson drunk who had just won the trifecta, and now he had come out with his new friend to see the wonderful antique car that was parked out here. Right then I knew this was what we were all waiting for, so I wheeled my black-and-white Ford down around the corner just as the four young studs were clustering around the winner, who was outraged to see that his new pal from the bar was helping his buds to the contents of his wallet.

'They were all so busy and happy with their victim, Sarah, he was protesting and they were debating whether to strangle him right there or gag him and put him in the trunk – oh, wait, we gotta get the cooler out first! – it was a walk in the park, really. I grabbed my shotgun off the rack and, you know, there's just nothing like the sound of a pump-action shotgun to get everybody's attention.

'And all that about me bringing in five bad guys single-handed – I had told Dispatch what I was watching, had him all primed so as soon as he got my call he sent me plenty of help. It's true I had them all lying face down on the gravel in The Spotted Pony's parking lot by the time they got there – that did make a nice picture, didn't it?'

'Beautiful. So now you're in homicide, is it the answer to all your hopes and dreams?'

'Well . . .' He did the hapless shrug again and they both laughed.

'Nothing's ever quite perfect, is it? What's the worst thing about being a detective?'

'The hours. On patrol you put in your eight or ten, depending which schedule you got, and when your shift is over you go home. Investigations sometimes go on and on.'

'That's true. Many a marriage has foundered after one of the pair got a job in homicide.'

'And on patrol I was just getting seniority enough to try for weekends off. Now I'm years from getting weekends and so far I can't even get two days together. Right now I've got Wednesday and Friday, and that may change on short notice.'

'Makes it hard to buy season tickets, hmm?'

'Makes it hard to keep a steady girl.'

'Guess you'll have to try being extra adorable.'

'Eee. Recent polling indicates that's not likely.'

They laughed together as they paid their checks. The other problem with detective division was that once out of uniform, cops didn't get much free pie.

'That's plenty of corned beef,' Sarah said. 'I'll take some more cabbage, though, and another potato.' The pie hadn't even begun to fill the vacancy left by the missed lunch, so she had been very glad to find a good meal waiting at home. 'This is a terrific dinner you cooked up for us tonight, Denny. What inspired you?'

'I'm celebrating,' Denny said. 'I took the last of the tests today for admission into advanced placement classes next semester. If I did as well as I think, I get to take computer coding in the spring.'

'Good for you,' Will said. 'You do well enough at those super-geek courses; maybe you can find the deposition I blew off into outer space yesterday morning.'

'I better not promise until I see if I can pass the tests.'

'Oh, you'll pass them all right,' Will said. 'If you can figure out all the moves to make a dinner like this, you can certainly conquer a batch of ones and zeroes.'

'Grandma helped me with this dinner,' Denny said. 'She *understands* vegetables, do you realize how profound that is?'

'Oh, my goodness,' Aggie said. 'Profound.'

'I mean it,' Denny said. 'Anybody can cook a meat loaf and a baked potato, but Grandma knows how to make a big dinner with many different parts and make everything get done at the same time.'

'You'll get it soon,' Aggie said. 'Be patient. It takes a lot of carrots and onions to get to where I am in the cooking game.'

'Which is a wonderful place to be,' Sarah said. 'But you're right about timing, Denny. It's the trickiest part of everything, isn't it? I spent all afternoon with another detective trying to answer questions we wouldn't be asking if everybody'd been in the right place at the right time.'

'Be a rare day when you achieve that in a police department,' Will said. 'Which detective was helping you learn that hard lesson?'

'Oh, the new one, the one they all call Bogey – Boganicevic.'

'Oh yeah, the one that brought in the street gang single-handed.' Will looked thoughtful. 'It's funny about that guy.'

'What is?'

'The way he's turned his career around. His first couple of years, he got kind of a reputation for messing things up.'

'Did he? I guess I never heard about that.' She finished the last of the potato and sat back with a sigh. 'Ah, well, but anybody can change, can't they?'

'God, yes,' Will said, 'I'd never have made it through seventh grade if that wasn't true.'

FOURTEEN

Tuesday

'I thought I heard thunder during the night,' Sarah said, coming out of her bedroom Tuesday morning. 'Is it possible we had some rain?' In a dry summer, they had all been complaining about what Denny was calling 'the little monsoon season that couldn't.'

'Sure did,' Will said, pulling open the front blinds. 'Look, puddles in the low spots!'

'Oh, I have to go outside and smell it,' Sarah said, and hurried out onto the front walk to stand with her nose in the air, sniffing, crying, 'Yes, yes, yes!' The desert gave off that wet-creosote aroma, and a cactus wren broadcast its creaky buzz of approval.

'Love it, love it, love it,' Denny crooned behind her. 'We should dance to show our gratitude!' She whirled into a mad caper of joy around the wet gravel, crying, 'Thank you, Mother Nature!' and nearly collided with Will when he came out to say breakfast was on the table.

'Easy there,' he said. 'You girls get kind of nutty when you're pleased, eh? Don't think I want to be around you when you win the lottery.' He held the door for them, chuckling, and they all sat down at the round table and poured milk over cereal and berries, and began grabbing parts of the paper.

After a few minutes' rustling silence Will took his head out of the Sports page to say he might be a little late tonight. 'Another one of those dismal board meetings.'

'Mmph,' Sarah said, behind the front page.

Denny said, 'I'll be right on time but I might need CPR. Our math teacher is going to dump on us today – a *killing load*!'

'Tell Aggie if the pain is serious,' Sarah said. 'She understands tween-agers even better than vegetables.' She got up and found her purse on the sideboard where she always left it, and loaded it with spare tissues, two good pens, a small flashlight, and her list. It had more than thirty items on it now, but most of them were crossed out.

'Try not to shoot anybody today, Aunt Sarah,' Denny said as she loaded her backpack.

'Never fear,' Sarah said. 'Today I'm going house-hunting.'

Denny giggled and waved goodbye. She knew her aunt was not going house-hunting; they already had this house that suited them fine, and besides this was a workday. So she didn't get the joke but she was in a hurry. And she knew she would find out tonight, if she asked (maybe even if she didn't), what her aunt had been doing all day. That was the grand thing about her situation now – she lived with three capable adults who weren't afraid of the truth. If she wanted to know what was going on with them, Denny thought, all she had to do was ask.

In her workspace on South Stone Sarah pulled up the database for car registrations and entered Amanda Petty's auto stats. It came up with her home address, 255 Jenny Mine Road. When she fed it into her Google map site and saw where it was, she stepped around the corner to Ollie's cubicle. He was sitting at his desk, staring at his computer monitor. Ray was behind him, looking over his shoulder. They both looked as if they had found some very good news.

She tapped on the thin wooden panel that outlined the doorway. Both men peeled their eyes slowly off the screen to face her, but their minds, obviously, were still on the monitor. Ray said, '*Que pasa?*'

Sarah said, 'I found this address off Ocotillo—'

'Good for you,' Ollie said. 'I've always wanted to do that. Haven't you, Ray?'

'God, yes,' Ray said. 'I told my bride yesterday, if only I could find an address off Ocotillo, my career would be made.'

Sarah stepped into the space beside Ray and stared at the screenful of gross pornography they were both watching. 'I see you're madly busy,' she said, politely, 'but could you spare a minute to come and look at my monitor?'

'Of course,' Ollie said, closing his screen as he got up.

'Why wouldn't I be glad to help a colleague when she's proving what a major pain in the butt she can be?'

Ray followed them into her cubicle, muttering, 'Although it's hard to understand what she's doing in the detective division if she needs help to read a map.'

'So are we trapped on silly street today?' Sarah asked them. 'Or what's made you both so frisky?'

'We finished all our interviews at the bank,' Ollie said. 'We don't have to listen to anybody cry today.'

'That hold-up was a big bummer, huh?'

'Hard enough to put up with the waterworks,' Ray said, 'but then we couldn't get any useful evidence. The bad guys all wore balaclavas so nobody knows what they look like, and they used some kind of freak accents and talked in high, piping voices so we don't have a clue where they're from.'

'And they were all gloved up and wearing slippers, so we're not getting any prints or DNA,' Ollie said. 'These guys are pros. The only thing that went *right* in this deal is that they didn't get the money.'

'Still, in a robbery that's a lot to go right.'

'Especially in a bank,' Ollie said. 'We do have happy bankers. So grateful to our fine police force, that's what the chairman of the board said.'

'The chairman did not say, but I believe it's safe to assume,' Ray said, 'that he was also pleased that he was not in the bank that day getting shot at and abused like his underpaid employees.' He did an elaborate stretch to ease his neck. 'Shall we stop talking about it now? I'm afraid I'll stop feeling frisky.'

'Good idea,' Sarah said. 'Let's talk about this address I want to find. I think it must be in this cluster of little streets out here in the desert . . .' She pointed. 'Do you know anything about that – is it a wildcat village or what? I suppose if I go west on Ocotillo—'

'Actually I think that's south,' Ray said.

'Oh, please,' Sarah said, 'let's not start that or I'll never get out of the building.' Built on the bias and around many hills, Tucson was a hard place to keep a fix on true north.

'OK,' Ray said, 'just keep your GPS on.'

'I will. Where's Bogey? I might as well take him along.'

'He's off today.' Ray smirked. 'Poor kid's got splits.'

'That's right, he told me that. No problem, this is basically sightseeing – I don't need any help. But tell me, have you driven that section of the desert much? Should I go out on Ocotillo?'

'You can do that,' Ollie said, squinting at the screen, 'or go on down the highway to Gould and turn west there. But remember, Sarah, west of Silverbell you're mostly out of the city limits.'

'I know. I'm not going to arrest anybody. I just want to look.'

'At what?'

'At whatever's on the lot at Amanda Petty's home address.'

'Who's Amanda Petty?'

'She's the steno, secretary, bookkeeper – *whatever* – at Fairweather Farms.'

'And that makes her yard interesting?'

'It wouldn't, except she doesn't want anybody to know where it is. The address she has listed at the company is a Mail Boxes address. She told her boss she's hiding from an abusive ex, and probably that's all there is to it. But I'm stalled out on this case, none of my leads has worked out. So I'm working my way back through my list, thinking I must have overlooked something. And the first thing I came to is Amanda Petty's home address, which I promised myself to verify, and then forgot.'

'Well, good luck trying to find it out there,' Ray said. 'I went out in that neighborhood once with a buddy, looking for an open spot to do some skeet shooting. We stumbled into that neighborhood by mistake and were totally lost for half an hour. All those little lines marked as streets? They're just gravel tracks – some are just dirt paths, and they all run steeply up and down hills. Old mine sites, mostly, and what look like storage sheds. Holes you can fall into. Good place to stay out of. You sure that steno lives in there? Must be some kinda girl.'

'Yes,' Sarah said, 'I think that's a fair description of Amanda.' She decided to take along her day pack, and began checking to be sure it held extra batteries, a county map, energy bars and bottled water.

Watching her take her phone off the charger and zip it into the outside pocket on her day pack, Ollie said, 'I'd ride out with you, Sarah, but I got two humongous reports to write, and Delaney wants them right away.'

'Hey, I've got an idea,' Ray said. 'I'm tight with the deputy sheriff, he's one of my thirty-seven cousins. Would you like me to call him and ask him to meet you out there?'

'Guys, I'm only going a few miles out in the desert, it's not the South Pole,' she said.

'I know, but some places out there are pretty desolate,' Ollie said. 'You got both our numbers handy on your phone?'

'Of course.'

'Good. And listen, send me a text when you get out there, will you? I'm going to be right here all day, typing my fingers to the bone.'

'Me too,' Ray said. 'So feel free to call us when you run into a ditch and can't get out.'

'You bet.' *When pigs fly, I will call you for help getting out of a ditch. What ailed them today? This was the condescension she had fought off years ago.*

She did double-check all her supplies, though, added a box of band-aids and extra sunscreen, and changed into the old ranch boots she kept in the office for days when she might want to walk a lot. For comfort, as long as she was taking the pack, she zipped her Glock into the holster on her day pack, next to the phone.

Tuning her radio to NPR as she headed out, she told herself, *It's a beautiful day, let's enjoy the trip.* And it *was* beautiful in the car, with the A/C cranking out cool air. The dashboard indicator said the outside temperature was ninety-five, and the morning news predicted Tucson would be around a hundred and three by mid-afternoon.

It was a small point of pride with Sarah that she seldom needed the GPS in her car. Having spent thousands of hours patrolling city streets, she stayed oriented in town and always knew the shortest route to wherever she was going. Her knowledge of the desert surrounding Tucson was mostly confined to major roads, except for her family's ranch, a few hundred acres north of town where she knew every track and slope.

But anywhere in the Tucson valley, she drove with the confidence of a driver who knew roughly where she was just by glancing at the mountains around her.

So she reviewed the map before she set out, thinking about the turns she would make to reach her destination, in the middle of the cluster of short streets she was driving toward. She decided to set her mileage when she left Silverbell, drive five miles west and take the next left turn.

When that took her to a sign on a padlocked gate marked, *Private Property, do not enter,* she took three tries to turn in the tiny space between two deep ditches, went back to Ocotillo and turned west again.

She took the next left and arrived at a fenced group of buildings with a small sign on a split-rail fence that read, *Goats for sale.* There were no goats in sight, nor any people. After she watched a small, empty corral for ten minutes without seeing anybody move, she went back, once again, to Ocotillo.

For the next twenty minutes, she took every possible turnoff from Ocotillo Road, no matter how sparse and unpromising, and found a small bird sanctuary, an Ashram (which she recognized because it had a sign that said, 'Ashram,') and rugs flapping on a line outside an apparent weaver's studio in what looked like an old barn.

All three of those establishments, and everything else she found, was interspersed with dead campsites next to the abandoned tailings of moribund mines. None of these amounted to much more than shallow holes hand-dug into the sides of sharp cutbanks – this community must have grown up around the rumor of some ore deposit that didn't prove out. The mining sites looked older than all of the cheapjack buildings that had been thrown up around them, and the whole neighborhood was clinging – and slouching and leaning – in hilly terrain strewn with rocks of all sizes.

'OK, technology gods, you win this round,' Sarah told her dashboard. She went back to Ocotillo, parked on the skimpy shoulder, and punched Amanda's address into her GPS. When she hit GO, the purple arrows sprang to life, directing her to continue driving southwest into the desert.

The road curved left when the arrow did, and presently she

was facing east, looking at the Rincon mountains, though still on Ocotillo which had turned ninety degrees. The device began to indicate a left turn in a fourth of a mile, then five hundred feet. When it told her to turn, she turned, saying softly, 'So *this* is how you get into the middle.'

She was on a narrow dirt track now, barely wide enough for her car, driving five miles an hour and occasionally muttering, 'Hope I don't meet a lot of traffic.' Lily Belle Mine Road, it called itself. The road, such as it was, traveled eastward from the entry point, but soon began to turn gradually left again.

Besides constantly turning, it was never level, but climbed up and down a couple of little hills and then up a steep hill, only to drop sharply down again. And down, and down, until she was asking herself how hard it was going to be to get out of here, and answered herself by climbing out in a tooth-gritting pedal-to-metal roar, clinging to the narrow track that filled the air around her with so much dust she had to pause and let some of it settle before she could drive on.

The hill she was stopped on afforded a view, so she got out to look around. As the air cleared, she was somewhat shaken to see that during the climb out she had driven past a mine shaft only twenty feet off the road. The opening was covered by a metal grate and surrounded by metal posts and chain-link fencing that carried hand-lettered wooden signs, *Lily Belle Mine, Keep Out.* All she could see through the grate was dark space, going down.

She watched her GPS carefully after that, and was happy to see that it was delivering good news – undaunted by rough terrain in its two-dimensional world, it was saying she was only three-quarters of a mile from Amanda's house. Which was fine while it lasted, but soon afterward the distance from her destination began to increase. She continued on Lily Belle Mine Road and soon was a mile and a half from Amanda's house. The road had curved all the way around a circle and was back at the entry point.

'This is crazy,' she muttered. She pulled out and parked on Ocotillo again, headed back toward town this time and dug her Tucson area map out of her day pack. When she had it folded into a convenient square she looked at all sides of this cluster of streets. The base of the area was Silverbell Road; it was bounded on the right side and the top by Ocotillo. On the left side was the obscure little street that Ollie had pointed out to her called Gould Road. Gould petered out, according to the map, before it quite intersected with Ocotillo.

'OK, lady, let's go around.' She was talking to the GPS now. Its gender established by a feminine voice, it had become a gal-pal in this adventure. She drove quickly back to Silverbell, turned right there and followed it to the inconspicuous sign for Gould Road. Ms GPS wanted to turn right there, and again a few turn-offs later, where a sign read *Crazy Mule Road*. In a cleared space just past the turn, a half dozen mailboxes were nailed to a peeled log.

'Oh, baby,' Sarah told her new friend as she set the brake, 'I think we're cooking now.'

The mailboxes all had names on them. None read 'Amanda Petty'. But then Amanda got her mail at Mail Boxes, didn't she? Sarah let the brake off and rolled slowly downhill on a better road than any she had seen before in this area, a proper two-lane road with gravel. A row of power poles followed the road down, carrying utilities to half a dozen small adobe houses on a terraced slope.

It was very quiet in this mini-village – the residents must all be at work in town, and the highway was too far away to hear. There was one old Ford pickup parked by the lowest house in the row. Fifty feet beyond it the road forked and became two narrow tracks. The tracks diverged into a little vale with a tangle of bushes and cactus between them. The GPS wanted to take the right-hand option so Sarah did, and in a few feet found a sign that read, *Jenny Mine Road*.

'How about that?' she said softly, pleased with herself.

The track wandered through thick brush and cactus to a clearing, where it dead-ended at a small stucco house with a fenced backyard. Outside the yard, an old barn and a dilapidated utility shed were separated by a stack of firewood. The power line had followed this track, she noticed, and all three buildings were wired. By the front door, dark-stained wooden numbers read 255.

There was a small hand-spaded garden inside the yard, with a row of corn just headed out, and the tops of some carrots and potatoes showing in neat rows. The whole rectangle was guarded by a border of marigolds. *Looks like she could give me gardening lessons*, Sarah thought. She imagined Amanda Petty's intent expression as she knelt by her garden plot, carefully dropping tiny carrot seeds into a shallow trench.

She pulled her phone out of its pocket, punched in Ollie's number, and sent him a text. *After twenty-five wrong turns tried Gould Road then Crazy Mule & found 255 Jenny Mine Road, ta-da!*

The answer came back in a few seconds. *Good show, Sherlock.*

She grinned at it, then sat looking past the garden at the outbuildings behind the house. *I would like to have a look in that barn.* But she didn't have a search warrant. *Could I get one?* Probably not over the phone, with the flimsy justification she could offer – being the steno at the senior living place that got attacked recently didn't amount to probable cause to suspect Amanda of anything.

She decided to take a picture anyway, in case some new piece of evidence came along. When she got out of the car, the air felt much hotter than in the car, but as she moved around, the dappled shade began to seem moderate compared to the highway.

The sky had been mostly clear all morning, with scattered clouds left over from the night's rain. But as she stepped out of the car a scrap of cloud moved across the sun. She watched it darken her surroundings and decided to wait until it moved on to try a photo. She dropped the phone into the back pocket of her jeans and strolled along the road a few steps past the car, exploring.

The area beyond the house was wild. Through a tangle of underbrush, she could see a sturdy fence of metal poles and chain-link fencing. She stepped closer and saw a metal gate, padlocked, with a commercially printed metal sign clipped firmly at all four corners that read, *Jenny Mine. No Trespassing.*

Well, I'm not, I'm staying on the road. Which ends here, by the way.

Everything beyond Amanda's house appeared to be no man's land, thickly overgrown and impenetrable. Just a few feet beyond where the road ended the ground dropped off sharply into a wild gully.

The sun came out from under its cloud then and the day grew hotter. Sarah moved back toward her car, ready to take her picture and go. The quiet house and garden had changed her feeling about Amanda. No wonder the woman was aloof and defensive, if she feared a stalker might find this peaceful retreat.

Well, I haven't touched anything, I'm only looking, she justified to herself as she walked back to her car. I'll just take my picture and go. She was looking up at the clouds again, judging the light, when a sharp metallic sound made her turn.

The old barn had a garage door on the gable end nearest the road and it was rising. Somebody had thrown a switch inside and stood now, his hand still on the power box, watching the door slide up. Behind him was a gray Dodge pickup with a missing license plate.

'Bogey.' She managed to keep her voice level, but she felt blood surge behind her ears. 'I didn't expect to find you here.'

'Sarah,' he said. A manic grin slowly lit up his face, turning him into someone she hadn't seen before. 'I wasn't exactly looking for you either.' He turned and picked something off the worktable to his left, folded it under his arm and stepped out into the light. 'What are you doing out here in the boonies?'

'Just verifying an address,' she said. 'I thought, isn't this where Amanda Petty lives?' She was looking past him at the pickup.

'Beats me,' he said. 'Who's Amanda Petty?'

'The steno at the senior living place where we first worked together. Don't you remember?' There was something seriously wrong with this conversation; he had never spoken to her in this way. Why was he grinning at her as if they shared some guilty secret?

He stepped out of the underbrush and across the little hump that formed an edge to the road she was on. He was suddenly close beside her – too close, so she stepped away.

'Bogey, what are you doing?' As she spoke, he swung both arms high to drop the bag he was carrying over her head.

She saw it coming and kicked as she ducked. They were both a little off, so her kick missed his groin but landed a solid crack to his right kneecap. She felt the jolt all through her body and saw that the shock knocked him down.

He didn't succeed at bagging her either. The bag slid off into the cactus, but the edge of his fist landed a painful blow to the side of her head. It stunned her and blurred her eyesight for a few seconds. She could hear him cursing somewhere below her.

When her vision cleared she saw him, curled in a fetal position at the edge of the road, cursing and cradling his right knee. His left foot was lying directly under her so she stomped on it, hard. The solid old ranch boot cracked his ankle and she judged from his awful scream that he would not be walking on it anytime soon. She turned toward her car then, took a step toward it and was reaching for the door handle when he roared, lunged, grabbed her rear leg and pulled her down into the underbrush with him.

They rolled over each other, grunting and yelling in pain, picking up cactus spines as they tumbled. She tried for a chokehold but never made it, scratched his face and drew blood but didn't hurt him enough to get free. That was her best chance – she had all but crippled him, he couldn't catch her if she ran. But his arms were so strong, she couldn't break his hold.

But then she did, suddenly. Because he had let her go – why? Then she felt him push her away – away from him, and over the edge, into the ravine.

As she went over the edge and fell, she heard him laugh. 'There you go, bitch!' he yelled. 'Have fun down there!'

She didn't fall very far – the ravine was perhaps twenty feet deep, but it was full of bushes. She lodged in a thorny tangle and lay panting, scratched and bleeding. She hurt all over, and urgently wanted to scream, sneeze and vomit. She forced herself to be silent, so he wouldn't know exactly where she was.

Or whether she was conscious, she hoped. She heard him

above her, panting and cursing as he dragged himself away from the edge of the ravine. Grunting and swearing, he tried to stand, twice, each time falling back to earth howling in pain.

After he rested a few minutes he began making small noises she couldn't at first identify. Then she realized he was talking very softly on his phone. He said a name she couldn't quite hear and began to give orders. He must have heard objections because he stopped and swore, louder, made vile threats, listened a minute and said, 'OK then,' and went back to his string of orders. She couldn't understand all of them but was pretty sure she heard 'gasoline can' and 'shovel'.

When he was finished phoning, he dragged himself back toward the road, swearing and blubbering, a little in pain but quieter than before. She heard him make it to her car, pull himself up and get in with a great deal of moaning, and start the motor. He didn't drive away. *He just wanted the A/C*, she told herself, and then thought, *So do I*. It was very hot in the prickly underbrush and she had a raging thirst.

Then she remembered. *He's got my Glock too.*

Tears flooded her eyes then and she only just managed to stay silent, shuddering, clenching her fists and curling her toes. Then slowly, pushing aside the pain and fear, her brain got back to work. And what it said was, *He's got my car but I've got my phone.*

FIFTEEN

Tuesday–Sunday

I t took nerve to move – she wasn't sure the bush she was caught in would hold her. Or how far she'd fall if it didn't. *How deep is this ravine?*

But she couldn't stay where she was – she could see light from where she was so she might be visible to anyone looking in. Bogey had her gun now, and he had proved he could cover the distance from here to the car if he chose. So there was nothing to keep him from killing her, and he had shown his willingness to do that, hadn't he?

I think so. I don't understand what his game is, but right now I believe it includes killing me if necessary.

So I've got to move. How? Her left hand felt free. She moved it toward her face. When she could see it she found a fair-sized branch to grasp while she slowly, painfully pulled her right arm loose from whatever nest of thorns was holding it. It hurt very much so she told herself to be glad she was alive to feel it. That and gritting her teeth got her right arm untangled.

Next came the sweaty reach into her rear pocket, telling herself, *If you drop this phone you're dead.* She could not stop sweating so she held the slick smoothness of her phone close against her body as she worked it through the brambles toward her face.

Now she needed both hands free. Letting go of the strong branch she'd been clinging to with her left hand felt like a crazy gamble. She thought it through, braced her feet against whatever they could find and opened the fingers of her left hand, leaving them close enough to grab again if she started to fall. She lay still a minute, breathing, telling herself *I didn't fall.* She began to realize the slope was not as steep as she had thought.

After that she was bolder. Shifting her body an inch at a time, she body-wedged upward and sideways, going for upright.

Don't move one foot until you have something firm under the other one. Once the ground under a rock crumbled when she put weight on it and she only just kept from crying out in alarm. She managed with a mini-yelp – and the slope she was on didn't crumble.

When she was almost sitting up, she stopped to breathe for a minute. Then, very carefully, begging her sweaty hands *please don't slip,* she moved the phone to her left hand and typed a text with her right: *Help, in a hole@255, Bogey bad, has my car & gun, hurry.*

Did that say enough? Surely he'd know she wouldn't joke about something so serious, wouldn't he? She debated with herself about adding *don't answer,* afraid the noise would give her position away. But she had to know if he got the message. And Bogey was in her car with the A/C working, so he couldn't hear her three dings, could he? He might get out later, but – *one thing at a time,* she decided, and sent the text to Ollie.

And after three minutes that felt like a week and a half, a text came back: *On our way, stay in the hole, bringing the cavalry – O.*

Perversely then, the wait got even harder to bear – to hang here in these thorns when her own cool office was so near! Then she glanced at her scratched and bleeding arms and thought how many hours of repairs and cleaning she would need before she was fit to occupy her workspace again. And every bite and scratch began to itch and sting.

Her discomfort grew so acute she thought that any action would beat just hanging here in the sweaty thorns. And she was still worried about being visible from above, so she put the phone in the front pocket of her jeans and began, cautiously, to try to move out of the bush she was caught in.

She found she could slither downslope, an inch at a time, without making much noise. The leaf cover got thicker with each move, encouraging her to keep going. Every time she moved, she turned her head both ways to explore her green nest. On her right, after a few moves, she found many empty half-pint gin bottles that a secret drinker must have hurled there in desperation. Nearby, on her left after the next two moves, was a heap of plastic doodads – toothbrushes, throw-away razors – bathroom trash.

Three careful downslides later came a moment of horrified clarity when she recognized that the gentle hissing she was hearing was coming from the nest of baby rattlesnakes she could suddenly see by her right elbow. She pushed herself back upslope faster than she'd come down and lay panting just below her original resting place.

Frantic little thoughts then: *Still plenty of cover.* As her breathing slowed down: *Lucky mama was away from the nest. God, we get grateful for small favors, don't we?* And as the wait stretched out again: *Wish I hadn't been too chicken to stay by those snakes and take a picture.*

Then with mixed emotions she realized that a motor had turned at the Crazy Mule sign and was coming down the road toward 255.

Certain she would die of curiosity if she couldn't poke her head up to look, she told herself she might die of damn fool-ishness if she did. Might die anyway if these were henchmen of Bogey's come looking for her. Was she really covered up enough? She burrowed deeper in the leaves.

The motor stopped by her car, doors slammed, and there was talk. Not Ollie and Ray. She shivered. More talk, along the lines of what the hell happened to you, man? Surly answers from Bogey, followed by thumping noises as they unloaded equipment from the vehicle they came in. The last thing they unloaded had a metallic clank.

What have I got to fight with?

The branches she had wished were stronger while she clung to them seemed even punier now. She broke off a couple of dry sticks while the unloading commotion above covered the little cracking noises. *At least I can poke them in the eye.*

The newcomers were inclined to make jokes about Bogey's injuries. He was trying to be stoic but was obviously in pain and angry. But when somebody said something like, '. . . shoot her and get it over with,' he said, 'no. It has to look like an accident.'

Yes, yes! Shuddering in her shelter of leaves and thorns, she told herself *He means to kill me but he doesn't want to shoot me.* It was very cold comfort but she went back to telling herself she could outrun him. The realist in her whispered, *what about his pals?* And the hero she was building herself into said, *pull them into this hole and scare them with the snakes.*

It wasn't much of a plan but it was the best she had and she was still embroidering it when a small parade of unmarked city vehicles came down the road from the Crazy Mule turn-off, and a half-dozen Tucson detectives jumped out and surrounded her car. They made a lot of noise, flashing badges and demanding that the three men they found there tell them where they'd put Sarah Burke.

Before the awkward fact emerged that they had no jurisdiction in the county, Sheriff Wheeler arrived with several of his deputies, including Ray's cousin Oscar. The space on front of Amanda's house was too small for their armored vehicle, so they parked it by the peeled log and walked down the graveled track, checking their weapons.

When they reached Amanda's house, they made three arrests, based on information provided by a Tucson detective whom they rescued from a hole in the desert.

Or so the story went on the nightly news.

At home, where she gratefully rested over the weekend after a day in the hospital and another in debriefing, Sarah had a somewhat longer story to tell. It came out slowly, interrupted by periods of rest and soaking in a hot tub.

'All right, I admit to an error in judgment,' she told her family. 'I should not have gone out there without a backup.'

Will said, 'Why did you?' He'd been horrified by how hurt she was when he first saw her in the hospital.

'Well, I really did think I was just going to confirm her address,' she said. 'But OK, I was angry, too – because my system wasn't working. Delaney handed me the Fairweather Farms case, and I did what I always do, made a list of questions and looked for the answers. Nothing seemed to fit with anything else, but I was sure I could break through all the clutter if I just kept checking, so that's what I did.'

'If it doesn't work, do more of the same,' Will said sadly. 'How many times—'

'Come on, don't nag.' She held up the tweezer. 'Right leg. Back of the knee.' She had been doing this all weekend, every time she found more cactus thorns that the hospital had overlooked. They had done a nice job on cuts and abrasions, but many cactus spines were tiny and hard to see. Sarah was going to be wearing her softest clothes to work for a while, and close to nothing at home.

'I still don't get it,' Denny said. 'The brave hero that arrested five guys at once, he turned out to be a bad guy? What about all that money you found together?'

'He planted that. Bogey, yes. While I was right there, but my back was turned. The guy's a master of deceit.'

'Why would he plant money on DeShawn, his own guy?'

'He saw a chance to get the little guys all arrested. He had to get them out of the way to clear the field for his deal with the Euros. He's amazingly opportunistic.'

'But the thumb drive, Sarah,' Will said. 'How could he know . . .?'

'He planted that too, don't you see? I should have known there was something hinky when he pretended all that interest in the ammo. There was nothing unusual about the two shots in the door. He pretended an interest so he could get into the van with Banjo and plant the dead drop that he supposedly found.'

'But how come he was carrying the right amount of money?' Denny said.

'Who says it was the right amount? He made the whole thing up, don't you see?'

'Ooohhh,' Denny said, taking two syllables to express her understanding, 'that really is adorably clever, isn't it?'

'Yes, well, I'm glad you're pleased,' Sarah said. She was a little testy; her pride was hurt.

'But what about that terrific arrest he made?' Denny said, 'The one you told me about before, with five men on the ground – he was an honest cop then, wasn't he?'

'No, that was the biggest con of all. He had his little drug ring going along nice, everybody happy with the extra money, when the big international thugs came to town and spied his action. They showed him some of their heat and said, "We're taking this turf, Dingbat, how many of you do we gotta kill?"

'So Bogey made a deal. Said he'd get his gang out of the way without a fight if they'd let him keep his policeman's badge, then there wouldn't be any big gun battle that gets the law involved, and he could protect us all.'

'That was good thinking,' Will said.

'Brilliant. And when the Euro-trash said yes, he went to his own gang and told them that those animals had got them outgunned so to make up their minds . . . they could be safe, out of the way with a couple of years in Yuma or could end up dead. So they staged that wonderful arrest on Kentucky Derby day.'

'I don't know, Sarah,' Will said, 'this all sounds pretty pie in the sky to me. What about DeShawn? Why is he always getting whacked?'

'Because he wouldn't go along. DeShawn was tired of running. He liked his job and he liked the nice little romance he was having with Amanda. He said he thought he could make a deal with the new guys, so he went to them and made his pitch, told them what a savvy guy he was, how he could please everybody and get them more customers. They evidently decided to take him quietly into the team and kill him later, and they've been trying to do that ever since. DeShawn seems to be a fraudster with a lot of luck.'

'Where does he stand right now?'

'In County waiting for the lawyers to decide what to charge him with. He's lost some confidence.'

'He'll get it back,' Will said. 'Con men always do.'

'I guess. One of the things I figured out while I was waiting in that ravine – the reason DeShawn quit talking to me in the hospital that day. Bogey had come to tell me about his phony search for the pickup, and he must have been standing in the doorway, looking for me. DeShawn thought Bogey was looking for him and right then he decided, *both sides want me dead.*

That was when he got more symptoms and slid down in the covers.'

'How does he do that? Get those symptoms when he wants them?'

'I wish I knew. DeShawn is a real piece of work. I can kind of see why Amanda couldn't resist him.'

'What about Amanda?' Denny said. 'She really didn't do anything illegal, did she? Does she have to take the fall for having that pickup in her barn?'

'What pickup? I think that's going to be her answer. I don't believe anybody can prove she knew it was there. I'm sure what happened is the Euros put the squeeze on DeShawn – "find us a place to store this truck" – even though they'd used it to try to kill him, but I guess they weren't 'fessing up to that yet. And DeShawn turned to Amanda and said, as he always will, to whatever woman is dancing to his tune at the moment, "Baby, I need your help." Amanda has unerring taste for men who will ruin her life.'

'One thing I've been wondering,' Will said. 'What was Bogey doing there?'

'Getting ready to drive the pickup out. He had a flatbed waiting on a curve at the top of Ocotillo, ready to haul the truck to a chop shop far away. The sheriff's crew picked them up. The sheriff already had the truck driver in chains when they came to rescue me.'

'Well, I sure hope you work it out so Amanda doesn't have to go to jail,' Denny said. 'That would be a shame, wouldn't it? After all she's just a' – she put her head back and warbled the last three words – 'prisoner of love.'

'Oh, pshaw,' Will said, getting up. 'I need some fresh air after that.' He went out and got his tools out of the shed, ready to start work on the patch in front of the carport.

The phone rang, and Jason Peete said, 'Is this the detective who likes to spend her paid vacations exploring the desert?'

'Anytime you hanker after exotic scenery,' Sarah said, 'call me. I know some very scenic places.'

'Are you hurt bad?'

'Nah. Still finding cactus thorns, but otherwise mostly healed – much better off than my opponent, I'm pleased to say.'

'Good for you. You want to hear the fun stuff I found by the dark of the moon?'

'You bet. You chatted with some staff?'

'Tammy might seem scattered to you, Sarah, but she showed me some devilish charm. She and a couple of her buds there, they know how to have fun in their time off.'

'You see, you just have a knack. Did you hear about anything stronger than weed?'

'Hard stuff's too expensive for the staff. Tammy's hoping you bring the hammer down hard on Mr Ames, though. It seems he has a serious Oxy habit, along with being a major pain in the butt.'

'I'll personally see to it that Mr Ames's habit gets the attention it deserves. Last time we spoke he called me girlie.'

'He what?' Jason erupted into laughter. 'Oh, Sarah, how did you keep from breaking his face?'

'Oh, you know the answer to that. I was interrogating him. I didn't even blink. How many times have you had to do the same thing?'

'Plenty. It isn't even hard anymore. I just stand there being glad I'm on the right side.'

'Except when it's Delaney.'

'It's different with him. I know you think it's racist but it isn't.'

'I know. You both want to be boss and only one of you is.'

'Very good; go to the head of the psych class. Listen, now that you've got all these big-time crimes to punish, you can forget about the pot, right?'

'Of course. Thanks for doing it, though. It helped me through the hiatus.'

After she poked *off* she stood listening to the drone of Dietz's motor for a minute, and then walked out to watch him work. When he stopped to rest she came and stood close to him.

'This is going to look very nice,' she said.

'Yeah, well, it's great that Aggie's cheered up and is getting along so well with that neighbor,' he said. 'She seems to be enjoying that plot by the kitchen. But here in front, I thought I'd like to do this one myself.'

She kissed his neck and began to whisper in his ear about the things around here that she thought needed no improvement. As her list of plenty good things grew longer and more explicit, Will Dietz began to blush with pleasure and, before long, he was putting his tools away.